SCISSOR SISTERS

Scissor Sisters

An Anthology Edited
by Rae Knowles and April Yates

To those who spent their youth amongst the library stacks seeking a mirror.

Content warnings are provided at the end of the book

Contents

Foreword by April Yates ... 1

Introduction by Paula D. Ashe ... 3

Gladys Glows at Night by Hatteras Mange ... 5

You Oughta Be in Pictures by Anastasia Dziekan ... 13

The Lady of the House on Legs by Ariel Marken Jack ... 23

To Wilt a Flower by Maerwynn Blackwood ... 31

Teratoma, Cacodaemon, Erinya by Avra Margariti ... 41

Torbalan's Gift by Grace R. Reynolds ... 51

Her Tongue, a Slippery Slope by Evelyn Freeling ... 57

Modern Art Curse, Mixed Media by Hailey Piper ... 65

The Flesh Grows Fonder by T.O. King ... 75

Pilgrim of Worlds by M.S. Dean ... 85

Gingerbread Red by Chloe Spencer ... 93

Buckskin for Linen by Mae Murray ... 103

Oubliette by L. R. Stuart ... 111

Conversations with Roe by Alex Luceli Jiménez ... 121

Our Lady of Devouring Violence by Cheyanne Brabo ... 129

Family Planning by Luc Diamant ... 137

Ungrateful Dead Things by Alyssa Lennander ... 143

Straight Flush by Anya Leigh Josephs ... 153

A Mirror Has Two Faces by Lindz McLeod ... 161

The Turner House Heritage Tour by Caitlin Marceau ... 167

Enamored by Shelley Lavigne ... 175

Lagniappe ... 187

The Call of the Sea by Eric Raglin ... 189

About the Authors ... 195

About the Editors ... 199

About the Illustrator   201

Content Warnings   203

More From Brigids Gate Press   207

Foreword

by April Yates

Who knows if by the time you read these words the dumpster fire that is Twitter will still exist, but without it this anthology—the entirety of the Sapphic Horror Series, in fact—would not. At a time when were both shopping our novellas (shameless plug alert) *City of Snares* and *Merciless Waters*, out now from Brigids Gate Press BTW, Rae sent me a message which basically reads, *Hey, why don't we write a tweet, proposing this as a series? Two novellas and co-write a third?*

The trap was set and Heather from Brigids Gate took the bait.

"What's your idea for this co-written project?" she asked us.

Reader, we did not know!!! Cue a frantic back and forth between Rae and I.

Fuck!

What were we going to say?

Not a Scooby!

After a few moments, I remembered an idea I had about fake lesbian mediums in Victorian England.

Perfect!

So, with only the vaguest inkling of an idea, we pitched it, Heather loved the concept, and we wrote what eventually became the novel *Lies That Bind*, out very soon from Brigids Gate Press (that was the last plug, promise).

After all that, an anthology showcasing other writers and their sapphic villains was the natural progression.

In much of the media I consumed growing up, simply being queer-coded—in large part due to the Hays Code and its lingering effects—was enough to warrant punishment whether they were villains or not. Both Mrs. Danvers from *Rebecca* and Martha from *The Children's Hour* suffer the same ultimate fate of death.

Bury your gays indeed.

It seemed to me that anytime I spotted a lesbian in horror literature, they were there simply to make a lecherous pass at the hero's girl, much to her disgust, and/or die. Rarely were there any fully fleshed out queer women who won at the end of the day.

This anthology is important to Rae and me as it presents an opportunity for people around the world to tell the stories they wish to read.

I shan't prattle on any longer and shall instead pass you over to the wonderful and talented Paula D. Ashe for what I'm sure will be more insightful thoughts than mine about the stories contained within these pages.

April Yates
December 2023

Introduction

by Paula D. Ashe

It was the summer of 2023 and for so many of us queers, it was a particularly demoralizing time to be alive. It was Yet Another Worryingly Hot Summer in Which We Were Reminded of the Precarity of Our Existence. We experienced and witnessed transphobia, misogyny, white supremacy, homophobia, ableism and fascism bloom across the ever-warming globe. Shit was (and still is) bleak. Every day there was something (or multiple somethings) new and terrible and overwhelming. At the same time though, every day also brought new ways to resist, new alliances and understandings, new glimmers and glimpses of joy.

It was in this milieu that the call for *Scissor Sisters* was first announced, alongside several other calls specifically aimed at various flavors of confrontational queer horror. I don't think this happened by accident. The last few years have seen not only a larger resurgence in Horror writ large, but a resurgence that is uniquely queer, inclusive, and revolutionary. The paradigm shifted from conservative horrors to the horrors of the marginalized. As a result, there were opportunities to play with and subvert the tropes that had historically been used to degrade, omit, and/or pathologize us, there were invitations to revel in our most unsaintly behavior, while others encouraged indulgences in (fictional of course) acts of unhinged sapphic villainy.

And here I have to give a shoutout to April and Rae, for curating something remarkable within the larger scope of queer horror. I'm certainly not saying it's the only subgenre of horror to do so, but I think that queer horror is unmatched at gruesomely illustrating the adage that the personal is political. And what better paragon than the sapphic villain to emblematize the vicious misogyny (and transmisogyny) so characteristic of our current age? When the personal becomes political, one surefire way to resist is by becoming the monster they already think you are. After all, the sapphic villain is everything a woman shouldn't be: predatory, selfish, vain, obsessive, driven, hedonistic, aggressive, morally ambiguous at best and immoral at worst. The sapphic villain directly challenges traditional structures and agents of power and authority. Her sapphistry challenges normative assumptions about sex and sexuality, while her villainy suggests that very few wish to resist her seductions. The sapphic villain is villainous largely because often, she must be. She must be the monster who reveals that the institutions most often charged with destroying evil, are the same ones that created it in the first place.

She does all that *and* gets the girl (usually).

Which is why so many of the stories in *Scissor Sisters* deal with monstruous transformations and hellish bargains. There are baddies aplenty: serial killers, demented monsterfuckers (bless 'em), vampires, sinister space travelers, vengeance-seeking ghosts, witches, and so much more, speaking truth to power or just burning it all down in the process. Because quite often—in the most basic sense of the term—every villain was once someone's victim.

It is the winter of 2023 and for so many of us queers, it is a particularly demoralizing time to be alive.

But we are alive. And we are not victims.

Let's be villains.

GLADYS GLOWS AT NIGHT

by Hatteras Mange

I am a thing the dark of night peels back from, a glowing number on the face of a clock—hooked like a two or a seven and always wiggly, as if I were painted with a scraggly brush.

I'm crooked and unsteady, things I never was in life. Not until the end when my hands began to shake, my hair got thin, and my teeth turned soft and loose. Not until I transformed into something awful.

There were girls who used to pray for that. I learned about them in Sunday school. They wanted to be nuns and saints instead of wives. They prayed for God to make them hideous and keep men away.

When they got tired of waiting, they did the work themselves.

They starved themselves until they lost the use of their legs, and their guts withered up behind their ribs. They mutilated their chests, hips, and rumps beyond recognition. Fasting Girls, people called them. Holy Anorexics.

That wasn't me.

I didn't want to be a saint. I wanted to smoke and drink coffee, sleep until noon, then go for walks in the park. I wanted to wear nice dresses with paste gem buttons down the backs. I wanted to curl my hair. I wanted to *live*.

To do that, a girl needs money, and for money a girl doesn't have many options. There's teaching, renting out dates, typing, and factories. For ease of entry, factories are best. The turnover is exceptional. There's always one hiring and new girls never ask why.

They don't have to. There are only a handful of reasons, all of which are tied in some way to men. Ingersoll wasn't different, but the agent of the violence there …

I never, in two-dozen lifetimes, could've imagined it.

I am a thing Mr. Gershwin mistakes for a streetlamp as he bisects 8th and Elm, leaving the factory. It looms behind him, a giant of darkened glass and steel. Inside are rows of workstations littered with brushes, all faintly glowing.

He doesn't notice the glow, or at least pretends he doesn't. He's made a fortune from the gift of oversight. He leaves the real work to the girls, preferring to spend his days drinking in his office and making social calls. He approves campaigns and consorts with shift leaders, senators, military generals. All men. The upper floors of Ingersoll reek of them.

I can only remember speaking to Mr. Gershwin three times in life. The first was when I interviewed for the job. I read in the Sunday paper that Ingersoll needed new painters. A batch of girls had recently left. I didn't think to ask why.

"You'll like it here," he told me from behind an antique desk that would've looked more at home in a library. "Best place for a girl to work these days. Great pay. Total independence."

Total independence. What a dream, I remember thinking.

The second time was when I reported for my first shift. I came in heavily coated, cold through my thin dress and pantyhose, and followed him around the painting room. For a factory, it was quiet. I could hear the faint thrum of machinery somewhere, but the room our desks were in was pleasantly still.

The station I was assigned to looked out over Elm Street. It was a nice, sunny spot lit by huge windows. The two on either side were abandoned, but the cluster was near a group of old hats who chatted over the crackle of a desktop radio while they painted.

On top of my new station was a set of freshly washed, thin brushes; a mounted magnifying glass; a few watch- and clock-faces to practice on; and a deep dish of paint cut with radium. Ingersoll's primary product, a modern marvel.

I'd seen radium watches before in mail-order catalogs and a few of town's nicer storefronts. Most of the supply was being shipped to Europe but some were commercially available. It was fashionable for men to play soldier, and strapping on watches was the safest form of dress up.

After being given my task and introduced to the neighbors, I began the competitive work of painting numbers. They had to be perfect, the others told me. Only the tightest lines would do.

One of them twirled her stained tool. "The trick is keeping your bristles stuck together."

It doesn't take Gershwin long to realize I'm not a streetlight. Streetlights don't twitch like broken tails, and their glow is contained, mimicking tame candles and torches. *My* glow is wild; my whole, desiccated body burns.

He pauses several blocks back from where I wait, watching him through eyes that tint the world lemon-green. My eyes must look like zeroes painted on the end of a ten to him. He stiffens in belated recognition and dashes across the street.

He thinks this distance matters, that it protects him, and why shouldn't he? This isn't the first time I've waited for him on 8th Street. Thus far, it's been a long and—for him—easy haunting. I've been patient. I've kept my distance. But I'm tired of waiting.

Glancing up often to make sure I haven't moved, Mr. Gerswhin tightens his coat and takes anxious strides. The soles of his loafers are noisy on the sidewalk. It's patched with ice, though snow has been swept from it several times. He doesn't look where he's going. He's more concerned about me than slipping.

When he passes under a streetlight, I see his eyes. They're bright and jittery, the fear in them clashing stubbornly with disbelief. His attention darts around, desperate to find proof that he's imagining things. But there isn't any. I'm no trick of winter moonlight.

He falters under the lamp at the corner of his street. Snow makes patterns like lace in his dark, coiffed hair. He's squinting in my direction, struggling to both deny and believe in me.

My shriek glasses the night. He swears, stumbling back from it, and runs.

⁂

It was nothing at first. At least, that's how it seemed. I felt nauseous and got headaches but that wasn't unusual. I thought the headaches were from eyestrain and asked for a larger magnifying glass.

My shift leader didn't put the request through. He suggested aspirin.

I took to keeping a bottle at my desk like the other girls. Their heads hurt too and so did their jaws and joints. Everyone kept something on them for the pain. When one of us was out, all we had to do was go trick-or-treating.

My favorite girl was Rosie. She was my age, formerly a typist. Our desks were close, and in the early days she was my helper. She'd come to Ingersoll from the library, which paid too little to cover her rent. She missed the books and warmth, but nothing beat factory compensation.

She liked the brushes too. Using them made her feel like an artist in a city more glamorous than ours. She taught me how to hold them: how to flick my wrist and make perfect zeroes; not to lock my elbows; to keep steady hands. She guided my first few strokes, and her fingers were so soft against my wrist that my own felt brutish.

Rosie smelled like freshly washed linen and peonies, the notes of her favorite department store perfume. She wore it daily, but never lipstick, because it ruined the brushes. I should give it up too, she had said.

You've got doll lips, Gladys! You don't even need it.

When she gave me lessons in plastering the bristles, all I could see was her tongue, dexterous and sharp and perfectly pink. "Like cleaning butter off a knife," she joked after slipping the dainty brush free of her lips. "Come on, you try."

I repeated the motion, grimacing at the taste. I wanted to spit, but she gave me a smile so sweet that I couldn't bring myself to. I would've licked every brush in the room to see that smile again. I would've licked all the paint pots clean if she asked me to.

She was a pretty, kind, and funny girl that I took to seeing socially. In the beginning, we met for coffee before shifts. Then came dinner and theater dates, trips to the library, bus rides for ice cream, and later: drinks in my little walk-up apartment.

Sometimes she stayed the night. It was safer, we agreed that first time, than her walking home alone drunk or hailing a cab. We didn't make excuses the second time, or any time after. It was enough that we wanted to lay together, whisper, and kiss.

It was the happiest time of my life, until it ended. Miserably. And it was always going to. I know that now. Rosie had worked for Ingersoll longer. She was one of the last remaining from the previous batch of hires.

The others had dropped off from Gershwin's without explanation, so Rosie never knew that they—and she—were sick. It compounded somewhere deep inside her, that sickness, out of sight, turning headaches to week-long migraines, violent vertigo, and nausea. She grew sluggish and disinterested. Her work got sloppy, her watch faces unsellable. She vomited on her desk one day, went home early, and never came back.

I visited her several times a week when it started but never for long. She was bedridden, her skin greener every time I went. She insisted on sitting up for me, though it was obviously painful. She could hardly speak without groaning and belching. Eventually, for her sake, I stopped going.

I kept to phone calls after that, checking in to keep her spirits up and to hear about her frequent trips to the doctor. I prayed for good news every night but it never came. She was losing too much weight and hair, too many teeth.

"They look like little stones on my pillow," she said one day, deliriously. "And I've swallowed some. They go down easy as rice." Her puffy tongue garbled the words, and I could hear her jaw cracking. It sounded like someone stomping on animal bones. "Gladys, am I dying?"

I let Gerswhin get ahead, let him think that he can outrun me. His house isn't far away, and he's made it before. All of the other nights he's seen me—whatever he tells himself that he's seeing—I've let him scamper inside, just in time, and lock the door.

His house, a handsome brownstone sandwiched between other handsome brownstones, all uniformly blanketed by snow, has been his fortress. He thinks he's safe inside it. He thinks he's safe from *me*.

Well, he isn't safe tonight.

I wait until he's nearly over the hill before I give chase. There's nothing to avoid, no bikes or walkers out this late. Gershwin's neighborhood is safe, but night is still night. It's frosty cold, with ice slicking the roads and clinging to windows still crossed with string lights.

It's quiet, and yes: pretty, picturesque, even. But winter is still winter; night is still night.

And I am still a thing that children hurry home from when the sun begins to settle low in the sky. They don't have a name for me, but in their minds, I'm *fear*. Something risen from its grave, reanimated by spite.

The last time I saw Rosie, she was in a hospital bed. The sheets were tucked and folded down over her chest. She was posed perfectly in the center, so still I'd have thought she was dead if not for her rasping breath.

I didn't touch her. I was afraid to. She was so bruised and swollen, and her face—*God*, it was awful. Her jaw was eroded, cheeks sucked tight against bone, her gums dotted with dry sockets. Only a few wisps of hair were left, as brittle as straw.

I sat next to her for a long time and thought about Fasting Girls, bound to their beds, enshrined in pillows, remembered only for their suffering. I promised then that whenever I thought of her, I'd remember kisses and swapping dresses. I'd remember that she smelled like peonies and try to forget *this*.

When I returned to work, my own sleepy sickness was worse. I still didn't understand it. I thought it was grief. My vision was blurry and my head pounded. My fingers were stiff and my teeth felt strange.

I didn't start to panic until one popped out.

"Something's wrong," I told Gershwin the last time he and I spoke. By then, I'd worked at Ingersoll for two years. More of my teeth were loose and my knuckles weren't cooperating. "I don't feel well, and Rosie—"

"You're upset," he interrupted, not bothering to look up from his paperwork. If he did, he might've noticed my seafoam tint. "I understand. She was your friend. Why don't you go home? Hell, take the rest of the week. I'll have a temp cover you."

"You aren't listening. I'm getting sick, just like she did! What if it's catching? What if the others—"

"Take the rest of the week," he repeated, waving for me to leave.

When I didn't get up, he had a shift leader escort me out.

⚜

Like Rosie, I spent the last weeks of my life in a hospital. A few factory girls came to see me, but it was too late to tell them what I wanted. My body was swollen and useless. I couldn't speak or write the words down for them. Any movement, however slight, was agony. Gershwin didn't come. I knew he wouldn't. He never came to see Rosie, or any of the others before us, I suspect. He's a thoughtless, greedy man, with eyes only for the glow of radium.

I wonder what he thinks of it now.

⚜

As he runs, his strides make neat plow lines in the snlow. Mine leave jagged gouges as I stumble, smearing yellow-green, lighting the street in streaks. He's nearly at his stoop when I catch up to him.

He fishes through his coat pocket for the keys. I hear them jingle and consider letting him get through the door, just once more, to draw this out a little longer, but—

No. I want to end it, here and now.

I shriek again, and the sound in my mind is a name: *Rosie*, who couldn't rise herself, didn't have enough hate to. Rosie, pretty and bookish, bad at dancing, with a whole life ahead of her before Ingersoll.

My scream is shredded, frothed with spit. It bounces off the matched-set houses. Gershwin echoes it, squealing like a pig. He fumbles the keys.

They sink in snow and as he bends for them, I snatch at his coat. My gnarled hands find his shoulders and I collapse, letting my weight drag us into a shoveled drift.

He lands face down and thrashes, squirming for air in the compacted ice. I hold him like that and consider letting him suffocate. But that isn't what I woke up for, not what I want, so I raise my body and let him wriggle around.

He gasps and falls onto his back, blinking clumps of frost from his lashes. His cheeks and nose are flushed, his brow is cut. Blood trickles down his temple as he gapes at my ruin—my missing jaw and blackish stump of a tongue; empty pockets where teeth should be; glowing skin sloughed off to show bone, and my eyes, dead and bright.

"Who are you?" he sputters. "*What* are you?"

I pant hot breath in his face, smelling the death on it, on myself. When it reaches Gershwin, he gags.

"Please, I don't have any—"

I let out a roar, splattering his face with spittle. I know what he wants to say. *I don't have any money!* It's a lie. He and I both know that he has more than anyone, but money, damn him, isn't what I want.

The reverb of my anger shatters something nearby. I hear it crack, delicate as the splintering of glass. Ice, or a window, or a bottle dropped by a drunk, walking home and shocked sober by the sound.

Gershwin's eyes make saucers as he stutters more pleas. I smell piss and feel warmth spreading beneath me.

"Let me go. I won't report it." He jerks his head toward his stoop. "I'll go in and forget all about it. No one has to know."

I shake my head so hard that the vertebrae snap, crooking my neck. He can't forget. He doesn't deserve to. *"God!"* he whimpers, *"God!"* and starts a prayer that I recognize. I learned it in church; I, too, thought of it at the end.

Gladys, I try to say, but it comes out as a mush of sound. He won't understand it, I know, but he isn't really listening. He's calling out to every angel in heaven, but only I hear him.

I force my fingers between his lips and smear radium. Like cleaning butter off a knife.

You Ought'a Be in Pictures

by Anastasia Dziekan

I only dream in shades of red. It looks like abstract art. Pollocks and Rothkos. Or like red chrysanthemums blooming, spreading their petals wide.

I think it's the memory of the contents of the inside of my skull splattering against my eyelids.

* * *

"Can you *please* stand on your mark?"

I follow Jezebel's gesturing hand and shuffle two steps to the left so that my feet are flat over the masking tape "X" stuck to the floor of her garage.

"You're being pretentious."

"I'm not moving the noose just because you can't hit your mark."

I glance up at the rope haphazardly dangling from the ceiling. "I still don't get it. Won't I be dead before you even start hoisting me up?"

"Ideally, yes."

"Well, how is that sexy?"

She laughs, sharp and clear, and in the enclosed space it echoes off the walls and surrounds me. "What do you possibly mean?"

"Killing I get. Killing is penetrative. It's evocative. Stabbing is the same as—I mean you're up in a girl's guts, or, electrocution makes sense, with the convulsions, and anything else active enough, you've got screaming and groaning and moaning and whimpering. All the noises. Money shot. O-face. Big moment. That makes sense to me."

"You've been hanged before."

"Sure, while I was alive. That I get too. Helplessness and breathlessness and whatever. But what's sexy about when I'm already gone? Just dangling there like some kind of limp fish? Who requested that?"

"No one. This is for my personal collection."

"That makes sense. You should've told me."

She rolls her eyes. "Oh, how does it make more sense if it's me?"

"Because you're a weirdo and a pervert. No offense."

"First of all," she says with a huff, "we're recreating a classic work of cinema—"

"Of course, we are. You fucking hack."

"Electrocuting an Elephant."

"And I'm the elephant? You sure know how to make a girl feel special."

"It was groundbreaking for its time."

"You're a freak, you know that?"

"I'm an artist. It's just that I never get to see you really dead."

"You get off on such disgusting shit."

"Our clients get to imagine, because the cameras cut, and you're lying on the pavement, but I watch you reform, and you're never even down long enough for me to get proper lingering footage. I've seen behind the curtain and my imagination is dead and I thought if I doubled up on methods, I might get a chance to capture you for just a few moments.

She wins, like always. Her excuses always manage to trump my concerns.

Still, I try playing my very last card: "And if it kills me? If it really kills me? In a way I can't come back from?"

She laughs again. "Then I know some people who would pay a lot of money to watch Eve finally die for real."

What's awful about the scam we run is that we both know this wasn't supposed to be a scam.

• • •

The ad she took out in the classifieds read *"Underground Filmmaker Seeking Aspiring Actress. Beautiful Young Women Wanted. Bring Headshot."*

And then it listed her address and a time. Not even a phone number to call in advance.

The first time I saw her, it surprised me to see that she was a woman. I expected to see the type of sleazy guys I now know as her peers and contemporaries: hair just a little too long, skin a little greasy, dark circles under the eyes like they've been pulling all-nighters.

But Jezebel was clean and sharp and put together. All tailored pantsuits and tightly cropped brunette hair with no flyaways. Standing at her front door, I could have imagined I was safe.

She didn't smile when she waved me in. Her demeanor was clinical, as if she'd been dealing with a long line of hopefuls all day, as if I wasn't the only one there. "Headshot?"

I handed it to her and she took it without even seeming to look at it. She had me follow her through the house to the garage I know so well now.

"Sit."

There was only one chair. I sat like a good dog. What else was I supposed to do? I was in it deep enough.

"This project is a horror film," she'd said, as if we were already midway through a conversation, as if she hadn't shrugged off the formalities of saying hello, or asking my name. "I don't know if you've heard of my work."

How could I have? She hadn't put her name or production company in the ad. If she had, I could have looked her up and stumbled on the world of extreme underground horror and made-to-order videos from a safe distance. I can let myself imagine that I might have stayed away.

"This is what's called a screen test," she'd said. "It's to see how well you work on camera. How well you scream, how well you emote, whether you look natural or fake, things like that. We'll do a kill scene. That's what I need to see the most."

If I had known better, if I hadn't been distracted by a beautiful woman and a film opportunity, I would have questioned. Wouldn't I need some kind of blood pack, some red corn syrup to spill out of the fake wound? Shouldn't I have been told where to look, what was wanted? Of course, I didn't. I just let her wrap the straps on the armrests around my wrists, tugged against them when she told me to try and get out, and felt warm when she smiled because I couldn't.

I watched her turn on the camera and trailed her with my eyes as she stepped around from there, until she was directly behind me, and I couldn't see her without tipping my head back. Then I saw nothing, just the red light. I had to feel the knife in my guts.

The pain tore through me, and no relief came. The constant movement of her hand drawing the weapon in and out, puncturing me, sawing me apart, left no room to even breathe. I stopped having control. I was a thing that bled. I was meat, leaking.

The next thing I remember is waking up groggy, flat on the floor, aside from my legs, which Jezebel had been using to drag me.

"Huh," she'd said out loud, mostly to herself. And then to me, she said, "You'll probably want to change your name. And your hair."

The men who watch our videos (and it is mostly men) prefer blondes.

That was Jezebel. She watched my skin stretch over open wounds and reform itself until breath and blood flow began again, and she saw dollar signs.

She'd never have to recruit an actress again. Never have to worry about safety or special effects or burying bodies. She'd been killing girls like they were disposable for months.

I hadn't known I could come back from the dead until I had done it. How could I? I'd never died before then. But as long as I got a cut of the cash and time with her, I was happy to join in her enterprise. And then my life was hers. My lives were hers. My essential belongings were in her house, and she helped bleach my hair over her bathroom sink, and we slept in the same bed, and on-camera I went by the name Eve, and soon enough that was my name off-camera too. She never stopped being Jezebel to me. And we were matching, and biblical, and quickly in love.

It's not a bad way to live, dying horribly. There's a level of celebrity to it. The people who watch me, the freaks, they adore me. I give them something they can't get anywhere else. To them, illustrious titles like *"Blonde Gets Beaten With Bat"* or *"Three Minute Chainsaw Murder"* … that's their favorite movie.

Pain becomes a memory quickly, and there're no scars left. The only lingering ache is that the first time Jezebel met me, she thought she was killing me. She intended to kill me. And I didn't know, until waking up on her floor, that she couldn't.

I am the only person who knows what she does. Or did. Who knows about the girls. The ones she killed that didn't come back. I'm pretty sure she slept with them too. Often. If it matters.

It's a bitter thought and it's the kind I try not to think. But it's true about your life flashing before your eyes, and my life has looked like her bedroom for a long while now.

※ ─────────── ※

She moves towards me, crossing into frame from stage left. It only takes her a few long strides before she's inches away from my face. She leans in as if to kiss me, then pauses, glancing back over her shoulder. Spying the blinking red light of the camera, she pulls back, reverses her steps, and flicks a button until the light goes dark and it's no longer recording.

That's one of her lines. Her rules.

I'm comfortable being looked at by men in ways that Jezebel is not, and though the lesbian mystique helps sell tapes, I've learned there are things she won't sell out for any price.

She'll gut me and hold up my entrails to the lens for a week's worth of grocery money, but the kisses stay strictly off-camera. That much of us is not for their consumption.

She approaches me again, now free of the Peeping Tom's eye of the camera and kisses me for real. It's short, and it's careful. No hands in the hair, despite one on the hip, nothing that could disrupt continuity. When she pulls back, she's examining my makeup, making sure she didn't pull too much off of my lips with her own.

Satisfied, she returns to the camera and calls out "Roll camera," and then "Roll sound," despite her being the only crew member. The lonely tripod and freestanding mic sit quietly, as always, but her pretentious tendency towards tradition and ritual is unflinching. She cues me with "Action," and a wave of her hand, and then makes an identical entrance of long, confident strides.

⁕ ——————————— ⁕

The world of extreme underground horror is tight-knit but not friendly. No one trusts anyone and really no one should. It's all lies. We call what we sell horror movies, but no one's watching them to get scared. They're watching them to get off.

Jezebel, at least, drops the artifice of plot, which makes her more honest than most. Her realm is the short film, and so there's not much space for plot and buildup, save for a line or two from off-camera before the action.

You wanna see a girl die in whatever special little way you request? That's what you'll get. Send an envelope of cash and a written description, and you'll get a tape in the mail.

The dread and hope among creators and consumers in these circles is that someone might have actual snuff. Something about the underground world of unchecked practices entices some to believe a level of ruthlessness. A lot of things look more real when they're worse, and there's an understanding that some things just can't be faked, or faked with our budgets. When I talk to other scream queens, they tell me stories about real duct tape on their skin and lips, real ropes around their wrists, real knives too close for comfort.

The people cannot explain the filmography of Jezebel Jolie. It's not abnormal for a filmmaker to have a series of girls who appear in only one film and leave. Once they realize what kind of movie they're actually in, they tend to flee and make themselves hard to find. And once you've got one that'll stick around, that seems to like or at least tolerate the business, she starts showing up in all your projects.

Still, the angry and scared part of your brain, deep in the back, an evolutionary leftover, knows that it's seeing someone die. Knows that it is seeing real death.

And that would be enough to start asking questions. That gut feeling. But there's two important reasons why no one does:

The first: it's the same girl over and over. The frightened part of your brain can scream all it wants, but the rational part of your brain knows better, and if you talk to other consumers or order another tape, you will see the same blonde, dying once again, which is something you can only do with effects. If you're the sort of person who really needs desperate reassurance that you're not a disgusting slimeball, you can request a sort of post-credits scene of the girl: smiling, waving, looking right at the camera and saying how fun the shoot was. Very alive. If you're really lucky, you can meet her at one of the little conventions where these filmmakers trade their wares. For forty bucks, you can get a photo with her.

The second: if one of them is doing something horrible, maybe the rest are too. Maybe your favorite is. Maybe you'd have to stop watching.

Can't have that.

⁂

She slips the noose around my neck and tightens it until my breath comes out as an involuntary gasp. And then to each of my hands, she clamps a jumper cable. Their metal teeth bite into the flesh of my palms and the pain is already excruciating. My best movie tears are already pricking at my eyes. I could have just held them, but the pain is nothing for me and everything for the viewer. In this case, it's Jezebel herself, and her tastes are not to be questioned.

The point of the placement on the hands, aside from the striking visual, is that the electricity will shoot itself across my chest and through my heart.

I'll admit it's one of the more creative ways she's tried to kill me and it should be relatively quick, which is a bonus.

She'd shown me *Electrocuting an Elephant* when we'd first gotten together. One of her favorites from her truly fucked-up and depraved collection. It became apparent quickly that she was obsessed with seeing real death on screen; animal death footage was the easiest to come by.

She liked the film because she deemed it classier than the kind of grindhouse slime that only butchers real animals because the fake ones turned out to be more expensive. The Coney Island people who made the film imagined that they were doing the right thing, thought that gentle giant Topsy the elephant had gone bad, thought after she killed a guest that the punishment should fit the crime, thought the world should be let in on the spectacle. They killed her three ways that day, in a promise to the ASPCA, to make the death ethical by making it quick. Maybe it's an act of care that Jezebel only chose two. Maybe she can't afford cyanide. Maybe if she poisoned my breakfast this morning I wouldn't even know.

⁘

I've never seen myself regenerate and Jezebel won't film it for me. She says there's some evidence you just don't keep, even if you intend to delete afterwards. She says that Hitchcock said that drama was life with the dull bits cut out. She says it's not fit for filming. Not artistic. Dull bit.

And so I frequently wake up, whole again, with no memory of how I got there. Often, this is still on the floor of Jezebel's garage, in the same clothes from the shoot, even frequently in a pool of my own sticky blood.

But when we're shooting in the woods (a favorite location of no-budget filmmakers, because you don't need a permit), I tend to wake up back at our place, laid on the couch, or on the bed, a blanket wrapped around me. I think she's afraid the ground is too unsanitary there, like as my wounds close, I might get dirt and twigs in my precious insides.

Those are the best times I wake up. Not because I'm in the soft bed, our shared bed, but because I get to imagine her carrying me home.

⁘

She exits from the same side she came in and settles herself behind the camera, rolling her shoulders like she can finally relax. She meets my eyes and smirks at me. There's not a question. She's not going to ask if I'm ready.

She winks, one of those casual little actions that lets me forget who she is, what she does, how we met. Effortless flirtation reminds me of how easily I fold. Anything for a beautiful woman.

The thoughts don't last long, interrupted harshly by Jezebel moving her hand quicker than I can see, and the burning rips across my body. I lose myself in the waves of pain, no longer a living thing, but a ragdoll being shaken, convulsions and spasms flailing my limbs in time with bursts of stabbing and horrible heat. I feel like I'm bleeding from somewhere, maybe everywhere, maybe it's just sweat, maybe it's a phantom sensation. The instinct is to scream through desperate breaths but the rope around my throat forbids the action, every sensation too intense and overwhelming for me to tell if that rope is tightening or if the flesh of my neck and my pulse pounding against it only makes it feel that way.

It feels like hours, but must be only seconds, before the scene in front of my eyes fuzzes out at the edges like bad letterboxing and then goes black.

I wake with my face wet. The shock of softness against my back is startling, the shift in sensations from pain to comfort too sudden to bear. I gasp and thrash before even understanding where I am, until a strong hand holds me down.

It's Jezebel looking down at me, her eyes too focused and intense for my having just woken up, having just died.

"Is it blood?" is the first question that comes tumbling out of my stupid lips.

"Is what blood?"

"My face is all wet."

She pouts in an expression of utter pity, and suddenly I'm awake and aware enough to feel embarrassed. "You've been crying," she says, "since you started coming back, you've been crying."

I realize then that the softness is our bed, that she carried me here, and a fresh sob starts in the back of my throat. I cough on it, finding myself still sore there from where she hanged me, and realize with surprise that I must have been more awake than usual as I rose from the dead and though I don't remember it, I feel like it will hit me later. Maybe in my dreams.

"You hate me, don't you?"

Jezebel flinches back, something I've never seen her do. "What?"

"You miss how things were before. Before me. You miss the other girls. You miss the way they'd die and be gone. You didn't have to think about them after. Always new girls and new ideas and not tied down and now, now you're stuck with me. And I won't even lie and say you aren't. I'm this awful THING that doesn't die. And I won't let you go. I won't. And you have to keep me, because I know what you did. What you still do to me. And I'll tell. If you get rid of me." Hiccupping sobs make my body shake for the third time that day. "I'll tell."

"Baby, that's—"

The use of the pet name only makes me cry harder. "You want me dead. You want me really for real dead. That's what this is. That's what you're trying to do to me. And I love you, so I'm going to let you."

In my haze, I don't realize that's the first time I've ever actually said those words.

Jezebel is silent for a long while. It's not her usual silence, all calm and confident, because she knows she doesn't have to say anything to command a room. It's awkward and unbalanced, a frightened and fragile silence. She, for once, actually seems unsure, like she's choosing her next words carefully. She makes a good choice.

"I love you too."

I stare up at her as my crying ceases.

She clears her throat. "I love you too," she repeats, firmer this time. "I love you, and I love killing you. I want to kill you again. I want to kill you for a very long time. You're beautiful when you die."

"But am I beautiful when I live?"

"Death is the drama," she says, "life is the dull bits. The tedium. The first act of the slasher that's all about getting to know pointless characters and prolonging the slaughter you actually came to see."

When tears sting at my eyes again, she says, "I share my life with you, because you open a space for death. I chose you because you make the in-between time bearable. Because just lying next to you, I get excited, thinking about what you are and what you can do." She sighs. "Loving you is the first time I haven't felt like I'm just seeking an ending."

I lean up to kiss her, wrapping my hand around the space on her neck where a noose was so recently around mine. She kisses back even though I know I taste like tears and sweat and snot and static.

She's somehow more romantic than she's ever been, and not romantic at all, and it's easier now to play our parts:

Me, giving her my body.

Her, stealing my breath.

The Lady of the House on Legs

by Ariel Marken Jack

No one has ever accused me of being raised right. Even so, I understand the importance of bringing a thoughtful gift when visiting a lady. A thoughtful gift—in opposition to a thoughtless gift—reflects the preferences of the lady in question more so than the convenience of the girl who is giving the gift. A thoughtful gift is specific and displays understanding. I have thought about this for months. I think I have thought about this for years. Now that I have come to visit the lady—*the* lady, you understand, not just any lady—I am flooded with doubt over the gift that I have chosen. I do not know if it will suffice.

Dressed in my festive solstice best, I stand outside the lady's gate with my heart pulsing hard and my breath catching in my throat. The gift drips crimson warmth down my freezing hands. Her fenceposts are topped with sun-bleached skulls, their eye sockets glowing with greenish light. I choose to interpret the color of their flames as invitingly warm. I paste on my finest smile. The lanterns chatter their gleaming teeth. I cannot translate the sound into welcome or warning. I chatter back. I do not know what I mean. The gate swings open.

Tonight is the longest night of the year. I have snowshoed through miles of darkness since the sun went away. My home—such as it was—lies far behind me. By morning, my tracks will have been erased by the wind playing in the snow. I unbind my feet from the snowshoes with one stiff hand, undoing both leather bindings and my impulsive wish that I had not given my rabbit-fur mittens to someone whose need—and desire—I had no right to refuse. My other palm is warmed by my gift, but the red drips freeze along the backs of my fingers.

The lady's house does not belong to the earth. I stand as tall as a creeping thing can and bend my head back to look up. And up, and up. The scales on the leglike pillars reflect the green light cast by the skulls turning on their posts to keep their watchful glowing fixed on my uncertain progress. My rising gaze finds at last the distant tops of the scaly pillars—and there, among the stars, above the atramentous tops of the silhouetted trees, her house. My dream.

In another life, I dreamed of another house. Another home. Another type of fire—warm and inviting, true, but mortal in nature—and another type of lady to tend its hearth. I think of that lady's small hands encased in my rabbit mittens as they stuffed her into the sleigh, the ring that encircled her finger hidden under the fur. I did not attend the ceremony. I could not bear to watch her vow to obey—to love—anyone other than me.

I cannot climb with the gift occupying my hands. I tuck it into my scarf to keep it warm as best as I can against my cold throat. It would not do to present the lady with the remains of a life gone cold. I refuse to acknowledge the voice that persists in reminding me that this is exactly what I plan to do. As long as the gift still beats, it will surely be good enough for the lady—despite the lack of anything approaching warmth that remains in the life it represents.

My ice-slicked fingers find no purchase on the pillars' frigid scales. I grasp to no avail, and fail to even pretend I do not feel the skulls' staring holes in my back. Their white teeth chitter, mocking my pitiful attempt to rise above my lowly station. I turn and glare. "Hush!"

Another round of insolent chittering.

"Hush," I hiss again, through frost-cracked lips. "Hush, or I will pack your sockets with snow, and you will see nothing to laugh at—nothing at all—until spring melts you free."

Silence. If the skulls thought they could unnerve me, they knew not who they witnessed. I have no time to play with dead fools—and fools they must be if their fate was topping fence posts. I tell myself that I am no fool. I will not share their fate. I stare them down, hoping their green-lit eyes are able to take in my meaning. The quiet holds, but they do not look away.

I did not look away either when I helped her dress, this morning, for her wedding. Those small hands shook as she held the veil in place while I stabbed the pins through her coiled hair.

"Nothing has to change," she said. "He travels so much. You can—you can visit me when he is gone. He does not know what you are to me. No one does. And no one will know what happens between us when he leaves us alone."

I tidied the shawl around her shoulders, twitched her layered skirts into place. "You look lovely," I told her. It was true, but when she asked me to kiss her—for luck—I could not bring myself to touch any part of her. "It will spoil your paint," I said. "We worked too hard to make you look the part of the perfect bride." She gazed at herself in the mirror. I could not read her expression. At last she pulled the veil down to cover her face.

As I try, again and again, to climb the pillars, I think of the way her hands used to feel when she slipped them into mine. She was always the first to seek connection, whenever we found a way to be alone. I always waited for her to ask for what she wanted. I would not take anything from her that she did not first offer. Her hands were so slender, I felt as though they would snap if I closed my fingers around them too firmly. She sought me out so often and asked so much of me. I never thought she would accept as much, and more, from anyone else.

I rub my hands raw on the icy scales, but I can find no way to hoist myself off the ground. She was always better than me at finding her way. That is, in this life, no small thing. I tell myself that I wish her well. My breath burns like acid against my cracked lips. I exhale crackling mist into the blackness of the still air wrapped around the lady's pillars. Something sticks to the scales. It must be from the blisters I did not realize were rising from my lacerated skin. I crumple into the knee-deep snow. The skulls click-clack at my back and I know the fools are laughing at me.

Because no one could ever accuse me of having been raised right, the last thing I have any intention of doing is asking anyone for help. I have always understood that a goal I cannot reach by my own power is a goal I have no right to even dream of reaching. I do not like to ask for help. I do not ask for permission or even forgiveness. I have always understood that if I cannot find the right path on my own, I should not even exist. That the only thing which matters is what I have to offer to others. I do not think I took the lessons of my childhood properly to heart—I still, despite all I know, feel some desire to ask what might be offered to me—but I know how to act. I lie in the snow among the claws of the pillars' feet and try to force my chattering teeth to slow, my hungry mouth to stay properly closed.

She did not share my fear of asking for help. I suppose she knew that no one would think to refuse her. I cannot imagine why else she would have asked me to wait with her before she married a man she knew I could not bear—though I suppose she must have known that I would be unable to bear any man she married. I could not feel my fingers then, as I fumbled through pinning the veil to her hair, and I cannot feel them now. I did not accompany her to the ceremony. I stood and watched as her father lifted her into the sleigh and her mother bundled in behind her, quickly, as if to block any possible thoughts of escape. I did not cry out as the white horses pulled her away. I do not want to cry out now, but my mouth falls open. The darkness all around me pulls something out of the darkness inside me. I howl. The skulls fall silent again.

In the stillness after my echo dies, a motion from high above shimmers a trail down through the night. The pillars fold toward where I lie, as neatly as a letter, as softly as a fine linen sheet. I cannot think about the sheets she must be sleeping between. At least, I hope she is sleeping. I hope he did not hurt her. I hope he was not rough.

It is too dark to see the house with any clarity. The skulls' green flames provide poor illumination. I think it seems smaller than I had expected—far from the palace I imagined for such a lady—but I am not sure my eyes are capable of seeing anything clearly in this moment. Still, when the door creaks open, I creep inside. My hands leave bloody prints in the snow, to show where I have been, how low my dreams have brought me in search of unknowable heights. No matter. The snow is still feathering down, in great soft flakes, and the evidence of my downfall will be buried long before morning.

The lady has lit no fire in her hearth. I cannot see well enough to stand, and so I remain on hands and knees as is proper. Her floor is made of stone. It feels as cold as hard-packed snow. I cannot see where I should turn to politely greet the lady. I cannot even see if she is at home. I blink at the darkness and hope for a clue—a hint of light, some sound that is not merely the harshness of my faltering breath. I reach out a hopeful hand, wishing for a lantern, but it lands on nothing save air.

I am falling already, unbalanced from reaching too far, when I feel the house begin to move. The sense of the sky rushing down past the open door must come from the pillars unfolding at some speed, anxious to bring the lady's home back to its proper place in the sky. My frostbitten lip splits against the angular edge of what feels like the stone of the hearth, bursting and leaking, a rush of warmth down my chin to baste the gift still nestled in my scarf. I do not mind being injured if my pain improves the suitability of my gift, brings it more in line with the lady's tastes. I lie in the darkness, bleeding, and find myself willing to wait for as long as it takes.

Because nothing in the way I was raised was right, I find myself unable to speak when—a lifetime later—a doubled light crawls across my legs. I find no words when the beams come to rest on my face with the click-clack of teeth snapping humorous anticipation. The skull lantern dangles from the holy hand of the lady and I am unworthy of being heard. I should not even look, but I gaze into her eyes, and see her smile. Her teeth are sharp and black as frozen iron.

The lady's face, as sharp-edged as her teeth, and faintly green from the lantern's flames—the flames that half blind me, so I must block them out with my hand so I can see her—is everything.

"Out with it, girl," she says, the grind of her voice like a pestle cracking bones in a cold stone mortar. "What is it—a man? A quest? A mother—or stepmother? A vengeance? A curse?" She pauses, inspecting my bloody face. "I see. Another girl, then. Far worse than a man." She smiles fondly at the skull in her hand. The flames in its eyes flutter and flirt, but she is already looking away.

I see that she thinks I am like every other who comes to her hoping that she will give them her favor. The ones who think to trick her out of the justly earned payment she demands in return for succor. The ones who believe they are special and will be spared. I think of all the skulls that light her fence. No wonder their greetings were tempered with spiteful insolence, such malign humor. No doubt they are eager to see me learn that the color of my bones is no different from any of theirs.

"My lady," I manage, at last, unearthing the gift with trembling fingers. "Please, this is for you. A gift. I ask nothing in return."

I hold it up to the light so she can see that it is still steaming. The layers of red on my ragged hands smell of rusted promises and broken oaths. I only want her to smell what I smell. I only want her to see in my eyes that I will ask nothing from her. I have no home to return to, no place to hoard and covet stolen goods and stories. All that I have is what I have given to her.

It is my greatest shame that I have never given before what I give to the lady. I do not know if that girl who is sleeping between that man's fine sheets ever knew that I would give it to her if she only asked. I could not bear to ask and be refused. I do not know, if I had asked, if she would have come away with me. I do not know if she would have been happy to walk the woods with me until we found a place where we would not have to keep our feelings hidden. I do not know, because I could not give myself, my heart, and my love away without being certain my gifts would be received with a grateful welcome.

We used to dream, as girls, about the stories we were told of the witch who lived in a house on legs in the untamed woods. The witch who lived wild and free, flying the skies in her great grey mortar, crushing her prey between the stones and her sharp black teeth. We used to fear her, this wild woman who did—and ate—as she pleased. We were raised to understand that a woman was never meant to do—or to eat—as she pleased. We wondered sometimes if the witch feared us, the women who lived in cottages like thatched stone cages and never once gave in to our hungers. We used to think that the witch would understand the hungers we felt. I lie now before her, the witch, the lady, in abject supplication, and know I was wrong to imagine her that way. She does not belong to my girlish dreams. Neither does she belong to anyone's nightmares. The lady does not belong to anyone at all.

The lady's iron nails curve into the shredded skin of my hands as she takes my gift. I am too cold to feel what must be the delicious agony of her touch, but I am trembling as much from the simple fact of her nearness as from the eternal chill of her house. She does not step back as she raises the gift to her lips and parts her teeth to take a bite.

Because it could never be said that I was raised right, the heart the lady eats is only my own. A proper gift should be a sacrifice. The thing I tore from my chest as I watched the girl turn around in her mother's grip to watch me—standing silently in the doorway, making no protest as her father carried her off to marry that man—is nothing I value. She waved at me, her soft palms protected from the cold by the mittens I ripped off my rough, strong hands to offer as a wedding gift. They were warmer than hers. I wanted her to feel as warm as she could on her way to what would surely be a chilly bed. I knew she felt nothing for that man. I wanted, too, to be rid of anything that would remind me of what I had not dared ask. The mittens had been her gift to me on the previous solstice, in the days when I still felt hope. I did not want to be left with a trace of her if she would not stay with me and be mine.

The lady bites into my heart like an apple. The juice spatters both her face and, beneath her, mine. I gaze, half-blinded from the light and the salty heat. Something inside me knots like a fist, or perhaps a welcoming noose. The moan that hums in the lady's throat as she devours me is everything. I feel my body grow colder as the pulsing object clutched in her fingers slows. I open my mouth. The lady's leavings drip into me like a rare and precious wine, my blood transubstantiated, made almost holy, by her hungry touch.

We were raised to fear our potential, the possibility that we might become as hated as the witch in the wood. We were taught that our only choice was to be witch or wife. We were taught, of course, that a wife was the only good thing to become. I do not know how I never learned that a good thing was a thing I wanted to be. I want to be free more than I want to be good. I was—I *am*—a bad thing. If I will never be a witch, still what is left of me finds comfort in knowing that I will never have to be a wife.

When all that remains of my heart is the wet on her lips, the witch wipes her mouth. I lie on the hearth, too cold now to even shiver. She clicks her nails together and flings a shower of sparks across me. The fire leaps to life, crackling with the eagerness of all insatiable things.

"Well," the lady says, her lined face aglow, "that takes care of that. I suppose you'll be happier now that you've gotten it out of you."

She picks her teeth with what looks like a young girl's finger bone, a pale blade, delicate and small, bleached and well bitten. I wonder what else she keeps in the pockets of her robe. She does not wear an apron, and the fabric is stained. I lick my own blood off my lips and wonder if the back of my dress is on fire. The heat is almost unbearable now that I have grown accustomed to the cold. The house is moving from side to side. Far below, the snow cracks and crunches beneath its steps.

The lady, losing interest, turns away. The lantern's light turns with her, and the fire casts dancing shadows on her back. She wears a lovely lacy shawl, woven from some golden and glossy material that looks like every shade of blonde hair intertwined. My blood dries tight and sticky on my neck. I am forgetting how to breathe. I watch the lady turn from me, and I surge to my feet and reach for the hem of her sleeve.

Because I was, in this one way, raised right, I do not protest when my boldness is properly chastised. I glue my lips together and make no sound. I know when I have presumed. I was taught to take whatever I was given, to be grateful if it was not taken back as soon as I thought it was safely mine. I have never been grateful for how I was raised, but as the lady casts me down I feel glad that I was trained to accept rough treatment.

The lady sets the lantern on the mantel. It clacks its teeth at me, whether in gleeful malice or in solidarity I cannot say. I wonder how long the lady kept the girl whose face that skull once wore beside her. I wonder if she ever truly loved that girl, or if she simply took what gifts she was given as her due. I wonder if the skulls on the fence posts were special too, if she laid them aside when she found a new toy. I wonder if she thinks of me as a toy, or if I am only a momentary annoyance. I wonder if I should have tried harder to be allowed speech.

The feeling of the lady's fingers further parting the rough-edged opening where I impulsively removed my heart is more than pain. I feel myself being unstitched, unmade. As she opens me up, I feel the things I was made to be slipping away. I find, too late, in the ecstasy of the lady's fingers working inside me, the will to grasp for a freedom truer than could be found in giving my life away.

The liver the lady draws from me is dark and rich like the bruise on a too-ripe fruit. She slices it into strips with her nails and swallows them entire. I watch her devour my kidneys, gorge on my lungs. I watch her feast until she eats my eyes, and then I listen to the chiming sounds her black teeth make when they meet in my vanishing flesh. I feel my blood pooling on the hearth stones and I hope it leaves a stain.

I wonder if the girl I did not offer my life to cut herself before she went to his bed, if she feared his discovery that his fingers were not the first to dip inside her. I wonder if she thought of me when his hands touched her skin. I wonder if I will become a light on the lady's fence. I do not think she cares enough for me to replace the one she carries in her hand. I wonder if the girl regrets that she did not ask me, that we both waited for the other to ask until another—a man, who could not be refused—asked instead and then it was too late. I wonder if she will grind my bones or suck out their marrow and cast their splintered shells into the sickly green fire. I wonder if the light she puts inside my skull will illuminate more of the world than I have previously understood. I wonder if anything of me will remain when the lady has eaten her fill.

I learn, as my body is taken from me—as my gift is understood to be far more than I knew I was offering—that there is no end to wondering even while life is slipping away into frozen darkness. It is the longest night of the year. A lucky night for a wedding. I wonder if I could have held my own wedding if I had taken the girl by the hand and run away into the shadowed woods. If I had asked for what I wanted instead of waiting to see if it would be given. The lady does not ask before she takes everything she wants. I think that if the ones who raised me could see how quietly, how obediently, I take what I am given at the last, they might be proud.

To Wilt a Flower

by Maerwynn Blackwood

Laudna, as she now calls herself, sits within a hawthorn brush. Its profusion of vibrant green leaves creates a shield, concealing her from prying eyes. She finds solace amidst the intertwining branches and thorny spines, feeling both protected and isolated.

The estate she is indentured to burdens her with unending tasks, and each day of penance feels like a lifetime. The grounds she cares for are an assembly of hedges, statues, and towering plants that twist and turn to create an intricate maze.

Sheds constructed from reclaimed materials dot the landscape, their exteriors weathered and worn. Greenhouses made from scavenged windows rise like hodgepodge glass castles, each filled with vibrant flora and thick, humid air.

A fortnight after Laudna's arrival, her resolve wanes, a blend of desire and pain clawing its way to the surface. Her restless thoughts torment her despite the ache of her muscles. Memory blurs the book in her lap.

Emmeline reclined in her bed, freshly plucked petals that Laudna had painstakingly gathered and sorted thrown about her nude form, gleaming under reflected light from a hundred colored bottles stacked on shelves.

Frustration melded with yearning at the sight of Emmeline's spread thighs. Laudna was rough with her. Two fingers slid inside Emmeline without teasing, her body wet with the pleasure of Laudna's anger.

Laudna did not stop pounding into her as she sank her teeth into the paint-splattered skin of Emmeline's shoulder, hard enough to break the skin. Emmeline cried out, gasping as she marked her. Demanded that it be her name that tumbled from Emmeline's lips.

"Why do you torment me so?" Laudna asked between nips, but Emmeline never answered, only begged for more—always longed more.

The sound of crunching footsteps and shouts of effort jolt Laudna from her reverie, and jealousy simmers on her tongue like acid. She yearns as she follows the serpentine paths, seeking silence.

The original greenhouse sits to the right of the manor, a testament to both the grandeur of the past and the ravages of time. Its once-stunning stained glass roof, adorned with intricate swirling patterns, has caved in, leaving shards of colored glass scattered amongst the ivy within. Sunlight filters through the gaps, casting kaleidoscopic patterns on the floor and bathing the untamed plants in a warm glow.

Laudna marvels at the beauty of the unrestrained *Epipremnum aureum*, heart-shaped leaves, deep green and variegated grown massive, covering the walls of the once-sturdy iron framework.

Ferns and pothos sit in planters around the perimeter. They thrive in the diffused light, their leaves reaching toward the sky as if in defiance of the ruin that surrounds them.

The air is heavy with the scent of damp earth and the sweetness of flowers and foliage. Sweat coats Launda's forehead and drips off her nose.

Beside a raised planter, beneath the ruined ceiling, Laudna's eyes narrow on an unfamiliar shape beneath a thick cluster of leaves.

She creeps closer, ignoring the sound of workers and the crunching wheels of a soil cart. The shape struggles to clear; her steps hesitate on the stone floor.

Full, pink lips between verdant leaves. Is there a painting hidden beneath?

Time is stationary as Laudna inches forward.

It is not a painting, but a woman's face and neck that lie tangled within the vines. Her eyes are closed, and the long lashes cast shadows on her still face. The cheekbones are high and pronounced, her skin too pale and tinged with a blue hue.

Mere steps away, Laudna's eyes trail down the curve of the woman's neck to her pert breasts obscured between the lance-shaped leaves. A nipple lays exposed, peaked and perfect. Excitement flares just as a wave of nausea crests her stomach.

Laudna's mouth fills with saliva, her body's desperate attempt to stave off the inevitable. She stumbles backward blindly toward the entrance, her movements clumsy and frantic.

Pothos shake and rustle, her hair catching their aerial roots in her panic.

Hot bile surges up her throat, and she clenches her jaw. Familiarity turns her insides into a churning cauldron, and her steps stagger over the uneven ground.

Laudna bursts out of the greenhouse, breath coming in ragged gasps as she races through branching paths until she is out of sight of the hothouse.

She collapses, her body wracked with violent heaves as she expels breakfast. Her eyes swim in a vision of her lost love.

Emmeline lay on the floor, her dark hair a sea around her face. The shop shelves stood bare, perfumes empty and scattered, their stoppers discarded. She wore a nightdress, her skin gone icy, and her body exposed to Laudna's gaze.

Her grief was veiled. Even in death, Emmeline's delicate beauty was striking. Laudna knelt beside Emmeline and looked into blue eyes that would never see again. Longing wet her thighs, and her popped mouth opened a small 'o'. Emmeline would enjoy this hold over her.

Laudna's gaze drank in the visage, Emmeline's nipples visible through the sheer fabric, crowning firm breasts that no longer rose nor fell. She traced them with a feather touch. The cold tantalizing, she continued lower, dancing over the curve of her waist and the swell of her hips.

The sweet, intoxicating aroma of Emmeline's perfume lingered, and Laudna leaned into her, inhaling deeply. God, she smelled good. Her hands went up and under the thin gown.

The path is known.

Laudna's fingers brushed against Emmeline's soft pubic hair, a whimper thick in her mouth. She needed this. Her fingers rubbed the flesh between Emmeline's thighs; the coolness of it sending a wave of clarity through her.

She jerked her hand away from the corpse and heaved onto the floor.

Bile and chunks of dinner erupted from Laudna's nose and mouth, and she choked on it. Gagging at the taste as she blinked away tears.

Emmeline's sightless eyes locked on Laudna's shame.

Days merge into an agonizing blur of sweat and broken fingernails. Laudna's mind is clouded.

The workers bustle around her with their trays of soil and carts of seedlings, becoming an incessant buzz, their presence a constant foe for her restless curiosity.

Each time opportunity arises for her to return to the crumbling greenhouse, fate intervenes with another tedious task. The days are a fruitless hell that offers no reprieve from her thoughts.

The faces of laborers blur into insignificance, their features obscured by the woman buried in foliage. Something dark stirs within her, something she cannot ignore.

Is it Emmeline who lies there, hidden within the leaves?

Barely dawn, Laudna slips from her shared sleeping room with electric energy that sets her nerves on end.

It is quiet save for the crunch of her feet in the dirt and the servant's soft murmurs through the manor's open windows.

A rich tapestry of ivy drapes the greenhouse gate, forming a verdant curtain of varying shades.

Doubt gnaws at Laudna. What if the woman is not there?

The soft leaves tickle her face as she ducks through the doorway. Laudna breathes in the sight, her mouth agape. The raised flower bed is just as she remembers it.

Basking in the warmth of the sun, the woman lies oblivious to the eyes fixed on her exposed form. She is a vision of loveliness—smooth stomach above gently rounded hips, her skin porcelain, tinged with the bluish-green hue of the lance-shaped leaves adorning her. Slender limbs intertwine with the vines, hidden beneath the thick canopy. Her long and straight fuchsia hair is crowned with blooms of various rosette hues.

Laudna's voice trembles, barely audible as she whispers, "Hello?"

The woman remains motionless, unyielding. Transfixed, Laudna gazes at her with reverence. Instinct extends her hand and gently rests it on the woman's arm, searching for any sign of acknowledgment. No flicker of recognition passes over the beautiful face.

Tracing her fingers down the flower woman's forearm, Laudna marvels at the blend of velvety softness and the supple resilience of the lanceolate leaves. Her palm rests against the woman's flat stomach, feeling its warmth and the gentle rise and fall of her breathing. With hesitant movements, Laudna continues stroking lower, her gaze trained on the woman's serene face.

Laudna pushes aside the foliage, desperate to see below the woman's hips. Clusters of pink flowers—*Dianthus barbatus*—cover her pubic area, concealing her from Laudna's searching eyes.

A cold sweat forms on Laudna's brow, her mind consumed by brackish guilt. The image of Emmeline shimmers before her, causing her hands to waver in their exploration of the flower woman's soft flesh.

A soft mewl escapes the woman's lips, piercing the air and sending a shockwave of terror through Laudna. Startled, she recoils, stumbling back in disarray.

A pot, holding a rabbit foot fern, shatters into a cacophony of splintering ceramic, littering the floor with a chaos of shards and soil.

Consumed by a suffocating wave of cowardice, Laudna flees. Her legs, weary and protesting from labor, propel her forward with desperate urgency, seeking solace from contrition.

The sun beats down on the garden maids in a spiteful display of radiance, the day not even half spent. Laudna carries two buckets of water to the orchid house, her muscles straining with the effort.

No thoughts bloom within her other than those of Petal. A seething mix of anger and frustration simmers beneath Laudna's flushed skin, fueled by the gnawing longing that has settled deep within her bones.

A wicked smile spreads across Laudna's sunburned face. With calculated recklessness, she allows her foot to catch on an uneven patch of ground, her body pitching forward as the buckets slip from her grasp.

Water splashes across the ground in a frigid cascade, and Laudna collapses, her knees buckling beneath her. She cries out in pain, her voice cracking in the sweltering air.

The force of the fall is genuine. A dull ache spreads through her knee, but she welcomes the pain. It frees her from the laborious hell with but a frustrated sigh from Taskmaster Ellis.

Laudna limps along the familiar path toward the manor, her pain replaced by a slick anticipation. She rounds the last corner, only to find the wrought iron door swung wide open. Silence urges her forward, her stomach sinking low in her belly as she realizes Petal is awake.

In her horticultural bed, the enchanting being stretches languidly, her flawless face lifted towards the sun. Petal's torso rises from the earth as she rests on her elbows, her hair adorned with living veils of flowers flowing behind her head.

Petal's eyes, blue like the afternoon sky, lazily shift towards Laudna, and she speaks with a voice as soft and melodic as a summer breeze. "I felt your touch before," she murmurs, her gaze unwavering. "It was … pleasant. I crave more." Her breathy cadence sends a pulsating throb between Laudna's legs.

Words threaten to remain lodged in Laudna's throat as she steps closer. "I need to know more about you," she whispers, her voice barely audible. "Do you possess a name?"

Petal's pouted lips curl into a slight smile. "I do not," she replies. "But you can give me a name."

"Petal," Laudna breathes, her name already chosen. "It suits you."

A warm blush spreads across Petal's high cheekbones as she beckons for Laudna to sit beside her, and Laudna eagerly obliges. She gazes down at Petal, who blinks back at her with eyes that hunger for pleasure.

"May I touch you again?" Laudna murmurs, her eyes on Petal's slowly grinding thighs and the answering sway of greenery.

"Yes."

Laudna's hand settles under Petal's left breast, the pad of her thumb gently stroking over her pebbled nipple. Petal's mouth pops open in a moan so soft it could have been a sigh.

Adrenaline courses through Laudna, and she pinches Petal's nipple hard. A shock of pleasure reverberates off the plant-dampened walls.

"Lower," Petal whispers. "Here."

Petal shifts, angling her hips. Her creamy blue thighs part slightly to reveal more of the delicate pink flowers that exude a familiar, sweet scent.

Desire turns Laudna's vision red around the edges. Her fingers tremble as she reaches out to trace the blush buds with a feather-light touch. Letting Petal's anticipation swell, Laudna lingers for torturous moments before dipping lower to explore the soft folds below.

Petal is wet and needy. The light strokes of Laudna's fingers cause a tumble of moans to unfold from her rosebud mouth. She lies beneath Laudna, eyes half closed in bliss. A thin film of sweat coats her beautiful body, and the flowers on her lower abdomen grow damp and fragrant with the spicy scent of her arousal.

Laudna leans forward, her mouth hovering over Petal's wiggling lower abdomen.

Petal's eyes widen. "Oh … I—"

Laudna doesn't hear Petal; instead, her tongue flicks out to taste the salt that clings to her skin. Laudna's fingers trace the outline of the buds, parting them to half reveal a perfect vulva. Petal's hips buck upwards and Laudna closes the gap in response, pressing her hot mouth against Petal's desperate pussy in a chaste kiss.

The greenhouse melts into obscurity. Petal writhes under Laudna's attention. Laudna flattens her tongue across Petal's open labia, licking slowly up and down, pulling her tongue away just shy of her clit in a merciless dance.

Petal writhes against her face, pulling Laudna's mouth closer until it becomes an altar of fervent devotion, worshiping the pinnacle of Petal.

Laudna attempts to guide Petal's legs apart, the peek of her dripping entrance breaks the last of the fragile composure Laudna has, and in a swift motion, she splays Petal's legs wide.

Amidst the rustling leaves, a grotesque crunch reverberates through the air. The sound of fibers splitting and roots tearing under the strain of abrupt movement.

Petal's eyes well up with unshed tears, and a sharp gasp escapes her trembling lips. She takes slow, shaking breaths as the mingled scent of crushed leaves and vanilla permeates the earthy air.

Laudna can only gaze down at her, lost for words, captive by a bewildering mix of emotions. Raw need trickles down Laudna's thighs, a primal ache that pushes her to continue. Tightness spreads through her chest and her vision tunnels, the periphery fading into a murky abyss.

"No, I'm sorry," Laudna manages to whisper, her voice barely audible above the clamor of her pulse. Laudna stumbles to the open doorway, her trembling legs wobbling under the weight of her desire. The world around her wavers, a distorted panorama of shapes and colors. Each breath is thick, a desperate struggle akin to drowning on dry land.

⚜ ——————————— ⚜

Emmeline. Emmeline.

Laudna's skilled fingers carefully plucked petals a vibrant shade of violet, her heart ached with each stroke of Emmeline's paintbrush, her lover's attention fixated on the curves of another woman.

It took weeks of trying and failing to create something unique enough to enrapture the wild spirit of her love. Morderebellis rubra. A flower whose scent is a blend of ripe fruits that conceal an olfactory concoction, one holding the power to awaken longing and wrap its tendrils around the heart.

This was the only scent for Emmeline.

Laudna combined its allure with the comforting warmth of vanilla and the exotic spiciness of cardamom. It was time to present her gift.

Emmeline stood before her work, slender fingers coated in brown paint. Laudna pulled her smaller body into her, crushing Emmeline against her chest. She was stiff, her face turned into Laudna's chest.

"Oh," Emmeline breathed.

She tucked her head into the crook of Laudna's neck, and her upturned nose brushed against the fragrant spot where the perfume had been applied.

"God, it smells good. Did you make it?"

Laudna's chest swelled. "I created it just for you, my love."

Emmeline flicked her tongue against the spot, and Laudna pulled back her restraint, a frayed cord pulled tautly. A moan escaped Laudna as Emmeline kissed the spot again, her mouth feverish as she began to suck and nip. Emmeline was hers again.

Petal consumes Laudna's every moment. Ellis keeps a firm eye on her as the large orders are carted and hauled away for shipment. With her body aching from days of exertion, Laudna feels the weight of her desperation pressing down, molding it into an idea.

Laudna drops her burden and searches through the nearby shed and wagons of discarded supplies. She does not find what she seeks.

The nearest greenhouse is teeming with white bougainvillea blooms, their pristine petals like freshly fallen snow. In a crate of broken tools, she finds her quarry—a pruning shear blade, severed at the joint from its twin.

Laudna eases the point into the crook of her arm and slices downward. White-hot pain shoots through her, and she grits her teeth, suppressing the scream that buzzes behind her clenched jaw. The gentle flora scent of the room mingles with the metallic tang of her blood. Her thoughts are far away, her lips already tracing a path across Petal's downy skin, tender in her adoration.

If each drop of blood could purchase a single moment with Petal, Laudna would willingly bleed herself dry this afternoon.

"Laudna!"

A cry shatters the stillness, jolting Laudna into abrupt awareness, the bloody object slipping to the ground. Her head snaps around to the entrance of the greenhouse, finding Ellis. Chest heaving, a mix of panic and disbelief is reflected in their gaze.

"You ... you need help, Laudna," Ellis stammers, their eyes darting between Laudna's self-inflicted wound and her wild stare. "Let me guide you to a place of rest. We can speak to Mr. Enfield upon his return."

Laudna remains silent, her weight shifting onto the balls of her feet, her thin lips pressed into a taut line. Paleness washes over Ellis, their arms instinctively reaching out in a gesture of peace.

The discordance of a barking dog ruptures the tension, and Laudna exhales with ragged breath, her demeanor softening.

"Do as you must. I will retire to rest," Laudna utters weakly, her voice calm.

Ellis does not trail Laudna toward the manor. Blood seeps steadily from the wound, its depth a testament to the quality of the blade. Her walk is slow, impeded by drowsiness.

Laudna's eyelids are heavy, the ground bobs up to meet her as the fading day morphs into another place and time.

Laudna sat at a heavy wooden desk scattered with glass stirring rods and pipettes, her hands stained dark green and trembling in the dim candlelight.

A bronze still was clutched at a distance from Laudna as she wafted the scent in her direction. It was divine.

Through a drawer Laudna rummaged, her fingers finding the small tin of beeswax. She applied it to the crook of her neck meticulously before doting the sweet-smelling liquid onto the spot.

The moments were slow, waiting for the burn of the oil, but it never came. Relief flushed Laudna's cheeks, the risk intoxicating. Precisely like Emmeline.

When Laudna opens her eyes, the sky is a blanket of darkness, pierced only by the faint glow of stars. She lies prone, feeling the dirt and grass pressed against her face. Her wound throbs in rhythm with her pounding heart. Distant shouts echo from somewhere in the darkness. She knows she must go.

Laudna stumbles along the uneven footpath, surrounded by towering hedges of English holly and looming trellises draped with ivy. Her name seems to reverberate from every direction, a disorienting discordance that blurs her vision.

Moonlight filters through the branches, casting eerie patterns on the ground. The greenhouse sits ahead, nestled neatly beside the manor as if concealing a hidden treasure. Laudna barely manages to stumble through the door before collapsing into a heaving lump on the worn floor.

Petal sits upright, bathed in the pale celestial light, her doe eyes filled with concern. "Laudna! What happened to you?"

"We need to leave, my love," Laudna pauses, taking a heavy breath to steady herself. "We can't stay here any longer. Things have changed."

Petal hesitates. "I … I want to be with you, but … what has changed?"

Anger flares in Laudna. Does Petal not love her in return? "I would never let anything happen to you, Petal. The truth is, I don't know why you are here or what is to be done with you. There are men out there looking for you." Laudna pleads, her lie flimsy but sweetened by the distant cry of Ellis.

Petal glances down at her abdomen, arched eyebrows furrowed. "Done with me?"

"Men are cruel to lovely women."

And Petal is so very lovely, her long legs slightly parted to tease Laudna as she approached. Laudna's urgency mounts as the shouts grow louder, but her aching body is slow to obey.

"We must hurry, my love," Laudna whispers.

Petal's hands find their place on either side of her makeshift bed, her frail arms quivering as she fights to lift herself. Faint breaths slip through her downturned lips, while a hint of surrender tiptoes near the surface of her eyes.

Laudna coaxes her forward, her words dripping with tender encouragement, as she reaches out to firmly grasp Petal's wrists, pulling with her with a quick tug.

Petal breaks free.

The sound of plant matter shredding fills the air as fibrous roots and tendrils, woven into Petal's now exposed spine and ribcage, rip apart.

The vines that twist around Petal's ankles snap, leaving trails of sap and blood. Beneath the skin of her backside, a lattice of vascular tissue pulses and writhes in time to the beating of Petal's heart.

Shock threatens to darken Laudna's world, but she shoves it down; she has to keep Petal, the damage has already been done.

Petal gasps on feet never made to walk. With each faltering step she takes, her body shrivels and decays. Vitality seeps out of her as if through a sieve.

Laudna grasps at Petal's broken waist to steady her, only to touch sinew and tendrils coated with a viscous liquid. The roots that held her anchored tear her muscles asunder in their death writhe.

A grimace of agony distorts Petal's face, her aquamarine eyes feral with terror. Guttural sobs force their way out of Laudna's throat as Petal crumples like jelly, slipping through her feeble grasp.

Hands slick with a mixture of Petal's blood and sap, Laudna rakes at the puddle of Petal. Her hands blindly claw in tangled, curly hair, the color wrong.

Emmeline?

Stars spin overhead and reality slips through Laudna's fingers as easily as sand. She plunges her face into the still-warm mass of her beloved. The sludge fills her nose and mouth with the taste of vanilla so strong it burns her eyes, forcing them closed.

Ellis's cries morph into mere whispers on a cold wind. Laudna's consciousness laps against the shore of her receding life, her airways filling with fetid plant matter that tastes like home.

Teratoma, Cacodaemon, Erinya

by Avra Margariti

The boil is tender at first, yielding-soft like a berry and subtly warm to the touch. It sits snug in the crook between Anastasia's neck and left shoulder. If she bent her head in its direction and let her ear rest against the reddened nodule—cradling the boil in the curved ear canal—she wonders if she might hear a susurration, like a seashell giving away the ocean's secrets.

But there is no sea here. The only shell is the life she contorts herself to occupy. No time for secrets, or for lumps fever-warming by degrees from the side of Anastasia's neck. She has a train to catch through her smog-washed city clinging to a past of stained, ancient marbles. An office cubicle to roast in under a broken air conditioner too expensive for her boss to fix or replace. She has the appearance of normalcy to maintain or else, *or else*. That was true even before the queer boil materialized overnight.

On the way to the office, a loop of the morning news plays on the subway announcements screen, cobwebbed with cracks and corrupted pixels like the rest of the graffiti-tagged wagon. The news anchor talks about the recently passed laws; it's all the TV and radio ever want to talk about, leeching the topic to a desiccated husk.

"We are so very close to a return to tradition, combating the low birth rates and the rise in crime and degeneracy."

There are other words, too. Not spoken, but breathed in the interstices of static, subliminal spaces where the past reaches festering fingers to infect the stagnating future. *Shame of the nation. A sin violating nature.*

The boil in Anastasia's neck—concealed under a fluffy turtleneck—sweats hot and throbbing all the way to the office. Anastasia wears a skin whose needs should go unnoticed, unremarked, *unfulfilled*, or else they risk drawing all the wrong attention to herself.

Yet she can't help sneaking an unsanctioned break to inspect her neck anomaly in the women's bathroom. Her haze of morbid curiosity is potent enough to make her careless as she bumps into Marina, her coworker.

They stare at each other with ichthyic-eyed awkwardness.

Marina looks away first, blinking as if her corneas burn. "About that company party last week … what happened there cannot be repeated. It's not safe, or right."

"I understand," Anastasia says, remembering the salty scent of Marina's core, as if she contained a small ocean between her legs. The blight on Anastasia's neck must remember, too, because it pulsates with the skin-memory of thirst.

Marina's hands tangle in her blouse before she catches herself, straightens out her creases. A pristine façade. "I need your discretion on this. Please."

It had been Marina dragging her inside a bathroom much like this one during the company party. Locking the door behind them. Making Anastasia kneel.

"I understand," Anastasia tells her coworker once more with a mechanical cadence, but she doesn't, not really.

Nothing has made much sense lately. In a way, the node on her neck is the least absurd thing to have happened since the new government, new legal campaigns, old fear not exorcised but made brand-new through the repetition of history.

"Wait!" Anastasia calls out on exhumed impulse. "Wait. There's this thing, on my neck, could you please check on it?"

Marina leans in, as if pulled by gut hooks. Yet her meek unease soon transforms into sneering disgust. "There's nothing here. It's just another ploy to get me involved with you. I knew it was wrong. You led me on."

Marina scurries away as if chased by the mythical Erinyes: winged, clawed enforcers of the natural order.

Anastasia is left standing in the doorway, lost like a stray. It strikes her then that the boil grew on the spot where Marina had last sucked a bruise, latching onto her neck with teeth and tongue after barely a drink and a smile. That same spot Anastasia's fingernails scratched raw afterward to keep the bruise longer. A mark only she knew was there.

⁂

In the morning light, the abscess coruscates with teeth and hair and eyes blossomed overnight. *A teratoma. There's no other word for it,* Anastasia thinks. The eyes are a mud-brown veined with crimson blood vessels. Spheres nestling in a bundle of hair that is less eyelash and more animal fur. The teeth protrude as milky little nubs, shining pearlescent in the gray-tinged dawn light.

Anastasia wonders if this is what the news mean about people like her getting what is coming for them. Some latent guilt resurfacing into the form of an Erinya—chthonic Fury born from the sins of her flesh, here to punish those who dare defy what is natural and moral. Anastasia's lymph nodes swell with it—but is *it* the personification of remorse weighing her down like in the old wives' tales? A leaden demon on her shoulder bending her double until she repents?

The thought of debridement is as fleeting as it is futile. She has no sick days left at her office job, no insurance-covered doctor to visit if the open wound turns into a bacterial playground.

Anastasia watches the morning news—a fear-born, flea-clingy habit she cannot shake. The new laws make public displays of affection illegal, but it's only certain people this affects. Only certain couples who get fined and imprisoned while others walk away with merely a warning. Smiling politicians orate with grandfatherly compassion: *the modern world has become so complicated, hasn't it? So why should we not make it simple again, free of guilt and confusion? Don't we owe our wayward children that much? Should we not guide our monstrous kin into the cleansing light?*

Anastasia brings a pocket mirror to her neck; the teratoma eyes watch the news as well. Fixed, unblinking from their thick thatch of hair spurting out of her straining pores.

She snaps a quick picture of herself with the eyes visible upon her body and posts it on her social media, but no one mentions the teratoma tumor in the comments. A friend from primary school asks if she cut her hair. Several unknown men comment *hello doll, hello beautiful, check your dms.*

Cancer took her father and great-aunt, but she suspects this growth is something else. Perhaps something saved not for pious relatives, but for transgressive daughters.

Marina 'likes' Anastasia's Instagram photo from her public account. Then, seconds later, she messages from the encrypted chat app they had been using. *If you don't stop pursuing me, I'll tell everyone you forced me into it. You turned me, like a vampire.*

The surplus eyes read the text above Anastasia's shoulder. They blink their crusted lids, the sound like arachnid legs scuttling across floorboards. It's not entirely unpleasant. She likes to believe the teratoma's fur rustles in something akin to sympathy against her ringing ears.

When Anastasia falls asleep on the couch after work, bathed in the TV's cerulean light, she makes sure not to squash the cells of enamel and keratin growing on her shoulder. Her teratoma Erinya has no full-formed mouth with which to speak, but as she drifts off, its whistling breath settles over her like a lullaby.

The next day, Anastasia's teratoma has grown a full head: a skull shrunken to the size of a nectarine but enlarging by the second. It brings to mind the anatomical sketches and old photos of conjoined twins.

She remembers being told as a young girl that she had eaten her identical sister in the womb. *That's why you are always so hungry now, so greedy,* Mother had pursed her painted lips and said, while Father watched on in silence. *This is why you are always wrong in your wants, your depraved appetites,* was implied. And it was true that in her dreams, Anastasia often saw that twin sister she had allegedly devoured. In those dreams, she did more than devouring. Amid an oneiric pink haze, her sister entered her body again and again, coiling inside Anastasia's under-developed womb, begging to be born anew as was her stolen birthright. A possession by the dispossessed.

In young Anastasia's mind, the guilt of having absorbed her sister in their mother's belly and the shame over her own belly stirring with undisclosed desire for other girls her age somehow interwove, wires crossed into fearful, lustful night terrors that no child psychoanalyst could extricate into coherence.

"Are you an Erinya manifested out of my wrongdoing?" she asks the stunted head. "My sister come back to haunt me from the infant asphodel fields?" No reply originates from the second head, only gentle, tuneless humming, like the gurgle of blood from a fresh cut.

When Anastasia stretches her neck in the opposite direction, she can still see the Erinya out of the corner of her eye, sprouting from the junction between neck and shoulder. Nestled in it like a small mammal. But tonight, Anastasia has a date to prepare for. It wouldn't do, in this political climate, to be seen not caring about her dating prospects with the opposite sex, or to be neglecting her appearance. Not at her age. Not with a target on her back. But how to hide a second head, if indeed it is visible? It's not as simple as hiding one's vices from the public eye.

She rides the train with her neck uncovered in a plunging blouse, yet no one spares her a second glance. From the droning news feed, a psychiatrist discusses the best ways to detect deviants in public. "Sometimes," she's saying in mock sympathy, "environmental stressors combined with a genetic mutation can cause a monstering of sorts. An unsophisticated method, regrettably, but still the best way to ascertain a person's unsavory tendencies at first sight."

Anastasia looks around the wagon, where everyone is focused on screens or pages, not paying a crumb of attention to her and the second, smaller head mushrooming from her shoulder. Pseudocephalus, theriocephalus. *Fake head, beast head.* She laughs. Someone shushes her without looking up from their paperback.

The diminutive skull nods gently along, pendulous with each rocking motion of the subway wagon. The crown of the Erinya's wan head smells like sulfur and marigolds. Anastasia catches herself breathing the scent in, the way one would do with an infant's curly hair.

Opening the matchmaking app, Anastasia checks on her date, who already waits for her at the grill house. He is earlier than scheduled, yet impatience still imbues his every text. She considers riding the subway to the end of the line. Her Erinya coos, as if catching the tail-end of her innermost thoughts. Still, Anastasia steps off the train and onto the platform when the time comes.

It would be foolish not to. It would be unsafe.

Her date owns a name with too many syllables and not enough personality to carry the legacy on his shoulders. Alkiviadis wants to know about her body count. How many men Anastasia has slept with in the past. "Two," she says, and it is not a lie. Two unfinished times, unfettered in their awkwardness. The number of women is a different story, unspoken but suspended midair like an aborted breath.

Her date wants to know if she plans to have any children. How many of them? Anastasia thinks about the news claiming queers are the ones responsible for the newest wave of anti-natalism. She thinks about the Erinya like an embryo crowning from her body, tissue growing from her tissue, and giggles into her wine glass.

"What's so funny?" Alkiviadis asks, chest puffed out at the perceived insult. "You need to ask these things early on. Weed out the weird ones and the degenerates."

At that last word, the guilt-demon on her shoulder seems to rouse from its half-slumber. It stays alert through the arrival of their orders, seared meats, and it unleashes cooing noises at the sound of Anastasia's voice. Soon, the two of them are harmonizing in a strange duet. When Alkiviadis dominates the conversation—about his job security, his wage and promotion, his two cars and yearly vacations throughout Europe—the teratoma bombinates furious hisses.

Alkiviadis excuses himself to the bathroom. Anastasia slumps in her chair, but her Erinya has other plans. It tugs and squirms until Anastasia's torso leans across the white-clad table, and the demon spits sizzling bile into Alkiviadis' wine. He drains his glass upon his return, his face soon turning jaundiced with the alien poison. Retching, he rushes to the bathroom once more. This time he does not return.

For the first time in years, Anastasia ignores the posters plastered all over the streets and subway; messages about thin pills and half portions of food to make oneself an attractive date mate. She scoops heaping spoonfuls of mashed potatoes into her mouth, then moves on to her runaway date's buttered steak, licking the plate clean. Anastasia swipes an unladylike fingertip through a glob of gravy. She lets the fat-coated finger hover above her shoulder, until she feels a warm, worm-like tongue lick it clean. The Erinya's tongue retreats, slapping the roof of a half-made mouth in toothsome appreciation.

After her cautious experiment, Anastasia grows bolder. She feeds the beak of the Erinya's mouth crumbs from her dinner roll, crunched between chitinous mandibles. Anastasia pets the curls matted against the Erinya's mishappen scalp as she finishes her meal at her leisure. For the first time in a long while, she feels no guilt for having eaten so much. No need to apologize for staying in the restaurant after her date absconded.

For taking up space in the world.

<hr>

The Erinya grows bigger. Grows stronger. No more an *it* but a *she*, as Anastasia knows one morning with clairvoyant clarity. Her skull no longer resembles a shrunken head specimen, or even an infant's soft-plated scalp. In fact, the Erinya's head is quickly matching her host's in terms of length and width, all but fully formed from the neck up. She has spiny teeth, deep-gouged blood-shot eyes, and hair spun from the night sky past its witching hour.

Conjoined, Anastasia thinks for the second time. Yet the larger the Erinya grows, the lighter she feels upon Anastasia's shoulder. Her presence no longer creaks her host's bones. Unlike the vintage illustrations of sinners plagued by cacodaemones, Anastasia isn't bent over double under the pulverizing weight of her guilt. Her spine feels the proudest it has ever been, she realized last time she admired herself and her teratoma creature in a shop's windows.

Not parasitism then, but symbiosis.

"Darling," Mother intones, snapping her fingers before Anastasia's face to earn her wandering attention.

Mother sits at Anastasia's sunken, secondhand couch with obvious distaste, watching the evening news to avoid looking around the tiny, cluttered apartment. Anastasia's demon hisses her own antipathy. Mother doesn't notice, or pretends not to. The television broadcasts more lies about Anastasia and those like her. Her mother eats everything up like tender morsels. Anastasia realizes she hasn't listened to the news in weeks, ever since she started nurturing her Erinya instead of starving her.

Mother clears her throat, swiping a finger down the coffee table overtaken by a foggy patina of dust and water stains. "You live in such squalor, my sweet. I don't know why you insist on singlehood. I told you, didn't I? The moment you find a suitable groom, the family home is yours and so is your trust fund."

Anastasia thinks about the shitty office job that pays barely enough for this fifth-floor studio apartment, ramshackle but hers. She thinks about her grandparents' two-story, the one Mother hopes will one day house a star-cluster of grandchildren. Anastasia remembers growing up there as an only child, a black sheep. The barren garden and drafty hallways. How everywhere she went, she felt watched, felt wrong. Overshadowed by the ghost of that so-called sister who didn't live long enough to disappoint her family like Anastasia had done countless times.

From her shoulder perch, the demon shudders in solidarity, as if some vestigial part of her remembers Anastasia's memories as her own.

"There's still time, Mother," Anastasia placates through the clenching of her stomach.

"Not if you're ever going to give me grandchildren," Mother adds, frowning at the discount-store tea Anastasia offers her. She keeps the used teabag on a saucer. Her Erinya enjoys gobbling it whole, throat bobbing snake-like on the way down. The demon murmurs her approval. She nuzzles against Anastasia's cheek, as if bolstering her for the conversation to come. "Your dating prospects will grow slimmer once you're past childbearing age. You'll be a government target, like those deviants. I know you had your little girlfriends when you were younger. But surely, you've outgrown all that by now?"

On the TV she hasn't willingly watched in weeks, a talk show discusses the Erinyes. The mythological chthonic deities, but also the psychosomatic manifestations of sin. Yet her own Erinya is visible only to her. Anastasia wonders if the powers that be are even certain of the beings' existence, or if they're trying to fearmonger those most vulnerable into conformity.

There's nothing scarier, after all, than a being you can't control growing from your body, gnawing on your nutrients.

Like a baby, Anastasia thinks, while mother drones on about future grandchildren. Babies stealing calcium, iron, folic acid. Embryos turning their mothers into brittle bestiaries to bear their fetal monstering. Bones weakening, clumps of hair and teeth falling like constellations of broken glass.

Yet Anastasia's skin, hair, and nails have never felt this healthy, this lustrous. Even Marina at the office noticed, her eyes lingering on Anastasia longer than necessarily. Hungry, too. Anastasia ignored her, instead leaning her head into her demon's netherworld warmth.

"You owe me a baby," Mother mumbles forlornly into her teacup, "after devouring your sister in the womb."

When Mother concludes her weekly visit with an air kiss and a dismissive wave, Anastasia marches to the TV. She doesn't switch it off, but unplugs it entirely from the wall, her Erinya rejoicing with mewls and toothsome lip smacks.

It's another week before Anastasia feels her Erinya—all grown-up now, not a cub but a crone—extricate herself from the fork between her host's neck and shoulder. Anastasia isn't afraid when that happens. In her midnight-drenched bedroom, she merely grits her teeth through the pangs of separation, the skin unfusing, the once-boil bursting open for her demon to crawl out of its sunken mound. The former abscess exudes a profound abattoir smell, permeating the small apartment. The entire process is neither brief nor easy, but Anastasia writhes exultant, encouragements falling from her lips as her demon births herself from her neck wound. The demon hums and croons, as if soothing her in return. Already Anastasia knows the Erinya is ready to fly the nest, and already she misses her somewhere diaphragm-deep.

Still, it won't be goodbye until dawn.

Soon the Erinya lies dewy and grub-pale on the mattress beside Anastasia, articulated limbs stretched out to match her full height. They face each other, Anastasia laden with perspiration, the Erinya with blood. They are both slippery things, one reaching for the other in mirror-image concert. And as they stroke wet fingers down each other's cheeks, Anastasia knows the Erinya isn't the twin she absorbed in the womb. She is a monstering all her own. A teratoma born not of punishable sin, but of righteous, repressed rage.

"I know you have a job to do," Anastasia says, "but I will miss your weight, your presence."

Her fingers push limp curls away from the Erinya's wildly protruding brow. She, too, runs her peregrine claws down Anastasia's face, thrusting a finger into the comfort of the mucus-ringed neck cavity. The same recess that had nourished her until the Erinya was viable enough to detach and survive on her own.

The Erinya leans forward and so does Anastasia, until their lips meet in the middle of her pillow. Her demon must have exchanged her beak for a mandibled mouth. Tendrils of coarse black hair coil around Anastasia's own, the iron and salt of creation shared with each string of saliva stretched between them everlasting. The Erinya coos and so does Anastasia, no longer in need of things so frail and fallible as words.

Her neck wound aches sweetly with each twist of taloned fingers, but Anastasia knows no infection will take her into its festering fold. The cavity recognizes the body it cradled for months, the foreign turned familiar. Anastasia's hands roam the Erinya's back, where ridges jut out from her shoulder blades. Tender pouches for vestigial wings, just beginning to unfurl.

When dawn draws near in strokes of mauve and magenta, Anastasia drinks in the sight of her slowly irradiated Erinya. A beautiful, grotesque commitment to memory.

At last, the Erinya squelches her hand out of the fluttering neck wound, offering its puckered edges a parting caress. One last spiked kiss is split between lips. The Erinya unravels a pair of leathern wings from the bilateral pockets in her back. She prowls to the apartment's cramped balcony and climbs, hunchbacked and clawed and naked, onto the balustrade. Anastasia trails her outside, though she knows she cannot follow her former symbiote skyward.

In the purple-plumed sky, several winged pinpricks fly toward the clusters of city lights not yet extinguished by daybreak. The darksome shapes are not birds, but other Erinyes like hers, so many of them it looks like the sky is foaming at the mouth. The news was correct about one thing. The demon once-perched on her shoulder was indeed a guilt-consuming being. Only, it was not *Anastasia's* shame the Erinya was created to devour, but the shame of the nation.

Anastasia remembers the old stories, before the media twisted them into new, self-serving configurations. How the Erinyes were the Furious Ones: Underworld deities meant to punish wrongdoing on earth; to shame humanity for committing crimes against its most vulnerable.

The winged being and the rest of her kind will feed and feed on the rot of the world—the sanctimony of it all.

Anastasia will be safe, as will be those like her.

She watches the Erinya borne of her flesh take flight. A peculiar, squalid grace permeates each flap of webbed wings. The taste gathering in Anastasia's mouth is a bittersweet one. Screeching into the night, the Erinya soars toward those with succulent guilt to spare.

Torbalan's Gift

by Grace R. Reynolds

Yana wasn't afraid of death; she was afraid of pain. Fearful of teeth tearing into her flesh, gnashing sinew away from the muscle. She imagined her bloody limbs stuffed and seeping through the linen sack on Torbalan's back. How many times had the creature ripped apart someone's body in the forest where no one would hear a sound? She arched her back and let out an ethereal gasp—

If this was death, then she welcomed it gladly.

Forget me, Yana wished, plunging into the forest. She prayed the fairies and woodland spirits heard her plea, but it did not matter. These woods were dangerous, and the jingling coins sewn into her saya dress did nothing to help conceal her. She considered stripping it off, but she needed something to keep her warm through the night. Something, perhaps, she could use to bargain until she found him.

Torbalan. She must find the monster of these woods. No one knew what he looked like. Perhaps he was a shapeshifter, a devil shrouded in damask, humors of the body oozing through its threads. Torbalan was a baby snatcher, a devourer of children who did not heed the warnings of their babas and dyados. Hunter of the lost, the never to be found. Yes, Yana would find this demon. If she didn't, she was sure that what awaited her back in the village was a fate worse than death.

Yana tore the red veil from her head. She rebuked the protection from presumed evils lurking behind spruce and birch trees. Her only hope—to be consumed.

The gaida's shrills from the wedding celebration propelled her further into darkness. They did not notice their bride's absence; there was still time to disappear before a search party came to collect her. She would not go back. She would not marry Damyan.

Her mother reminded her more than once that Damyan was handsome and well-off, a good match, but Yana heard the rumors. Women did not survive long in his keep. Where had his first wife, Vasilka, disappeared to? And did Ginka, his second, really die from a weak heart? Yana wasn't willing to find out what would happen to her as the third.

Sweat dripped at the nape of her neck. Yana's heart hammered against her ribcage. If monsters could exist in the village, why could they not exist in the forest? The cold closed in, suffocating Yana like weighted fabric on her body. She stilled. The woods pulsated through miles of mycelium under her feet. They urged her to run, but Yana could not. He was there, just as she hoped.

The towering figure loomed from above. His body was twisted and gnarled like the trees around him; the ruddy sack on his back the only indicator of who he was. It leaked, putrid with the scent of rotting meat under a hot sun.

"Stop." A grunt echoed from his throat. He held a hand up, shifting his weight underneath the sack. "Do you not know what I am, child of the forest?" he asked, his voice low and tenebrous.

"I know what you are, who you are. You're Torbalan, and today's the day you'll kill me."

Torbalan stood, unnerved by her presence. Could he not see the pain stabbing Yana's heart? Did he not hear the urgent, raspy call of the chukar bird, spreading her news all the way through the valley? How the forest dormouse squeaked from its burrow, fearful of what lay in wait for her? The gadoulka's strums quickened, its melody, buzzing with fury, cut the tension like a knife. The forest's whispers reached the hollow pits under Torbalan's temples where his ears should have been. His gaze averted to the tree line from whence Yana came. If there was understanding, it did not show.

"What are you waiting for? Will you kill me? Or will you allow them to force me to fulfill the role of the wife I do not wish to be? I don't want to be a homemaker or bear children for a man who's more likely to murder me than love me for anything more than what my body's capable of." Yana fell to her knees. "That's all I am to them, a body. And that's what I am to you, I suppose." She wiped away the tears welling in her eyes. "So, tear me apart already! Erase me from this earth because I don't want to exist in it anymore as I am."

"And what is that, exactly?"

"As woman," she seethed, "one that does not conform to what is natural of my sex. One that will submit to no man. One that defies what nature intended for me."

Past cuts and bruises that mottled his face, Yana saw the pain in his eyes as if she were the one that plunged a blade into him.

"And what is it that nature intended for you?"

Yana grimaced and let hot tears stream down her cheeks. She looked into his sorrowful gaze once more and said, "That I am to love a man. Submit to him. But I will not. Cannot. It brings me no pleasure to think about his naked body on top of mine." Yana paused, considering her next words carefully. "I yearn for pleasure elsewhere ... from women, like myself. My mother knows it. The priest knows it. My husband-to-be knows it, too; and still they have sold my freedom to love and be loved by whoever I want for a God I do not even know exists."

Torbalan paused before he drew nearer. "They took your freedom from you?"

"Yes," she breathed. Torbalan lay his hands on her shoulders. She braced, her heart hammering against her ribs like a bird trapped in a cage.

"I will give you your freedom back if that is what you want," he grunted.

"In exchange for what?" Torbalan plucked the saya off her shoulders, leaving her in nothing but a tunic beneath. Yana froze as claws cupped the small of her back, lowering her to the ground. Incredible and sharp, pricks of their cutting edges traced the curves of her body, scraping the sides of her breasts. She did not need to look down to know they pebbled under his touch.

"I will help you harness your power if you let me." A knowing look rested between their eyes, an innate trust. Yana nodded, and Torbalan sank between her legs. He leaned in, his breath hot against her sex before gliding his tongue along the folds of her inner lips. Yana's back arched, wanton with desire. She ached to drown him in the taste of her as she grabbed a fistful of his hair.

Yana never wanted a man in the way she wanted Torbalan. He was not a man, though. Her mother, the priest, Damyan—all said her desires were monstrous, that she was an abomination. So too, would she be monstrous with Torbalan, and they would fall into ruin together.

"Don't stop," she breathed. The crisp earth on her back and the heat of Torbalan's tongue flicking against her clitoris made her circle her hips and push her pelvis further into his gaping maw, begging him to enter. She wanted him to devour and consume her right there as she ground against his tongue once more.

"Speak your intention, Yana. What would make you free?" Torbalan sucked, bringing her closer to her peak.

Yana threw back her head and released a moan. A raven flew above her, its silhouette cutting the twilight. Death was nigh. Yana felt it hovering from above, waiting to descend upon her like a carrion bird ready to pick at the scraps of flesh Torbalan would leave behind.

"I want to fly, Torbalan; I want to be free of this form forever!" She rolled her eyes back, intoxicated by the rush of pleasure. All she could think of was that bird circling above and wished nothing more than to be as free.

Yana was breathless—the peak of her orgasm flooded Torbalan like a tidal wave of magic pulsating from her body through the woods. She floated, forces of ecstasy and mystery shaping her into something new. Yana didn't know what it was, nor did she care. Transformation was something to be savored.

The crackle of thunder. Bones shattering under the weight of claws. Teeth grazed Yana's skin and stripped away ribbons of flesh. Claws that cupped her breasts buried into her chest cavity, squeezing the heart pumping life through her veins. What remained melted and slid off her skull and digits to make room for new shapes. New angles. The pain was horrible and beautiful; feathers sprouted, and a deep ache burned her entire body.

Yana was overcome with wonder and fearlessness, a feeling she expressed with a loud croak. She was different now, something whole. Invincible, even. As Yana emerged from the gristle and viscera of her old form, she stretched out her arms to take flight. Yana looked to Torbalan, satisfaction written on his face.

"Go, Yana! Fly! You have wings now; fly to freedom! Let the winds carry you to wherever you wish. To whomever you wish. These woods will not hold you here, child. You are as nature always intended you to be."

Yana nodded the tip of her obsidian beak in thanks. She looked toward the heavens and flapped her wings. The thrill of another first prickled under her feathers as excitement beat through her chest. No going back now.

Yana kicked back in the dirt and took flight.

⊷═══════⊶

Where is she? Where is that bitch? Damyan leaned against the stone and stucco of a nearby house as he stumbled through the village in a drunken stupor. His baba warned him about Yana, that she was different, but he didn't care. He would straighten her out, bend her to his will like a blacksmith hammering steel.

The shrill of a bird, a raven circling in the last rays of twilight above. Dusk descended upon the valley, a chill settling with it. The villagers warmed their spirits with rakia, and Yana was nowhere to be found. "Come dance with us!" someone called out to Damyan as his family prepared for the horo. He waved them off, taking a bottle with him, and found himself on the forest's edge.

He stared into the darkness, willing her to return. This is where she would have gone, the only place no one dared venture through. Monsters lived in these woods, but she, too, was a monster. There was nothing to fear for her here. Damyan leaned his head back and downed the last of the rakia before crossing its threshold.

Birch trees reached their scraggly limbs and tugged at the frieze coat he wore. Damyan swatted them out of his way, his ears hot, a fire smoldering in his chest.

"Come out, Yana! Stop hiding, you bitch!"

It was no use, his voice deafened by the woods that encircled him. The hoot of an owl, the brush of leaves somewhere from the west, and the unmistakable outline of a giant standing thirty paces before him, secluded by the shadows.

"Who are you? Come closer, coward!"

The figure didn't move. The stench of rotten meat permeated Damyan's nose. It made him double over and retch until he could breathe once more. The croak of a raven neared, and the figure stepped toward him. Damyan got to his knees, ready to barrel into the stranger with all his strength.

"So, you have found her then, yes? Good." Damyan spit on the ground. "You can have her. She's a disgrace to her family, to her culture, our village, our God—"

The glint of obsidian talons—piercing hooks into the soft whites of his eyes. His corneas and sclera eviscerated. Screams caught in Damyan's throat. The world was dark, and warm liquid trickled down his cheeks. Gravity betrayed him as he felt his body lifted off the ground, unaware of who or what held him in its grasp.

Bones splintered through skin as Damyan's body folded backward from the harsh impact on the earth. The smooth sheath of a bird's beak thrashed the nerves and muscles of his eye sockets. Viscous. Determined. Hell-bent on plucking out the gray matter of his brain.

"How does it taste, Yana?" Torbalan asked as he stroked her feathered skull.

Yana thought it tasted like mercy. It tasted like freedom.

Her Tongue, a Slippery Slope

by Evelyn Freeling

If hell has nine circles, her fingers are the first. Gently, they urge me toward my eternal destruction. Their tips graze my ankles, yet her touch ripples through the rest of me, everywhere and all at once. They trace my skin, inch by delicious inch, as she slides my linen gown up and over my head.

Her oil slick eyes are the second, dark yet gleaming in the dormitory's shadows while they devour my form now laid bare.

With the third circle, her palm, she traverses my swollen belly and paces around me, never letting go, nails clawing my flesh possessively, claiming the unborn child I know she cannot have. Her arm binds me against her. Her breasts beneath her black habit press into my back. The fourth and fifth, respectively.

The sixth trails up the column of my neck, her nose breathing me in deep and stealing the air from my lungs. The seventh circle belongs to her velveteen lips pressing into my skin, the eighth her sharp teeth nipping at my ear.

But her tongue, my God, her tongue is hell's center.

With every dart against my skin and word whispered in my ear, she slides me headfirst into damnation. Each night inside these sacred walls, she devotes herself to my destruction. Each day, as I pray my rosary, I promise our Father in heaven that I will do the right thing and march to Mother Superior's office, that I will put my eternal soul and that of the unborn child inside me before my selfish desires, and yet …

And yet.

I tumble down, shuddering from adrenaline as her legs entwine with mine and our most intimate of places kiss in a mockery of a pilgrim's prayer. Even the fear penetrating my veins as her mouth twists into that demonic grin cannot cool the molten heat she summons between my thighs or dry the well of desire dripping from me.

"Say it," she demands in a voice deeper than her own, a voice that echoes and reverberates through the room, not one but many. "Say it."

My lungs tighten as if the evil lurking within her is fisting them, wringing the words out against my will. They escape my lips at the precise time her slickened channel sends me hurtling over the edge.

"It's yours, you can have it," I say, though it sounds more like a scream.

I collapse to the bed, panting, skin pearled with sweat. She sprawls next to my pregnant belly and traces with one finger strange shapes that burn long into the night like brands. She whispers to the unborn child inside me, speaking a language I cannot understand, or an amalgamation of many languages that bleed into each other.

"Tell me again," I say over the susurrus of her nonsense, but it continues unimpeded. "Tell me where we'll go after this. What we'll do," I try again.

Still, she ignores me.

"Why do you want it?" I ask instead.

Slowly, her head turns toward me, swiveling on her neck a hair too far, as if the thing lurking within her wants to remind me. The corners of her mouth curl upon themselves too severely, not natural, not human.

"I want what I can have," she says.

"And me?"

Her grin never falters. She crawls down my body, hooks my knees over her shoulders, and vanishes behind the pale hill of my belly as her tongue parts me and sends me sliding to hell.

⁂

She feeds me, spoonful after spoonful of bland noodle soup until I'm bursting. In the bleak light of day, under the watchful eyes of the sisters and the other so-called fallen women, the evil tucks itself away. She almost looks the way she did the first day I arrived at the convent—feet aching, shivering and soaked from a hard rain. No glint of malice haunts her eyes, though they're still darker than the chestnut color I recall. Her smile curls gently …

But the evil reappears when I refuse another spoonful of soup. Then, she wets her bottom lip, silently promising my reward if I'm obedient. The same way she did all those months ago, when the first circle of hell still taunted me with accidental touches. A brush as we passed in the hall, a lingering squeeze of my arm after I perfectly recited a scripture. A bite of her lip that could have meant anything.

"You're eating for two," she says, her voice seemingly her own.

Mother Superior nods her approval as she stalks the cafeteria tables. "Very right, Sister Theresa," she sings more than speaks.

The other fallen women shuffle into the cafeteria with their necks bent, beige uniforms stained with sweat and steam, backs permanently stooped from toiling over laundry. Some prostitutes, others runaways or unwed mothers with their stomachs now deflated. Mother Superior catches me staring and raps her cane on the table.

"Pay fallen women no mind," she says. "You have hope yet."

Sister Theresa lifts the bowl to my lips, forcing me to drain its last drops and giving me a glimpse of the ingredients she's secreted into it: nail clippings, one of her hairs, and I detect a distinct coppery tinge. The hair catches in my throat and I gag, but I don't pry it from my mouth. She's tangled inside of me already. Her smile twists into that rictus grin as she uses her thumb to wipe my lips, dips it in against my tongue, and permits me to suck.

My thoughts should be of the unborn child inside me, but my toes curl at the perversion, flaunting our sins in plain sight. I am the picture of control. Mother Superior displays me each week the priest arrives to check upon the convent's good work, her proof that reform can be successful. Calm, serene, surrendering to my lot in life with my chin held high. Supposedly, that's me. Yet, I'm spiraling.

Down.

Down into the widening pit of the hell that is my tormentor's maw, her tongue its slope.

* * *

Mother Superior watches me from beneath the habit shrouding her head, hands clasped atop her desk. Stained glass windows loom behind her and dim the daylight sifting in, but as I settle into the chair, the effect is less like a small chapel and more like a nightmare I might've had some time ago. Shadow slants across Mother Superior's perfect face. She's held her title for twenty years, yet her skin is a smooth canvas for the darkness, not a wrinkle or a sunspot to give her away. Ageless as a statue. A guess anywhere from thirty to sixty could be accurate. Pale blue eyes regard me under fans of blonde lashes, but she says nothing, only waits.

"You wanted to see me?"

"Yes," she says, "I thought I ought to check in on you. How you're doing."

"You want to know how I'm doing."

"The baby is due any day now," she reminds me. "Usually around this time the unwed mothers come into my office to beg for their babies. 'Please, let me keep him.' 'Please, don't give her to strangers.' That's what I like about you, Marianne. You're so empty of pride."

Jesus's gaze from his crucifix high over her head weighs heavily on my skin.

When I say nothing, she continues. "You haven't even asked who they are, what they're like. Your faith in us is something special. That you believe in God at all amazes me, after everything you've endured."

She searches me. Whatever she finds makes her click her tongue. "To be used like that," she says with a shake of her head. "I'll never forget that tale. Oh, you must think I judge but yours is every woman's story. Opening your legs to a man because you chose his love over the Lord's, only to discover the hard truth: men's hearts are fickle. Only the Lord's love is everlasting. That was how it happened, wasn't it?"

My lie is a pair of nails being driven into my ears. They clang through me with every hard hit of the hammer. Still, his silhouette moves in the darkness of my room whenever I close my eyes. When I lurch awake, breathless and drenched in a cold sweat, it's not because I've dreamt of falling, but of his hand on my shoulder, turning me over. His eyes scanning me in my Sunday best the next morning, his thigh pressed against mine in the pews as he sat between Mother and I.

"It was," I say.

She smiles, but I can't tell if it's sad or knowing or perhaps something else. Perhaps both.

"You mustn't feel guilty that you don't care what becomes of your baby," she says. I flinch at the phrasing, at the possession of it, but she doesn't notice. Or maybe she does. "You're doing what you know is best. You will be rewarded for that. Normally, after an unwed mother gives birth, she joins the other fallen women in the foundry, but I want to make you one of us. Would you like that?"

"I haven't thought much about what comes next," I lie.

Each night my hell encircles me, so too do its promises, ones made months ago that first night Sister Theresa stole into my dormitory. I didn't know then what I know now, hadn't yet seen her rictus grin, and yet the truth has done nothing to loosen my grasp of fanciful possibilities. Growing old together beyond the convent walls.

"You believe in God, don't you? In heaven and hell?" she asks, tilting her head at me as silence stretches into a fragile thing, broken by the muffled footfall of sisters beyond her office door. "Well, it's something to consider. Your soul is eternal, but this life is long and the world is full of monsters. You're protected here."

"They are good people," I say, "aren't they? The parents."

She chuckles, but the sound never quite reaches her eyes. "Oh, yes. I think so. Well, only God knows a person's truth, but they seem perfectly acceptable according to the church."

⁕⸺⸺⸺⸺⁕

Dark shapes ripple over Sister Theresa's body. Shadow transforms her into a night-cloaked sea, fathomless and unknowable. Her tongue dips. Her fingers dig into my flesh, never penetrating me where he once did. I try to throw myself into the pleasure she offers, but each time my eyes roll into the back of my head, his silhouette moves in the darkness.

I know what it is to be used. To be turned into a thing not of your own making. A person degraded into the rag doll of a bored child, tossed aside, handed over to another who will eventually grow tired as well.

I unhook my legs from her shoulders and pull away as much as my swollen belly allows. Every movement is tedious and slow under the burden of the unborn child inside me, though. Sister Theresa pins me by my hips. Her mouth curls into something like a snarl, more animal than human.

"Where do you think you're going?" she asks.

"You can't have it," I say.

Her laugh is low and sardonic and erects every hair across my body. It makes her larger than she is. For all the circles of hell her body holds, she's several inches shorter than me, and with this creature growing in my womb, at least thirty pounds lighter. But her dark chuckle rumbles my dormitory walls and suddenly she dwarfs the entire room.

"It's too late for that," she tells me. "You're mine. Your choice is sealed."

"Choice," I spit back at her and struggle to roll onto my hands and knees, to hobble up from my bed and ignore her saliva oozing between my thighs like juice from poisoned fruit. "What choice have I ever had?"

She prowls toward me while I stagger away, but her voice is saccharine, bidding me closer. My feet obey. At first, they root in place, but then they drag across the cold stone floor, step by step, as if my body is not my own. The first circle strokes my cheek, the seventh kisses my neck, the ninth licks in a long line up to my ear where it whispers, "I do not relinquish what has been given to me."

My hand moves of its own accord, and I only realize what I've done when my palm stings and the clap of flesh against flesh rings against a leaden silence. Her head swivels on her neck, and for a terrible moment, she doesn't move. She only stares into the dormitory's shadows, her mouth ajar. When she looks at me again, her oil slick eyes are lighter—a chestnut brown gleaming with tears rather than wicked delight. A sharp gasp draws between trembling lips, and she releases a keening sob that makes me stumble back a step.

"Marianne?" she says. Her gaze darts down my naked body, then hers, brow pinched with what looks like genuine confusion. "What's happening to me, Marianne?"

She buries her face in both hands and wails. I'm not sure what I expected, but it wasn't this. My arm is rigid as I reach for her, forcing myself to pat her on the shoulder, but it does nothing to calm her crying. I step closer, the rat that I am, lured into her trap so easily.

In a single movement, she closes the distance between us and presses against my pregnant belly painfully. Her lips envelop mine, her tongue forcing my mouth open. Liquid, rancid, yet cloaked in sweetness like the reek of a corpse hidden behind bouquets of roses, pours from her and into me. It chokes its way down my throat, its path through my body cold and acute. I try to jerk away, but only when she lets go am I free. Red sludge, dark and clotted like menstrual blood, sputters between my lips. It splashes against her pale form, but she lays herself down, laughing as it splatters her body, and she spreads her legs.

Laughing as she massages it into her, as her back arches into a bow and she brings herself to a climax while I continue vomiting.

⁕⁕⁕

Jesus stares down from Mother Superior's wall, but every stolen glance finds the tears streaking his hollowed face as dark as the blood that gushed from my throat last night, and I can taste it all over again. Smell that rancid, sweet reek cloying in the air as if she has stained my skin with the same permanence that she's sentenced my soul.

I am hers. I accept that, but the unborn child inside me has hope yet, even if it is born from a tainted womb.

Mother Superior watches me from beneath the grim shape of her habit, hands clasped patiently atop her desk. But where to begin, how to explain that one of her own is possessed or perhaps not. Perhaps it's simply her. Beasts dress themselves in their Sunday best once a week, secreting themselves into pews like wrong ingredients in soup.

"You asked me if I believe in God," I begin. "I've seen the devil. I've seen devils all my life. If hell's real, then heaven must be too. I don't want this child, but maybe it deserves a chance. A better chance than I ever had."

"I'm not sure I understand," she replies.

"It's Sister Theresa," I say, and that seems to be enough because Mother Superior nods as if she suspected as much all along.

A drawer sighs open and she places on her desk a knife so small it could be a letter opener, but its metal blade winks in the dim light. It sits between us, waiting as patiently as she did moments ago.

"And if thy hand causes thee to sin," she says, "cut it off. It is better to enter life crippled than with two hands to go to hell. And if thy foot causes thee to sin …"

She trails off as I return her nod. The silence is taut, unbroken when I pick up the blade, certain what I must do, interrupted only by a sudden burst of warm liquid splashing between my thighs as I stand. Murky liquid, yellow and tinged with red, spreads across stone.

"It's time," Mother Superior says as she rises. "Are you ready?"

She paces around the desk, but she doesn't usher me away in a panic, only opens her office door and sweeps an arm out toward the hall. I waddle through the convent's narrow corridors, Mother Superior trailing like a shadow in my wake. My hand trembles around the dagger clenched to my belly, and I fight the contractions panging through me. One by one, sisters fall behind Mother Superior. All is quiet. Only the sound of feet and habits whispering over stone accompany my hammering heart. My knuckles tighten, my decision made.

We find Sister Theresa in my dormitory, undressed and sprawled on my bed, limbs spread and daring me onward as if she has known all along what I'm here to do. My shadow looms over her, but her mouth curls into that rictus grin. Her heart is right there, hidden beneath flesh and bone. And yet, she was the one who dried the tears God never touched.

She stands and I try to back away, but Mother Superior and the sisters are a wall behind me, penning me in. I don't know if Sister Theresa takes the small knife from me, or if I give it to her. Either way, my hand is empty.

Mother Superior pulls my gown up and over my head. "We never would've let this happen to you," she says, breath hot on my neck.

This slope is slippery. I've been tumbling down all this time. The first circle brushes my aching belly. I land in the seventh as Sister Theresa presses a kiss to my neck, in the eighth as her teeth claim my skin with a bite, the ninth as her tongue flicks against my ear. There is no love in her touch. Once, I convinced myself there was. I needed her to be different, but I know now.

All beasts are the same, devils and gods alike.

MODERN ART CURSE, MIXED MEDIA

by Hailey Piper

If you loved her more, she would still be alive. She would've been home at night instead of wandering that warehouse in search of inspiration.

Or maybe if you loved her less, that might have saved her instead. She would've taken her broken heart out of this brick-and-smog city, driven a thousand miles away, and never met whatever monster took her life.

Either way, her death has to be your fault. You need that semblance of control while sitting in this cramped interview room with a detective who doesn't care.

"Well, I think that covers everything," says Detective Apathetic, handing you his card. "But let me know if anything else comes to mind."

You take it, but he's asked you nothing. Where's his partner? Why isn't someone checking your whereabouts last night, taking samples, verifying an alibi? Don't cops investigate the significant other first? Her girlfriend should be suspect number one.

Not because you did it—that would have taken more effort than you've put into this relationship in a long time—but the absence of suspicion feels sexist. Or homophobic. And if Detective Apathetic can't manage the basics of investigation, how's he supposed to find your girlfriend's murderer?

There's a hitch in your throat, the first physical manifestation of misery since you found out you won't be waking up beside her tomorrow. Cough past it. Get angry. *Demand* he suspect you, then rule you out.

Detective Apathetic listens and then smirks. "Whoever did this is strong, and you're—you. No offense."

<hr>

You recount this to your crowd of friends at the bar that night. There's nowhere else to be but home, and you can't go there. Not yet.

"But she was so tough," your friends say, as if to deny the murder.

"Cops say she put up a fight," you tell them, rubbing your hand against your forehead. It smells of dust. "They asked about enemies, jealous exes. But we're friends with you all."

The gathered friends nod. All exes of each other, and you, and she who can't be here.

"Maybe it's someone from before she knew us," the friends suggest.

You entertain the possibility there has been someone in your girlfriend's social circle whom you don't know. Or don't know as well as you think. The entire world might writhe with girlfriend-slaughtering shadows, the kind to beat her half to death and then finish the job with a blade to the eye, stealing her life, future, and dreams.

The tears come hot and sudden. You thrust your hands over your face, and the friends herd close with sympathy and cooing and a shout for another round of drinks.

You slosh into the apartment like a rolling barrel of alcohol, the drink filling your gut, your skull. Your clumsy hand misses the light switch, but you go on stumbling. Bang your shin on the coffee table. Catch your hip on the sofa, spin around, and then tumble hard onto the floor.

She would laugh to see you this way. And then she would lift you in her tree trunk arms and carry you to the bedroom. She made love seem easy, even when you didn't make it easy. Always badgering her to clean up her workspaces, keep her art out of the living room and kitchen, shoving away her paintbrushes, stained aprons, and the magazines and newspapers she tore apart for scrapbooking and mixed-media pieces.

You harass her absence in her place, shouting through your empty apartment to clean up this marble countertop, that corner stacked with issues of *Harper's Bazaar*, all of it. Get your house orderly. You march drunkenly as if ushering the mess to follow until you reach her art studio.

Your hand manages to hit the wall switch, lighting the cramped room. Newspaper pages mat the hardwood floor. Paintings of mountains, rivers, and naked women in relaxed positions dot the walls, offering windows to sweeter worlds. Junk flows from every corner.

At the studio's center stands an easel, where a once-white canvas now drips garish colors and oily menace.

Her final painting, *Lady of the Dark Hand.*

Black paint wreathes the edges, while the background glares with bright magenta, sickly gold, and resplendent turquoise. The painting's center hosts a tall figure in a cardinal-red coat. One black-gloved hand hangs almost daintily at her side. The other clutches a glass blade alongside a great white grin, aimed at the small wasteland of black crackle paste where your girlfriend meant to paint a face and finish the painting.

But she never will. Its completion is out of her cold lifeless hands.

Another round of crying fights the last round of drinks, and the latter wins. You make it out of the studio and halfway to the bathroom before vomiting in the hall.

⊶⊶━━━━━━━━⊷⊷

Finish it.

The thought hits alongside a hangover as you blink at the first dawn alone. This bed is too empty, but you keep yourself together by repeating that thought.

Finish it.

Everyone will expect you to juggle the morticians, the wake, and the burial once the police eventually release her body, the one you could hardly look at. A dead woman with a horrible wound in her left eye, abrasions across her body—what did that have to do with your girlfriend? In circumstances so dire, how could anyone expect responsibility of an alcoholic bookworm who uses tidiness to cover her failure of self?

Too soon, they'll expect you to get over it. Your coworkers and boss at the accounting firm, your friends at the bar, anyone who hears of the tragedy and goes, *I'm so sorry*—they'll demand a convenient woman. Back to normalcy, quickly.

They treat this loss of life as purely an absence, but death creates a new fucked-up presence to weigh on you, made worse by the circumstances.

Her death wasn't a blameless heart attack or a collision brought on by a deer in the road. Someone made the conscious decision to repaint her in violent red and then replace her with this waking nightmare. You can hardly stomach it.

But that thought—*Finish it.* You can do that. She always wanted one of her art pieces to be remembered. A creation to outlast the creator. Why not *Lady of the Dark Hand?*

Would it be best remembered as the unfinished masterpiece of a murdered woman? Or would it capture hearts and live forever as the project completed by the devoted girlfriend after the artist's passing? Not simply a last art piece, but something you and she made together.

A goodbye in brushstrokes.

You struggle out of bed to take a piss, wash last night's drinking from your mouth, shower, decide how to proceed, when you stop at the mirror.

The glass is fogged. Like someone has just been breathing on it.

You study it until the moisture dissipates, and you feel like you might throw up again. Could last night have been a bad dream?

"Honey?" you sing into the hall.

Too much to hope, but you barrel through the apartment, breath reeking, bladder full, heart battering your rib cage. Check the living room—no one. The kitchen—nothing.

In the studio, you hope to find her perched on that stool, its skinny legs tearing through the newspaper and scraping your nice hardwood floor, while she obliviously sweeps a paintbrush from palette to canvas, her muscles rippling at every movement.

There's nobody inside the studio. Only the paintings on the walls, the one east-facing window bleeding hopeless orange sunshine into the room, and *Lady of the Dark Hand*, grinning beneath the shadows of a crackling wasteland.

When you've finished crying again, you fetch Detective Apathetic's card. Odds of an update this morning are practically zero, but you gave up practicality when you ran through this apartment shouting for a girlfriend you've already seen dead on a slab.

It takes several tries to get through to anyone who even knows the detective. "Think he went home around midnight," says a tired-sounding woman. "How about he'll call you back?"

You hang up and try to figure out what the hell you're going to do with the rest of today.

Better than trying to figure out what you're going to do with the rest of your life.

Leave the painting as is? Finish it?

You text your friends, but they aren't much help. Their answers are contradictory, elusive, and then they surrender to collective apathy as if they've become detectives themselves.

"We'll support whatever you decide!"

You would crush this phone in your fist if you could. Too much responsibility, so many expectations—why can't someone tell you what to do? Control is a noose. You're crumbling inside, and no one wants to put you back together, but they're ready to cheer for you when you pick up the pieces yourself. Don't they know you at all? You're a rule follower, a number counter, someone who colors within the lines. Likely that drew you to your girlfriend's chaos. Within her artistic catastrophe, she knew what she wanted.

And she wanted to finish the painting. Take up her direction then. Finish it.

You drop onto the stool and study the paints, hoping to absorb understanding through the eye. Don't know what you're doing? No one really does when they get started. The brush feels heavy between your fingers. Try sliding a dark color along the black streaks at the painting's edge. That's your testing ground. No harm you do here will taint the figure at *Lady of the Dark Hand*'s center.

Slowly, confidence builds in your brushstrokes, as if a strong hand encircles your forearm and guides you.

As if you're not alone in her art studio.

To fool yourself is a kindness, but you imagine she's sneaking around the apartment, only pretending to have died. You can pretend, too, that she's creeping through the hall. In the doorway.

That if you glance over your shoulder at just the right moment, you'll catch her.

Oh, you got me, she'll say in her casual goofy way. She'll toss her hair back, stick her tongue out, carry you to bed. You'll burn with the need to climb her tower of a muscly body until her mouth dips between your legs. You never did this for her, too much the pillow princess, but she never complained before, and won't have the chance again. She's hungry for you, and you're ready to be devoured by the scream she'll paint inside you.

Right before she slides your jeans and panties down, she'll look up and flash that confident grin, all pearly-toothed, and then—

Your eyes open, the fantasy melting away. There's no one here but you.

No grin but in the painting. *Lady of the Dark Hand* tenses her black-gloved hands, one against her red coat, the other at the glassy blade aimed where there is no eye.

You stare into that darkness. Harsh breath seeps in and out. Were the canvas a bathroom mirror, you would have coated your reflection in white mist.

The sound of rattling jolts you backward. You kick out in surprise, knocking the easel. It bangs hard against the floor, and something flakes from its front on impact. You grab the legs with panicked hands and right it to standing, and then you charge into the living room to catch the still-quaking noise that startled you.

Your cellphone. You grab it from your purse, but you've already missed the call. There's no name. You're not sure who it was, but you have a hunch.

The phone quakes in your hands again. Keep your cool this time, and answer it.

As you suspected—hoped—it's Detective Apathetic. An irrationality in your heart hopes again for a mistake. Or a miracle. *She had a twin, didn't you know?* the detective will ask. *Life's like a soap opera. These things happen.*

"I need to tell you about your girlfriend," he says. His voice is shaky and dry, like fear has sponged up all his spit. "Her unusual circumstances."

You ask him when the cops will be releasing her body. Doesn't he have anyone he cares about? How would he feel if their remains were kept from him? You pace the apartment as you lay into him, and you only stop when you've returned to the art studio, hearing a cry in his voice.

"I'm sorry," you say. "Tell me."

"Her knuckles," the detective says. "They were raw from hitting somebody pretty hard. A struggle. The killer must have used leather gloves, we found bits of leather in her teeth, covering against a scream. So, no fingerprints. And the murder weapon—it was a glass knife. The gouge in her eye? It went through, and then the killer broke it off, and it shattered when her face hit the warehouse floor. Looked like any other glass shards you'd find in an empty building. Couldn't have known."

You swallow hard. "How do you know now?"

"I've been told." The detective sighs into receiver. "I shouldn't be sharing any of this."

But you're grateful. And confused, too, because you know about black gloves and a glass knife. You're looking at them right now.

At their likeness in *Lady of the Dark Hand.*

The detective's voice slides from the phone, growing distant. "I did what you wanted. Now let me go home and see my kids."

You don't understand what he means. You call out for him to explain.

His voice rises in a frightened gasp. "No, put that down! Let me g—"

There's a collision as his phone smacks a hard surface, and then his voice shatters into a guttural scream.

The call ends.

You wait in silence through the afternoon for your phone to quake again. The detective will tell you he had the TV on too loud, or mixed himself up in another case. That he dropped his phone.

Because you can't have heard what you think you heard.

Because then the detective might be dead. Over your girlfriend's case. Meaning he might have been targeted, which would mean she was targeted, her death not a random encounter or a mysterious ex from the past, but a focused intent.

Meaning you might be targeted, too.

You can't be alone right now. Your thumbs plod over your phone screen, drawing in your friends. They'll have to come; you're grieving. Tell them to bring beer, box wine, anything. You don't want to think. You want to drink.

But your thoughts don't care what you want. They guide your gaze to *Lady of the Dark Hand*, desperate to absorb understanding as if your eyes are gateways to knowledge. The black edges, the vibrant background colors. Those dark gloves, the red coat and glass knife, that grin beneath shadowy crackle paste. Flecks of black have fallen away from that faceless void as if the figure has grown new teeth.

You leave the art studio to tidy up the living room and await your guests. Anything to avoid this mess in your head.

They fill your glass again and again as you repeat the detective's phone call, how his description of events fit the painting. Each wanders into the art studio to see it, but you stick with the group. Part of you isn't ready to inspect the damage you've done in kicking the easel over, and the rest of you hasn't had enough to drink yet. Don't worry; you'll get there. You always do.

A couple of friends suggest the killer must be a fan of your girlfriend's work. Others propose she might have been a latent psychic experiencing a premonition of her own murder, which she mistook for inspiration. It could happen to any artist.

You doubt a murderous art fan plunged a glass knife into your girlfriend's skull, and you doubt psychic powers even more.

"But you believe someone killed her," your friends say. "Someone who fits the painting."

Your belief in her death is irrelevant. If belief could be your friend, your girlfriend would have appeared this morning when you thought that breathy residue on the bathroom mirror might've been hers.

The murder is a fact. Same as the murderer.

As you listen to your friends squawk out theories and pontificate on extrasensory perception, you start to wonder—do you actually like these people? Or are you more interested in their skill at inebriating you without guilt as a chaser?

Your girlfriend could never do that. She worried, always worried. Cared about you. She wasn't someone who'd *yes* you to death or support any decision you made without question.

Are these really your friends solely because you dated them once? Or are they sycophants with plentiful alcohol, and you're the right addict to appease?

She would hate to see you stewing in resentment. But you're having a hard time understanding what she saw in you in the first place.

⁂

You're well on your way to hammered when you stagger from the rumbling living room conversation, into the studio. You manage to hit the wall switch again, and golden light washes across *Lady of the Dark Hand.*

Black gloves. Glass knife. It doesn't feel possible. Your girlfriend couldn't have foreseen her murder any more than she could have guessed you would kick over the painting like a panicky rabbit. You've never hurt her art before, except in demanding she clean it up. Crackle paste has broken from the above-grin void, and the pale spaces jab guilty teeth into your heart.

And then you notice a mark jutting from edge of the damage.

Your vision swims as you stumble closer to the painting, nose inches from canvas. The shape is unmistakable.

There are letters hidden beneath the crackle paste.

With no thought toward the sanctity of the art, you press a fingernail into the pale space and dig beneath the crackle paste, peeling away another painted flake.

The word *create* stares out at you in tiny yet readable font.

A sober you would think twice about further damaging your late girlfriend's final painting. Maybe you would call on an expert, or bring it for an X-ray. Isn't this creation supposed to outlast its creator?

But you're far from sober, and there's not enough good judgment left in your skull to keep from digging your fingernail in again and tearing away the adjoining specks of crackle paste. Further words appear.

to create a

You plant yourself on the stool and set feverishly to clearing away the non-face region about the painting's grin. A black crescent builds beneath your nail, but you don't halt to clear it. You don't even grab a tool to help you. The message is for you, you're certain of it, and you must unveil it by hand.

Confidence again guides your movements. You sense someone else in the room, but you won't fantasize this time. She isn't here. You won't see her again, same as you're certain that detective's family will never see him, either. But they don't have access to a secret message from the dead. You're different. You're the lucky one.

The crackle paste flakes away bit by bit. If necessary, you can repair this part. The paste doesn't look difficult to apply, and besides, this section was always unfinished. *Lady of the Dark Hand* has never truly had a face.

to create a

presumption of

Hope briefly falters in your heart as you remember how she liked to layer in pages from *Harper's Bazaar*. This might be a paragraph about spring fashion or a celebrity interview.

Ignore doubt. There's a message for you. Has to be. Keep going, and you'll be able to read it. Pour all your focus into the work. Let it slosh like the drink in your gut, but keep your gaze hazy. You don't want to see the message until it's revealed.

And you want nothing to distract you. Not the sounds of commotion from the living room as rumbling chatter breaks into surprise. Not the muffled struggling, or the stark silence to follow. Anyone who isn't dead has fled, but you keep working.

Open your eyes; you're almost done. The small text is cramped above *Lady of the Dark Hand*'s toothy grin, but your girlfriend fit a brief note into that featureless wasteland. Its edges now bare black paint and pale canvas.

You've unveiled all there is to find. Read it, and take in your reward:

My love,

I offer an act of creation in destruction. This creation will outlast me.

No one will remember the genuine harm. How I'll beat my hands against brick and then wash them. How I'll bite into a leather glove. How I'll thrash at my legs and sides with a lead pipe. The stabbing will be the hardest part, driving the glass shard into my eye while I lean at an angle to fall and shatter it.

But I believe in the work, its intent and consequence. This is the challenge of making a death by my own hand resemble death by another's. To fake a murder and insist on a murderer. The art is in making room for the suggestion. A negative space where a murderer is expected, this presumption of monstrosity. The space will be filled, like the universe finishing a painting.

Absorb it through your eyes, and you'll understanding this thing we'll have made together. Through my death. And then through yours.

The studio light snaps off, dousing the painting and its message in dim shadow. You lurch back, toppling the stool, struggling in your half-drunken stupor to comprehend this final note, its intent in the past, and its consequence in the present.

The consequence that is me.

I don't have to let you know I'm in the room. I've been here most of the day, leaning behind you, breathing you in, shadowing your movements, and you haven't noticed, not even when I returned from ambushing that detective. I could've killed you without a sound. Without a sign.

But to fake a murder is only the beginning of suggestion, and here in the end, I want your awareness. This is about completion.

The universe will finish a painting, even when you can't.

I keep you standing, one arm tucking your shoulder to my chest, the other reaching higher, where this lady's dark hand claps over your mouth. You twist and fight, tangling your legs in my long red coat, bellowing against the black leather squeezed against your lips. A shock runs through you—I can feel it—when you see the glass knife.

You're trying to turn around, but I don't want you to glimpse this face. You should know me instead as you have always known me.

Look ahead, on the destruction within the creation that will outlast the creator. The painting appears mostly black with the lights out, but I squeeze your face as the glass blade rises to meet your eye, keeping your gaze locked on the art.

Absorb understanding where the pale flesh bursts, drooling wet white paint down your cheek. See *Lady of the Dark Hand* as it is. Realize that compulsive thought—*Finish it*—had nothing to do with the painting and everything to do with *me*.

This thing you and she have made together.

The Flesh Grows Fonder

by T.O. King

Beneath Flora's fingers, the petals of the corpse flower pulse warm. They remind her of flesh: living, breathing, running with spoiled nectar like blood. She knows the flower isn't made from human skin, just a fable devised from the scent of the thing—rotting body, viscera spilled out to bake in the sun—but there are no bodies where she is. No humans to touch, to commune with. So she spreads her palms along the bloom's length and revels in the way it makes her feel less alone. Less forgotten.

Flora took this assignment because she would be alone. An empty manor home far from any village, any train station, any place for strangers to ask her why she is there, who she is.

Mother is dead, she recites. *Mother is dead amongst all her flowers and books; and so I mourn her loss by sinking my own fingers into the soil and giving the trees their names.*

The university promised it would be the best place to continue her studies away from all the prying questions, the looks of sympathy, the concern for her wellbeing.

Aren't you afraid of dying just like your mother?

Perhaps the plants are not your friends.

Flora shakes her head, closes her eyes to clear the cobwebs. Plants are her *only* friends. They might've taken her mother, might've turned her body to frost, sunk thorny vines into the soft hollow of her throat, but Flora only feels at home amongst the green and growing things. So she draws her hands from the corpse flower's petals and digs deep into the dirt at the roots. Grounding herself, in a way, against all the chaos, all the noise, until it all turns to silence.

Sound echoes out in the corridor, shaking Flora's bones. She turns to the greenhouse door where the shadows curve sharper. Her breath hitches, a gloss of sweat skimming her forearms and chest.

She is alone.

They promised she would be. The gardens untouched, her time and studies unbroken, the rarest of plants hers and hers *alone*. But there are footsteps now, footsteps striking the tiled floor behind the arched glass, and Flora feels her heart beating a tattoo against her ribs. She draws her fingers, one by one, from the soil, the dirt crumbling to land beside her feet. Palms shaking at her sides like downed birds, the footsteps close in, a hooked shadow spilling beneath the door.

She is *not* alone.

The brass knob jangles and twists, creaking like old bones. Flora feels all the warmth drain from her body. Was this how her mother felt, when the final leaf had loosed itself from *Dendrocnide moroides* and sunk teeth into her skin? Was this how it felt when her mother's life's work betrayed her? Flora steels herself, nerves crackling like autumn leaves.

The door swings open, letting in skifts of golden light and Flora's chest contracts. A woman stands in the doorway, a woman she has seen before. Only in swirls of paint, though she would know that twist of a smile anywhere. She has studied the portrait over and over, tracing her finger along the slip of the woman's jaw, wondering at just *who* exactly she is. Her hands shove deep into a pair of black slacks, and dark curls spill down along her angled brow. Flora's fingers find their way back to the dirt, soil skimming her skin until she can breathe once more. *Focus.* The woman takes a step closer, eyes drinking in the whole of her, hungry, ravenous like a starved beast.

"Hello, Ms. Heywood," she croons, voice slick and dark as a crystalline night. "I've been expecting you."

⁕⁓╾━━━━━━━━━╼⁓⁕

Flora's knife slips against the meat, juices spilling out like the sap of *Sanguinaria canadensis.* Bloodroot. She remembers the first time she saw it, dripping wet lines across her mother's palm.

There'd been no blood when she'd found her mother wrapped in vines and spiked leaves, the smell of death and decay, turning blue on the floor of her study. Her mother, who once felt like spring, but is now nothing more than a cold, lifeless shell.

She takes a bite, chews, the meat turning to threads in her teeth.

"Are you often this quiet, Ms. Heywood?"

She looks up from her plate, half-forgetting the woman standing above her, pouring wine into her glass. The woman who should not be here. The university had promised.

"The owner of the house, a Ms. Whitley, will not be at home."
"Overseas research."

They had lied. Or, they hadn't known Lilith Whitley was a woman of her own whims and fancies, to hell with all the rest. Flora studies her through the candlelight, curls shining, slightly damp with oil that smells of geranium. Her white shirt unbuttons to the curve of her breast, a glimmer of pale skin spreading there like snow on soil. Flora grinds a slice of meat between her teeth and swallows, fighting the urge to get lost in the way Lilith's eyes seem like endless pools. A siren song.

She draws a fingernail sharp across her thigh. *Stop. Focus.* She rolls wine on her tongue. It tastes of apple, thick and summer-fresh. "And do you often drop in when you are supposed to be away?"

Lilith's brows arch, a pair of twisting snakes as she moves for her seat. "It is my house, is it not?"

Flora smiles, slipping the fork against the roof of her mouth. She tries not to focus on the glimmer in Lilith's eye, the smirk on her cherry-bruised lips. This woman is a stranger. An unknown. And Flora thinks this is what entrances her most. For years she has studied plants, tracing the frills of flowers, the length of roots, sketching out their images and writing their names in crisp, little lines. But it is always the species of unknown origins, the plants that come bearing no name, that spark a flame in her chest. And this woman—Lilith Whitley—who should not be here, ignites a fire of unknowns in her belly.

Flora's fingers clench around the edge of a napkin, the fabric soft, and wonders if Lilith's skin would be softer, more taut. She spreads her pink lips like *Nerium oleander*. To seize the bones.

"The university said your gardens hold rare specimens. I was wondering"—she cuts a demure smile, lowers her dark lashes through the haze smoldering above the candle flame—"they said you even have slipper orchids hidden away somewhere."

Lilith grins, silver rings glinting on her knuckles. "The university doesn't know what they're talking about."

Disappointment blooms across Flora's face like blood on snow. A cold bead of sweat rolls down her spine and she shivers, feeling foolish. But Lilith does not laugh, does not make fun or dismiss her; only continues.

"I have things beyond slipper orchids, Ms. Heywood."

Flora lifts her eyes, the hunger in her belly no longer for the food bleeding on her plate. Her fingers itch for the soil, the rough bark of twisted roots. She swallows, studying the curve of Lilith's jaw, the tight, full lips like bee stings.

"Show me," she says. "Please."

The cut of the stone path glows opalescent in the moonlight. Flora's heart stutters on the edge of excitement, the thought of something new pulsing beneath her fingers. But it isn't plant life or the dark wetness of soil, it's *her*. Lilith. From behind, the woman is nothing but shadow. Dark clothes and black hair and the scent of buried things left in her wake. Flora wants to breathe in great mouthfuls of the stuff, dig fingers into Lilith's flesh and unearth her as some discovery. Some *unknown*. She swallows, throat jagged, and tries to calm the blood in her veins.

All around them, night settles and gathers in low places, the air kissed with chill. Flora shivers, the cold breeding in her bones.

"Where are you taking me?" she asks, surprised as her own voice breaks the silence of the gardens.

Ahead, Lilith stops and turns. There's that wicked twist to her lips again, and Flora has half a mind to sink her teeth into it, note how it tastes. How *a woman* tastes. *Actaea pachypoda*. White baneberry. A taste so sweet it stops the heart.

"You asked to see the slipper orchids," Lilith says. "I'm only giving you what you want."

But suddenly, Flora does not want slipper orchids or white baneberry or the sweet reek of corpse flowers. She wants *more*. She takes a step closer to Lilith until all the air she drags between her lips is heavy with the strange woman's scent. A garden of perfumes. Flora's eyes flick to the full mouth, the sharp blades of Lilith's jaw, down to where the white skin begs to be ravaged. Flora's chest heaves, breasts pressing against the thin cotton of her blouse.

"Show me something else," she breathes. "Something I have never seen before."

Lilith's eyes trail along Flora's body, lingering where skin disappears beneath fabric and up to the curve of her lips. Her smile deepens, teeth glinting white in the darkness.

"Oh, Ms. Heywood." She laughs. "I do not think you're ready."

Flora's skin flushes hot. Lilith is wrong. But she doesn't care, she is already fighting the urge to sink her fingers into the woman's flesh, and she can see Lilith is fighting it too. Sees it in the veins pressing out on her jaw, beating staccato above her brow. There's a depth in her eyes now, a glimmer of something Flora has seen before. The same hunger that carves hollows in her own belly. A hunger for specimens undiscovered. For experiences unknown. Her palms tingle, but she holds them at her sides.

"Fine, then show me whatever it is we've come out here for."

Lilith tips her head, cheekbones dusting with shadow, and turns. They continue down the path until the moonlight reflects on panes of glass. Another greenhouse, this one smaller, more square. Lilith fits a key to the lock and swings the door open.

"After you, Ms. Heywood."

In all the wisps of night, the greenhouse pools in jungle hues. Flora inches a toe inside, breath catching at the tip of her tongue, words forgotten. She comes alive here, amongst all the roots and leaves, all the things gasping for their own breath, their own life. She leaves Lilith behind, only wanting to feel the soft velvet of petals, the slip of dew on stems. Lilith laughs as Flora twirls, fingers brushing spikes of night-blooming cereus, the butter-smoothness of chocolate cosmos. A tree twists up against the glass wall, leaves licking at the condensation rolling like sweat. *Malus domestica*. Apples. Flora reaches out a finger to trace the scarlet fruits.

One, two, three, four, five, six.

Lilith comes up behind her, breath lingering hot on her neck as she bends and hooks a hand over Flora's, fingers reaching into soil. Flora's belly aches, a throbbing that spills down along her legs and suddenly she's turning, chest heaving against Lilith's, and that is all they are in that moment. Two sets of lungs, two beating hearts, breath mingling and dancing with the scent of all the green and growing things around them. Flora's lips part and she bites down, the iron tang of blood filling her mouth. Lilith's eyes train on the single red bead, dripping like a ruby down Flora's chin, her throat, puddling in the hollow there just above her breasts.

She stares at this strange woman.

Actaea pachypoda. But she doesn't care, just wants to taste Lilith. Interlacing their fingers amongst the dark soil, Flora lets her lips part to reveal her tongue and teeth, blood still dripping. Lilith moans, her mouth quirking.

"*Ophrys speculum*, Ms. Heywood," she whispers, dipping her head until their lips are mere moments from each other.

Mirror orchid. Luring prey with the promise of sex. Lilith nudges Flora back against the glass wall, their fingers still dripping soil. The air spins heady and unchecked and for the briefest of moments, Flora remembers why she is here.

For Mother.

But Lilith lowers her lips to Flora's neck, already slick with sweat. Her breath is moist, earth-damp fingers brushing the dip of Flora's shoulder, the length of her arm, the curve of one breast. Flora exhales, stomach ripping with ache, a pulsing warmth at the center of her. To open this new part of her, unearth what lies beneath. Lilith's lips press up her throat, tongue flicking out to lick the blood, to taste her like freshly fallen dew. A tremor cascades down Flora's legs and her mind goes hazy. Hazy with desire. To *know* Lilith, to lay her out and lay her bare, and discover who she is beneath it all.

Breath deepening, Lilith lifts her hand to circle Flora's breast, soft and slow as her nipple beads against the touch. And then Flora surges forward, skin searing, to crash her mouth against the cherry-bruised lips. Lilith tastes just how Flora wants—wine left to chill in cool earth, nectar sucked from the brightest blooms, and something dark. Darker than anything else she's tasted in her life. Lilith's tongue flicks out along the roof of Flora's mouth, and she bites down, tasting the sucked-penny slip of her.

"You're a hungry thing, Ms. Heywood," Lilith breathes, withdrawing her lips.

Flora's fingers glide up the front of Lilith, undoing the buttons one by one, the pale skin there shimmering with sweat.

"Show me," Flora says. "Show me more. I *know* there's more."

She can still taste Lilith in her mouth, threads it between her teeth. Lilith's hand comes to rest on Flora's waist, eyes still lingering where her blouse slips from her shoulder, fabric loose and wrinkled.

"Do you know where the seeds are sown?" Lilith presses hips against Flora's and smiles as she shudders with ache. Lilith nuzzles Flora's neck, tongue dragging her throat.

Flora moves her hips, urging the woman closer, deeper. "Show me."

Without a word, Lilith untangles from her, leaving her breathless against the glass. She reaches out a hand, earth staining her fingers, and leads Flora out into the night.

⁂

Flora tells herself it is safe. The way her skin throbs for this woman she hardly knows. A woman whose home she has entered and claimed as her own. She thinks of all the warnings her mother taught her, the bright colors of pitcher plants, but Lilith Whitley is all shadow, all blurred lines. And her mother is dead.

Lilith carves a path back through the night-drenched gardens and down a set of stone steps crumbling into unkempt hedges. For a moment, Flora is sure Lilith is leading her to death, and she wonders if she would even mind. Death by those hands might be a miraculous thing. But then the path opens, and a door comes into view at the edge of a stone wall. Flora's heart thumps like a mad thing.

Open me, open me, open me, it seems to say. *Let me show you my secrets.*

Her fingertips tingle in Lilith's smooth palm and before she can ask what lies beyond, before she can utter a single word, Lilith has her again, pressed against the wall, moss and stone etching patterns on her back. Lilith looks at her, eyes glinting like some delicious devil, and she should be afraid, should scream out into the reaching darkness, but all she can do is shake beneath these hands. They mold her body, starting low at her hips and creeping up her waist to cup her breasts, run the length of her throat, smudge her lips. Flora tries to breathe, but the air in her lungs turns to cotton and all she can do is gasp as Lilith dips a hand against the hem of her skirt, pulling it *up, up, up.*

"Tell me how much you want it," she croons. "Ask me to go beyond the gate."

Behind them, the night gathers solid, and Flora is sure that if she reached into it, her fingers would sink into something cold and lifeless. Mist hangs in the air, like sweeping curtains of spider silk, and she shudders against Lilith's fingers, come to tease the skin of her thigh.

"Ask me, Flora."

The sound of her name, the name her mother gave her, strikes a flint in Flora's guts, fire slicking the pink folds there like oil. She lashes out, tongue and teeth and lips, until the very air this woman breathes out coats her lungs. Lilith's fingers glide small circles, teasing strokes that leave Flora breathless and damp, cursing and wanting more in the same whisper. The fire in her stomach turns molten and she bites down again, wounded lip cracking. The blood trickles, but Lilith is already lapping it up, sliding her finger closer and closer to Flora's center as she utters a moan up to the moonlight.

"Ask me," Lilith purrs, gliding her finger inside. "Flora."

Flora cries out, hands fisting into the stone at her back, nailbeds filling with soil. The shuddering ripples cascade through her like bursting blooms. Shoots of spring grass, undone there, in all the starlight and shadow. Her fingers come to tangle in Lilith's wild hair, and she pulls her face up to meet her own. There is something darker now, in the hollows of Lilith's cheekbones, in the depths of her eyes. A shadowed mask. She reaches up to touch Lilith's cheek …

How did this woman know her name?

She opens her mouth to ask, to form the words on her tongue, but Lilith's lips are moments away from hers and she can't think, she can hardly breathe as the scent of the woman—geranium and something else now, something sickly-sweet—floods her senses.

Her hips roll toward Lilith, wanting more, *gods above*, but the woman laughs. "You didn't ask. You must ask me, Flora. You must ask to go beyond the door."

"Please," she moans. "Show me."

And so, Lilith does.

⊹⊶══════════⊷⊹

Flora tells herself it isn't real. The things she is seeing are not real. Beyond the door, the garden—*Lilith's* garden—smells of rot. Of overripe fruit slurring in the sun. But there is no sun here. There is only a darkness she has never seen before. It *moves*. Twisting like serpents, the shadows swim through the garden, their corrugated bodies undulating in the crepuscular hues. She looks up, eyes searching for the moon, the stars, anything that is known. That is real.

But they are gone. Vanished.

So, what is making the light?

It is not a true light, not a natural one. It beats a sickly yellow against Flora's skin. Her breathing hitches as she watches the darkness moving against her feet, casting pointed shadows on the ripped fabric of her blouse, the wrinkled hem of her skirt.

What ... what has she done?

Mother tried to warn her.

She turns to leave, to run back to the house, but Lilith stands there.

No. Not Lilith.

A breath-stealing thing of night.

Cheekbones stand out like cuts of diamond, eyes like darkened pits. Lilith wears nothing but snakes of smoke twisting about her pale flesh. Flora's chest contracts, heart lunging up into her throat. She reaches out to steady herself and her fingers sink into something warm. Something pulsing. Her skin swims with sweat, the fear rising from her body like heat.

She looks down.

A flower blooms at the edges of her feet, breaking up from the earth and spreading out toward the ether. Flora's eyes hang on the folds of the petals, the blue veins running along their pale gleam. She bends down, nostrils filling with the rotten scent, and strokes a finger down the thing.

The flower reacts to her touch. The blue veins beating *one two, one two, one two*. She falls back, scrabbles in the dirt, trying to get to her feet, but Lilith's hand is already on her shoulder, pressing her *down, down, down.*

82

"You asked for me to show you, to reveal things you have never seen before." Her voice is silk and midnight oil. "Look, Ms. Heywood. Don't you see?"

Flora's throat seems to fill with cotton; and she tries to swallow, but the skin turns jagged. She threads saliva between her teeth, leans toward the throbbing bloom, fingers itching as the curses leave her tongue. This was what killed her mother, wasn't it? This incessant need to know the unknowns, to discover things no one else has ever seen.

The petals sponge beneath Flora's touch, springing forward as she lets go. The blue veins pump, and the flower almost seems to *breathe*. She draws her hand back.

"What is it?" she asks.

But she already knows the answer. There can be no mistaking it. Though to speak it out loud, to acknowledge the existence of the thing … Flora shudders.

"Flesh." Lilith's hands are on her now, hauling her up, squeezing her jaw so she can see every blossom, every petal that oozes the sickly yellow light. "Living flesh."

Flora's scream curdles in her throat, slurrying in her belly. But Lilith's mouth has found hers, and she sloshes beneath the delicious weight. Knees give out and heart races. Her hand falls away, drifting back to the petals of flesh at her side. They match her own pulse as Lilith's fingers come down around her waist, pulling at her skirt.

"Don't you see," the woman whispers against the curve of her throat. "Don't you understand? There is no one else like you, no one who matches my hunger. Not even your mother, Flora. There is only you. Only you can tend the flesh."

Something like sour milk gathers at the back of Flora's mouth, but Lilith's tongue swipes in between her teeth, stealing it away. Gods, she wants this. Wants *her*. Everywhere. All around her.

Tend the flesh.

The flowers of living, breathing flesh. It shouldn't make sense. It should be impossible, but Lilith's mouth is trailing lines down her breasts, and even the air around Flora feels suddenly *possible*. Isn't this what she has always wanted? To know something new. To sink her fingers into something she cannot explain and make it her own.

Lilith's mouth is on her stomach now, fingers loosing the buttons on her blouse. Flora arches against the touch, feels the flower behind her quiver.

"Stay with me," Lilith croons, a soft groan against Flora's skin.

Yes, yes, she must.

She wrenches Lilith's head back and spreads her legs wide. Lilith's eyes gleam wicked black, breathless pleas caressing her skin.

Flora's skin tremors. "And if I say no?"

Lilith smiles, dips her head low between Flora's thighs. "You can say whatever you want. You are not my prisoner."

Flora's legs clench as Lilith's mouth finds the place where her finger was only moments before, one hand cupping her hips, raising her up against a flower. It is warm beneath her.

Gods above, she will not say no. She will stay. Her hands, slick with sweat, tighten on the edges of Lilith's bare shoulder. Lilith groans, a murmuration against the center of Flora. A low moan breaks from her lips.

"Yes, gods, yes. I will stay."

Lilith's tongue flicks out and Flora's body shudders like the burst of a dying star. And then, in one fluid motion, Flora presses Lilith to the earth, draws her body closer until they both are enveloped in wisps of shadow. Flora feels it circle her skin—cold as ice—and then Lilith is against her, so warm and so full and everything she has ever wanted.

Not alone.

Never again alone.

Lilith fills up Flora's veins, the blooms of flesh beating a rhythm around them with every stroke, every touch, every cry that tears from their lips. Lilith drips with sweat like oil, pulsing against her again and again.

"Yes," Flora groans, fingers digging into Lilith's skin, teeth threaded with geranium. "I will tend the flesh."

Lilith's back arches, shouting Flora's name, vibrating as their bodies skim and shudder. Around them, the flowers brighten, their sickly yellow light turning a brilliant, honeyed gold as they buzz and burst with nectar.

A cry escapes Flora's lips, her tongue edged with sounds of pleasure; and when they are finally undone there, covered in the juice of the flowers, she lets the words roll around on her tongue until they slip from her lips like poisoned wine.

"Show me how," Flora murmurs. Her fingers itch to know. To feel.

Lilith kisses her hair, pulls her up on shaking feet. They are both naked now, wrapped in velvet night. Lilith grins, a wicked thing.

"Like this," she says and places Flora's sweat-slicked hands on the pulsing tissue of the flower at their feet. It shudders beneath them, petals stretching as it drinks the moisture from their bodies.

Flora's palm flexes, every sense heightened as she strokes the blooms that surround them, the night coming to steel across her body. She smiles, watching the hellfire in Lilith's eyes as the flesh grows fonder.

Pilgrim of Worlds

by M.S. Dean

On the night before hazefall, a family of bats stole into Rahm's cabin. Rather than spend the night chasing them out, Rahm swung her sleeping bag onto the roof and slept under the moon and stars. It would be the last time she would see them for weeks.

Rahm had spent all day fixing up the trails, making sure the signs were upright and legible, making sure new trees hadn't sprung into the paths like they sometimes tried to do. She was sore and tired from a hard day's work, and fell asleep just as the stars began to dim.

By morning, Rahm could barely see her hand in front of her face and had to feel her way off of the roof and into the cabin by touch alone. The bats had fallen asleep in the rafters, and she was able to pluck them off one by one. They were so soundly asleep from the haze that they didn't wake even when she set them gently outside. The mountain was utterly, unnaturally quiet.

Then all Rahm could do was wait for the pilgrims to arrive.

The glade had room for forty people to camp, but in all Rahm's time as a caretaker, there had never been half as many. At last year's hazefall, there were twelve pilgrims. This time, only nine.

Rahm saw the lanterns first. Their blue copper light was the only thing that shone reliably in the haze. Firelight had a mind of its own, a tendency to mislead. Anyone who stepped off the trail would never be found again.

The first out of the haze, like always, was Evy. She led the group of pilgrims to Rahm's glade and directed them in setting up camp. After seeing to her pilgrims, Evy introduced herself to Rahm and clasped her hand. Rahm held on for a second too long. Long enough for Evy to look Rahm up and down.

"I'm Rahm," she told Evy, as she had told her many times. "Welcome to the crossroads."

After they set up camp, the pilgrims went to the spring and drank from it. A hazecatcher flower floated on the water in full bloom, its blue petals open to the haze, releasing in turn the heady aroma of dreams.

Rahm stayed a respectful distance away. She was no pilgrim, no worldwalker. She was just caretaker of these interstices, this safe place between vanishing visions.

There was something desperate about the way the pilgrims sank with their bellies to the grass, drinking from the water like animals. Even Evy seemed lost to her thirst, gulping frantically from her cupped hands, water dripping down her throat.

One of the pilgrims was a young girl, perhaps nineteen or twenty. Tremors ran through her body like the involuntary movements of sleep paralysis. She reached over to the hazecatcher and crushed it between her fingers.

Evy, quicker than Rahm could see, turned and tackled the girl into the long grass, forcing her to release the flower. They fought; Evy overpowered her. She hissed something into the girl's ear, and then the two of them returned to the spring to drink. The girl's eyes had gone glazed with dreams once more.

Rahm let out a breath, shaken by the sudden outburst of violence and how close they'd all been to oblivion. Crossroads were delicate sanctuaries, after all. If the girl had destroyed the flower—the nexus—it would have broken the paths and they'd all be lost, wandering the space between worlds forever.

It was a close call, thought Rahm. But then she caught the suspicious look Evy gave the girl as they all finished drinking. This wasn't over yet.

⁕⁕⁕

When Rahm grew too impatient to wait any longer, she invited Evy to her cabin and asked if she had brought any tea.

Evy looked surprised. She took a sachet of tea leaves out of her pack and gave it to Rahm. "I always bring tea along all my travels," said Evy. "But how did you know?"

Rather than answer, Rahm began to brew a pot. She breathed in the strange smells, letting herself imagine distant, unfamiliar lands. A world beyond the one she knew.

"Where is it from?" Rahm asked.

"The Bay of Salts," said Evy. "The continent of Khorasa."

Rahm murmured the strange names under her breath, savoring the way they felt on her tongue. She loved hearing the names of places that would never exist for her, even as they filled her with longing. Such was the curse of one who cared for the crossroads.

As they drank, Evy gave Rahm long, studying looks. Warmth gathered in Rahm's belly, but not from the tea.

"It's curious," said Evy. "Every time I walk these paths, they seem to narrow. All my futures collapsing. All my worlds condensing. Like some hidden destiny is anchoring me. The journey from here will be a trial, I think."

"You could always stay," said Rahm.

Evy tilted her head. "This isn't the first time you've asked me that, is it?"

"No," said Rahm. "I've seen many versions of you pass through here. You're older sometimes, or younger. You're always a pilgrim. You always leave."

"I think," said Evy, "I've dreamed of you."

Rahm shivered. She wanted to ask after the nature of these dreams, but by the dark look in Evy's eyes, she thought she knew. She remembered the insatiable way Evy had drunk from the spring. She remembered the ease with which she'd sprung on her fellow pilgrim.

There was something dangerous about this Evy, some missing warmth. It didn't matter. There had been hooks long laid beneath Rahm's skin, and they were tugging.

"Stay with me," Rahm said, and for those next hours, Evy did.

Later, they drank their now cold tea in Rahm's bed and Evy asked her, as she had asked countless times, how Rahm had become a caretaker of the crossroads.

"I was a pilgrim once, a very long time ago," Rahm explained. "One day, our group came to a crossroads. Out of the fog between worlds, out of the valleys of abyss with oblivion tugging at our ankles, I saw this great big sanctuary. This mountain. This crossroads. There was a caretaker here, and she and I fell in love. I stayed, even after she left me behind. She wasn't done being a pilgrim yet, like I was."

She always liked studying Evy's face when she told this part. Sometimes Evy didn't react at all. Sometimes she blushed or looked angry on Rahm's behalf. Sometimes, like this Evy did, she turned jealous.

It amused Rahm. "Did you think you were my first and only love?" she teased.

"Yes," Evy said, flat and angry. She rolled back onto Rahm, upsetting their tea, and took Rahm's mouth again.

The haze thickened and the long night continued. When Rahm and Evy emerged from the cabin, they found that a pilgrim was dead, lying face down in the spring. The young girl with tremors. Bruises ringed her neck.

Rahm couldn't help but look at Evy, and though she didn't mean it as an accusation, Evy's expression still darkened.

"I was with you, wasn't I?" said Evy sharply.

"Of course," Rahm said. "I'm sorry. I've never had a pilgrim die on my watch before."

She gently touched Evy's arm to summon the softness in her once again, but softness did not come easily to this Evy. She left Rahm's side to go help the others construct a litter for the body out of branches. It didn't take them very long—they had clearly done this before.

"What sort of world do you and your pilgrims come from?" Rahm asked carefully, as Evy wrapped black cloth around the dead girl's eyes.

"You're asking me how often I've seen death," Evy said. "If this is the first body I've blessed."

"You seem," said Rahm, "unfazed."

Evy pressed her thumb into the girl's forehead hard enough to dimple and bruise. "The world I come from isn't kind," Evy said. "Maybe that's true of most worlds. You'd know, as someone at the crossroads. Are there kind worlds out there? Do I ever come from them?"

There was an awful, hungry hope in Evy's voice. Rahm hesitated. She had come from one of those other worlds once. It hadn't always shown her kindness either.

She put her hand on Evy's shoulder. "Kindness exists," said Rahm. "It is, unfortunately, not the only species."

***

Evy and her pilgrims carried their fallen fellow into the haze. Rahm did not ask where they would put her body. There were only two places left under hazefall: the trails, or the endless plains of oblivion.

Filled with nervous energy, Rahm walked her rounds through the crossroads to make sure everything was in order. She discovered that an oak tree had sprung up in the middle of one of her trails. Its roots were gnarled into the ground like it had stood for centuries, even though it had not been there yesterday. Such was the way of this mountain—it liked to defy her.

The oak was an old and noble thing. Rahm put her axe to it and chopped it down.

It took a long time. Every swing of Rahm's axe built a new violence in her until she was almost snarling, sweat pouring off her. It wasn't fair. It wasn't fair that the girl had died where she should have been safe. It wasn't fair that she had almost certainly been murdered. It wasn't fair that once the haze lifted, Evy would leave Rahm behind like she always did, and that Rahm would be alone again.

When the tree finally fell, it should have shaken the entire mountainside. Instead, it swung into the haze outside of the path and only terrible silence followed.

"It looked like you needed that."

Rahm spun around. Evy sat on the ground further up the path, barely visible through the haze. After a moment of stunned silence, Rahm joined her.

"Tell me," said Evy. "Do we always fall in love?"

Rahm curled her fingers restlessly around the handle of her axe. "Yes," she said. "There are constants, even in the infinite worlds. You always find me. We always fall in love. You always want to be a pilgrim."

"I didn't want to be a pilgrim," said Evy. "In fact, it was the last thing I wanted. I wanted to settle in the world I was in. I wanted a family, Rahm. And yet every time I tried, something went wrong. In the end, the only path left to me was the one that led me here. To you."

The bitterness in her voice shocked Rahm. She had never heard Evy speak like this.

"What will you do with the stump?" Evy asked. "Burn it away?"

"It can't stay there," Rahm said. "The path must be clear. Otherwise—"

"Otherwise, it'll lead somewhere else," interrupted Evy. "To some other crossroads. Some other caretaker. Isn't that right?"

It finally struck Rahm that Evy was angry with her. "It's not like I forced you here," she said, confused.

Evy made a derisive noise. "Who do you think hooked all my paths, all my worlds, and converged them here at this crossroads? Who do you think kept calling all my fates to your feet? It's your fault I keep ending up here."

"I love you," Rahm said, growing desperate. "I loved you enough to want you to return to me."

"Maybe that answer would have meant more to a different version of me," Evy said.

Rahm felt like she'd been slapped. She could hear the quiet voices of the other pilgrims further into the haze. They weren't alone.

"I want to show you something," she told Evy, getting to her feet. And perhaps Evy's fate was tied to hers after all, because without hesitating, Evy followed.

They climbed the mountain to where the haze was thinnest. Here the skin of the crossroads was the barest wisp of a barrier, the veil so fragile Rahm could sometimes hear someone else's breath as if they were standing right beside her.

"I only found this place last hazefall," Rahm explained. "I didn't have time to bring you. So you're the first Evy I've shown this to."

She could tell that this pleased Evy. They both looked with awe up at the sky. Unfamiliar stars and mysterious planetoids passed overhead, just visible through the haze.

Like the breaking of a dream, a beam of sunlight shot through, lighting up a patch of grass with an almost blinding intensity. Exchanging a breathless look, Evy and Rahm ran to it and lay down in the light and warmth. A window to other worlds was open above them—they could hear birdsong, taste desert dust.

"I am the last Evy you'll bring to this crossroads," said Evy, her fingers curling in the grass. "Promise, Rahm."

This was the first time Rahm had ever seen Evy in the sun, all the flecks of gold glittering in her eyes. And for it to be the last?

"You don't know how lonely it gets," she said.

"Then why have you stayed?" Evy asked.

"Someone has to," Rahm said. "Without a caretaker, the crossroads are swallowed up. How many pilgrims get lost in the haze every year? How many more if I wasn't here?"

Evy was quiet for a long moment. Even before she spoke, Rahm knew, her heart sinking, what she would offer. "Then let me stay," Evy said finally. "Go, and I'll stay. I know I can protect the crossroads. I've done it already."

"You did kill that girl," Rahm whispered. "Didn't you?"

"She would have brought oblivion down on all of us," Evy said. "It's what had to be done."

Rahm had always adored Evy's practicality, her ambition. It only occurred to her now how often that went hand in hand with ruthlessness.

She brought her axe up. Evy was ready for it; she had been waiting all along for Rahm to strike. She knocked the axe easily out of Rahm's hand and drove her knee into Rahm's stomach. Rahm gasped and doubled over as all the breath left her lungs. She was helpless as Evy took her by her shoulders and dragged her to the edge of the cliff.

The haze was thin here. Oblivion waited beneath them, but so did windows to other worlds. Which would Rahm fall into, if she fell?

"Don't you want to know," said Evy, "what else is out there?"

Her lips were pressed just beneath Rahm's ear. It was almost tender, the way Evy held her there at the precipice and kept her from falling. Rahm shook and clung to Evy, not ready yet to let go.

"What if I keep falling?" Rahm said. "What if it's just emptiness, forever?"

"And what if you find a new world to land in?" Evy said. "A piece of infinity for you to bear witness to? Isn't that chance worth it?"

Rahm's feet kept slipping back on the slope. Her heart was so full of terror that her heartbeat felt loud enough to shatter even the oppressive silence of hazefall. This was the most alive she had felt in decades, perhaps centuries. She'd spent too many hazefalls here.

"Let go," Evy said gently.

Rahm loosened her grip. She fell.

She fell.

After an eternity, the air began to smell like salt. Below her, a sea spread to the horizon and waves crashed onto a shore. Rahm held her breath, looking forward to the waiting world.

Gingerbread Red

by Chloe Spencer

Pristine, red, raw; with marbled fat glistening on the bone. That was exactly how Briony preferred her meals—but since it was winter, she opted for something hot to warm her belly. Her favorite parts? Typically the ribs, but the thigh bones had the juiciest flesh. It'd been a few months since she caught worthy prey, so tonight she decided to indulge. A feast of flesh, sizzling pound after pound into her cauldron, and two little feet perfect for pickling.

Crunch. Briony frowned and opened her mouth, reaching her spindly hand into her gullet. She removed a small bow, one that had been in the child's raven-blue hair. With a frown, she tossed it into the crackling fire. Her familiar, Bram, squawked and flapped his wings in disapproval. He was always so upset when she didn't share.

"What? It's nothing you would've liked."

She picked up the discarded pieces of clothing lying beside the hearth. Into the fire they went—they weren't worth repurposing. They always reeked of piss. Children couldn't exactly control their bowels before being eaten. That was the one downside to consuming them: no matter how perfectly you planned their demise, it was always messy. At the very least, the scraps would serve as excellent kindling for the fire, and it would mean she wouldn't have to go outside into the cold tonight, where yet another winter storm raged on. By the way the wind sounded—howling and mournful like the child she tore apart hours ago—it was far too treacherous to step outside her warm gingerbread walls.

Bram squawked again. Briony reached into the scorching cauldron and carefully fished out a sizzling finger, then tossed it to him. He guzzled it down. She rolled her eyes.

"Don't say I never did anything for you."

Bram blinked in response and preened his feathers. Briony migrated over to where her mirror stood, its ornate golden frame reflecting the fire's glowing amber light. Each step she took towards it, she felt her joints loosening, her muscles stretching; breathing new life into her ancient skeleton. Already she looked younger and fresher; the red returning to her blossoming cheeks and the wrinkles disappearing from her eyes and mouth. With a vivacious smile, she ran her hands over her hips and noted how her breasts lifted, how her bat wings disappeared. Green eyes, no longer dead like a fish's, but vibrant like the surrounding forest. One dead child to be drop dead gorgeous. She would never tire of seeing herself as she was hundreds of years ago.

Normally, the rest of Briony's evenings would pass by in peace. She would reorganize her witch hazel and dried mandrake roots, meticulously sweep the floors of her home, and maybe partake in a spiritual ceremony or two. But right now, she longed for nothing more than to curl up beside the fire in her favorite shortbread chair, to inhale the sweet yet spicy scent of her home, and stroke Bram's feathers until they fell asleep.

But tonight Briony would not get what she wished for, because soon after sitting down, she heard a loud knocking at the door. Her back arched, and her nerves prickled in fear. It'd been a long time since anyone found her cottage. She'd carved protection emblems on numerous trees throughout the forest to hide it from the common folk, but perhaps the marks needed to be refreshened. Every rite had to weaken at some point.

A coarse, feminine voice called out. "P-please! If anyone is there, let me in! I'll catch my death!"

Bram ruffled his feathers; unnerved. Stupefied, Briony stared at the door.

"I can see the fire through the windows!" The voice sounded annoyed now. "I know you're in there!"

Briony squeezed her eyes shut as anxiety rumbled in the pit of her stomach. She folded her hands together and pressed her lips against them, mumbling a prayer to her Gods Far Below. Then she rubbed them over Bram's body, and beneath her touch, he transformed into a cat. Bram yowled disdainfully, but he put up with it, nonetheless. She stood up and wrapped her cloak around her body, then opened the door.

A flourish of icy wind obscured her vision for a few moments, before finally, she saw a young woman. Her curly copper tresses, too free-spirited to hide beneath the hood of her coat, framed her round face. And, Briony noted, a plump, curvaceous body. She was a beautiful woman, and no doubt, would make for a beautiful meal. Too enraptured in her greed, Briony didn't even notice she was on the verge of drooling. The young woman didn't seem to either.

She rubbed her tired eyes and blew into her chapped hands. "Please, can I come inside?"

Briony stepped aside and the woman shuffled in. The ends of her cloak, already thin and threaded, tracked in mud and chunks of snow. For a moment, she stood there, basking in the light of the glowing fire, allowing the snow and dirt to slough off her body and onto the floor. Now that she was inside and in the light, Briony could see her face more clearly. Bruises. Scars. Scratches. Her split lip had scabbed over; leaving a ruby red crust on her otherwise frosted pink lips. She helped the woman remove her dripping cloak and offered her the chair by the fire.

"Thank you," she murmured, her body shivering. She rubbed her hands together and placed them dangerously close to the smoldering embers. "For a moment I was worried I'd have to break down the door."

"Thank you for not doing that," Briony replied. She continued to stare, fascinated. She couldn't decide on the more intriguing fantasy: how the woman would look roasting over a spit or rolling in the sheets in her bed. She took a seat across from her on a splintered stool. "I didn't realize there were many who lived in these parts."

"Neither did I." She looked around the home and Briony could tell she was already enraptured.

The home was built to mystify, and the various enchantments Briony created had helped to seal the deal. In truth, she could've just made a normal home from hay and stone, and manipulated her prey into believing that it was made of candy—but while Briony was a cocky witch, she was also a cautious one. When she first erected her home, she took painstaking effort to construct all the details: the dark-chocolate crown molding, the crackled peanut brittle ceiling, the sugar-striped candy cane columns. The textures and colors were real, but the tastes were very much fake. Candy, after all, would melt or grow brittle—but these enchanted woods would only burn.

"It looks delicious." The woman blinked, her sapphire eyes curious and innocent. Only the obvious rings of exhaustion on her face betrayed her youth. Life had not been kind to her.

Briony drifted over to the kitchen and retrieved half a loaf of bread along with a bowl of freshly churned butter. She wordlessly passed the food to the woman who began to eat, glistening droplets of butter rolling down her fingers and melting in the fire's heat. Briony noted the scratches on her hands; the red rimming her nails. She felt something stir within her—pity?—but she should have none.

"Careful you don't choke," Briony said, sitting down again.

Bram hopped onto her lap, and she stroked the cat slowly, keeping a watchful eye on the woman. She licked her damp fingertips and wiped them on the skirt of her tattered dress, leaving greasy stains.

"I apologize. I haven't eaten in days." She wiped the crumbs from around her lips.

"Looks like it."

The woman flinched. Briony couldn't help but smile softly.

"What's your name?"

"My name is Gretel. Gretel Weber."

"Briony Wyrm."

"Are you married, Mrs. Wyrm?"

"Widowed."

"Ahh." Gretel fell silent. Stared anxiously at the floor. "I envy you."

"I bet you do." Briony took that as a cue to stand up and fetch the wine. "Care for a drink, Gretel? You sound rather parched."

"Oh, well, yes … because …" Gretel loosened the upper strings of her shirt, uncovering her neck, which was also bruised. That explained the hoarse voice. "I would love a drink. Water."

"I only have wine."

Gretel flinched. "Wine then."

Briony didn't know for certain why Gretel felt unsafe. Maybe the woman was still reeling from recent events, or because she realized that it was unusually sinister to meet a young widow living in a gingerbread house in the woods. But Briony didn't push, only poured two glasses of red wine. Gretel took a small sip, and a faint smile teased across her lips.

"It's so rich. I've helped myself to a pint of ale here and there, but I've only had wine on my wedding day."

"How long have you been wedded in unfortunate matrimony?"

Gretel shrugged. "I was still young. Maybe a few moons after my first bleed."

"And you've grown up around here?"

"On the outskirts of this forest, yes. Ivorycombe. And yourself?"

"Far, far away."

Gretel's eyes shimmered with excitement. "You mean in the Capital?"

"Close enough." Briony took another sip. "Ivorycombe. Quaint place. Every once in a while, I set up shop at the merchant's market. But there's not a lot of extra income to go around in that little town, I've noticed."

"Oh, yes!" Gretel's mouth dropped open, as if she suddenly recognized her. For a moment, Briony wanted to panic. "You're the toymaker?"

"Yes." To occasionally earn money for trading, Briony built toys. It was a useful trade when she was in contact with those wealthy enough to afford them, and otherwise useful when it came to trapping small children. The back room of her house was entirely dedicated to her workshop.

"Makes sense as to why your house would look like this. Do you run your shop from your home?"

"Only when there're passersby. What does your husband do?"

"He's a blacksmith. Just finished his apprenticeship."

"Just finished the apprenticeship?"

"He wanted to be a farmer. But when the well ran dry a few years back, we had to abandon our homestead." Gretel took a long, deep swig from her cup of wine.

"And I imagine he takes those stresses out on you." Briony sighed. "Men are such troublesome creatures when they can't get their way."

"Your husband was the same?"

For a moment, Briony forgot she had told the lie. But then she smiled and nodded. Gretel mumbled a little prayer under her breath.

"I shouldn't speak ill of the dead."

"The dead aren't around to hear. Their ears are full of dirt."

Gretel let out a hiccupy laugh. She glanced down at her cup and saw that it was empty. Without asking, Briony poured her another glass. Gretel looked outside, and for a brief moment, the fear crept back into her face. Briony waved a hand dismissively.

"Even the dumbest of brutes wouldn't go out in a snowstorm to hunt you down. Tell you the truth, I don't know how you found this place."

Gretel laughed softly. "I don't know how, either. There I was, treading through snow and through the woods, and then I saw the little lights through the trees. It was almost magical."

<hr>

Briony prepared a bed for Gretel in her guest bedroom. She had a cot which was regrettably rancid—but Gretel, too intoxicated to protest, had curled up right away. Briony tucked sheets in around her body, and once again, her fantasies ran wild. Those plump thighs and breasts. She didn't know what she would want more: to bite them or kiss them. But she quelled those thoughts, scooped up Bram in her arms, and went to sleep.

In the morning, she found Gretel in front of the fireplace, preparing tea by placing the kettle in the embers of the fresh fire. Outside the world was calm, covered in a shimmering blanket of ice and snow. At first, Briony felt aggravated with herself—she should've made sure Gretel could not escape—but then she felt immensely grateful she had stayed. Gretel bowed her head respectfully when they locked eyes.

"I know that I shouldn't overstay my welcome. But I couldn't leave without thanking you for taking care of me. I wanted to prepare breakfast, if that's alright with you? I saw you had eggs, and I—"

Briony held up her hand. "It's alright."

Briony sat and watched as Gretel prepared breakfast in her cast-iron pan: consisting of eggs and thick slabs of meat ... human meat. Inside, Briony broiled at the idea of her precious food being consumed by a mortal, but she stopped. Gretel could have one last meal. It would only flavor her more.

"You've got a nice little homestead here." Gretel carefully moved the pan over the flames and sprinkled a handful of salt over the crackling eggs. "Fresh eggs, big fireplace. Plenty of food. You'd think we weren't in the middle of a famine."

Briony slowly nodded. By this point, she knew Gretel was suspicious of her. But she had to remain calm; play it safe. Prey were best taken when they least suspected it. Scaring them into fleeing or fighting back always made it worse.

Once the food was finished, Gretel plated the breakfast. She presented Briony with her food and sat across from her. Briony cautiously took a bite of the eggs and watched as Gretel broke up the yolk, mixing it in with the slabs of meat. But Gretel did not eat. Instead, she pinched a slab between the two fingers and held it up, examining it closely.

"Is this what grants you your powers?"

Gretel's blue eyes bore through her soulless husk. Her expression was calm, but her shoulders were stiff. She was afraid, but beyond that, she was curious. Briony couldn't find the words to reply. Gretel laid the bacon on her plate.

"I met you once when I was small." Gretel took a bite of her eggs. "You were older back then. Wrinkles upon wrinkles. I think we were the first you had come across in a long time."

Gretel's eyes met hers, and a chill trickled down Briony's spine. Although she did not remember their names, she remembered their eyes. Twins. Dirty faces. Crying eyes. Hungry mouths. They were the first she had caught in nearly a year. The boy went into the embers of the oven, screeching as children always did. The girl escaped from the chicken coop. In her weakness, she had gotten sloppy. But it didn't matter—she had gotten what she needed. Children had escaped her before. Children would escape her in the future.

Children had never returned.

Frozen, Briony watched as Gretel brought the bacon closer to her face, examining the scorch marks from the pan, the lacy ribbons of fat running like rivers through the juicy red flesh. Tentatively, Gretel bit into it, and slowly chewed. The bite was small, but delectable. Her eyelids fluttered and rolled towards the back of her skull, and she murmured sounds of pleasure, sending a delicious chill down Briony's spine. Still, Briony reached across and slapped it from her hands, back onto the plate.

"Don't do that!"

Gretel licked her fingers and sized up Briony with a sultry smirk. Briony watched as the bruises and dark circles faded underneath her eyes, as her skin became as dewy as fresh spring grass. She placed her hands against her cheeks and giggled girlishly at their soft texture.

"Why are you scared?" Gretel asked, her voice low and teasing. "Was it not you who stained these gingerbread walls red?"

"Why are you here?"

Gretel smirked again. She drifted over to where her still-damp cloak hung on the wall and reached into its deep pockets. After rummaging around, she withdrew a wilted piece of parchment paper with familiar symbols scrolled on it. A charm to break rites. That's how she found the house. It wasn't by chance, or a hole in the magic.

She had been looking for her.

With a heavy sigh, Briony crouched and picked up the still sizzling pan. She turned to face Gretel, but to her surprise, saw Gretel reaching for Bram. She snatched the cat up by the scruff and he yowled, desperately trying to escape her clutches.

"Put down my cat, gutter rat. Or I'll show you how a witch really fights."

Gretel chuckled. "You don't fight. You trick. You cheat. You *lure*. You're just as cowardly as I am. But if you're going to kill me and eat me, I might as well take your cat down with me."

Briony swallowed, tensely. She placed the pan back on the open flames. "Are you here for revenge?"

Bram howled mournfully, his black eyes wide with fear. Briony pointed to the floor. Reluctantly, Gretel put the cat down, and Bram scrambled over and up into Briony's arms.

"A long time ago, I was. I ran from here, naked and screaming, through the forest. Found my way home. Begged my father and stepmother to take me back in." She hugged her arms around her body, her eyes mournful but burning with malice. "And it was after they took me back in, that I realized that it would've been better if I died. Because my life was not my own regardless. Sold from home to home until I ended up with his family. And then betrothed to their son as soon as I could birth a babe."

Haunted, Gretel sat down and stared into the flames. Briony sat as well. Gretel's eyes were wet, and she kept shaking her head over and over again. She folded her hands in her lap, but they trembled as she spoke.

"But then I saw you at the market, with all your trinkets and toys. Living your life. And beautiful. Beautiful and young. I knew it was you when I saw your eyes and when I saw your dress. It was the same one that you had worn when you found us." She spoke fast yet soft. "And when all this time I had felt hatred, now I felt nothing but envy. Even now. *Envy.* And I thought about what it was like, and what it meant to be you. Free. Beautiful. Powerful."

"Powerful? This life's but a mere curse, mortal. And the reason I chase it is because I am unworthy for the afterworld in the eyes of the Gods Above."

"You killed my brother. And ate him."

"I owe you nothing, if that's what you're implying."

Briony blinked, folding her hands in her lap.

"And I will not help you when I do not have much to give."

"You view it as having nothing. But I've come from nothing, and I know that you have *everything*," Gretel's voice came out in a brutal growl, but then it warbled; wet. "I risked my life to make it here."

"What are you talking about?"

Suddenly, Gretel was unable to meet her gaze. Wordlessly, she examined her cuticles, her bloodied nails. Realization slowly filled Briony's body.

"You killed him, didn't you?"

"It was either him or me." Gretel swallowed back an obvious lump of tears. "So, if you'd rather cast me away than help me, at least kill me now."

"Where's the fun in that?" Prey was best killed in the heat of the moment—not during a feeble surrender. "What was your plan? To find me, grovel, and demand that I show you the witching ways without giving anything in return?"

"I think you know what I have to give you in return," Gretel said, her voice low. "Or is that no fun for you either?"

"Well, it takes away the game of seduction and chase."

"You seduced me the moment I saw those green eyes." Gretel crossed over to Briony and straddled her lap. "Besides, why expend energy on those things when you could use it in other ways?"

She moved Briony's hands to her thighs, and the witch could not help but squeeze them firmly, causing Gretel to shiver in response. Briony nipped at the tender flesh on Gretel's freshly healed neck, savoring the salt on her skin. Tenderly, Gretel tilted her head upwards, finally meeting her lips. Briony softly bit down on her bottom lip, pulling ever so slightly. Gretel entwined her fingers in Briony's hair and pulled downwards, forcing the witch to lock eyes with her.

"You," she said firmly, her smile vivacious, "will be gentle, understand?"

"Make me," Briony replied mischievously, and Gretel pulled on her hair again.

A violent shiver, delicious and swift, coursed down the witch's spine. Gretel kissed her neck as she slowly unbuttoned her nightshirt. Her soft hand caressed Briony's tender breast, and the witch in turn dug her fingers into her thighs, feral, her voice a low, rumbling growl. It was at this moment Gretel realized taming this beast would be a tremendous challenge, but a welcome one. There was a part of her that enjoyed the pain; that felt a pleasurable wave flood her body whenever Briony dug her fingers into her flesh. The witch's body was tense, every muscle poised to strike and tear her limb from limb, but she would not succumb to her animalistic desires.

In turn, Gretel rewarded her with gentle kisses, eliciting soft moans from her mouth. Briony's fingers slipped beneath the skirt of her dress, brushing along the inside of her thighs. Gretel firmly placed her hand on Briony's, guiding her fingers inside her body. She hissed in delight as Briony entered her, and eagerly rolled her hips forward, trying to move with the pace of Briony's fingers. Gretel could feel her humanity crumble beneath her as each wave of pleasure wracked her body, clouded her mind; and it was Briony's turn to reward her for her aggression. Gretel's kiss was as voracious and violent as the moans escaping her body, and in the heat of the moment, she firmly bit down on Briony's lip. Briony gasped in wordless pleasure as she felt the soft flesh rupture and the beads of blood trickle from the wound. With a satisfied smile, Gretel licked up the morsels, her pupils dilated, her mind succumbing to this act of sin; to the absolution of her humanity.

Briony had enjoyed many a meal, but she had never experienced anything as delicious as this.

BUCKSKIN FOR LINEN

by Mae Murray

The river was high when we needed it to be high and the river was low when we needed to pan crawfish from their mucky burrows. We were often hungry, but we were always fed.

When the French came, they built their church upon the unsteady ground of the Misi-ziibi, swaying to-and-fro like a cattail in the wind. When they took us virgin 'Indian' girls into the church, we traded our buckskin for linen and covered our dark hair. Our beds lined the four walls of a single room, their wooden legs scraping across the floor by half-inches depending on the lean of the church. We would climb from our beds in our white gowns and move them back in place, stifling fits of giggles. Then the Mother Superior would come with a flame in the night, and a hush would fall over us; even as we were whipped with the thin green arm of a young redbud tree, we did not make a sound.

Our tongues were forced from our mouths like when stern mothers squeeze their child's cheeks to expel a poison berry. In their place, we were given French tongues, imperfect and stumbling like fawns over their incomplete consonants and invisible vowels. We were given French names; I was to be called Sister Paulette, and my little sister was to be called Sister Josephine, and my cousins Sisters Angélique and Marie-Thérèse, and the other two from a tribe further down the Big River were to be called Sisters Éléonore and Jeanne, and together we were the Indian Sisters of St. Joan of Arc.

We did not know where our mothers, fathers, and brothers had gone, or our sisters who had already had children, nor did we know where the toddlers and infants had gone, and we were forbidden that knowledge and told we'd be punished should we ever ask again. We were taught the French letters and spent our days transcribing our own Bibles from the Mother Superior's book, and we studied the passages endlessly until they became a blur of hellfire on the page, the strange script sharp and jagged as a stone blade and the ink runny as blood. We were forbade reading anything else, and soon our dreams were populated by red seas and salt pillars in the shape of women, arms ever-reaching and breasts white as stone. But one night our dreaming was broken by a whisper from Sister Marie-Thérèse, quiet as a fox paw in the dark.

"Sisters," said she, passing each of our beds and squeezing our feet. "Sisters, I have something to confess."

We stirred under our quilts, for we rarely slept, spending most of our nights in silent contemplation, willing the minds of our Sisters to hear our thoughts. Rarely was that silence broken.

"What is it?" Sister Angélique sat up, her voice so low it could barely be heard.

"I am the eldest at nineteen, and as such I have taken it upon myself to form a plan of escape. These twelve nights past, I have gone in the early hours of the morning to the Mother Superior's quarters, and I have seduced her. The first night, I simply watched her as she slept, until she awoke and found me there. She was frightened, but she did not send me away. Each twilight, I have crept closer and touched new parts of her body, and this morning I will place my mouth on her and speak our 'savage' tongue until she cries out."

We sat in stunned silence, clutching our quilts to our chests.

"How does this serve us?" Sister Éléonore stood, an imposing figure. "You've done little but satisfy your own lust." Marie-Thérèse may be the eldest, but Éléonore was by far the largest of we six, with wide hips and broad shoulders.

"And there is nowhere to escape to," I added.

"Because," said Marie-Thérèse, "Mother Superior will grant us leniency if I continue to come to her each night, and there are many ways to escape. Or shall we continue to spend our days in quiet recitation, being whipped for speaking and then whipped again if we whimper from pain?"

We considered this, then gave our approval, fearing hope equally as we feared failure. But the following night, Sister Marie-Thérèse told us to stay awake until the light went out in the priest's window, which we could see from our own in the church's loft. Then, together we descended the steps, passing the Mother Superior's door. It creaked open and we paused, one blue eye peering from the crack and swiveling to look upon each of our faces, then landing finally on Marie-Thérèse. The blue eye was set in weathered white skin that seemed to tremble at the sight of her. Marie-Thérèse blew the eye a kiss and the door shut quickly, and she motioned us on our way.

Our land was a wild land and St. Joan's sat in the overgrowth as if she had dropped from the sky. From outside, even in the darkness, it was evident that nature had overtaken her, silent as a snake. The weeds had grown up high as the stained glass windows, their stalks wet from the marshy earth and following the lean of the building. We stood there looking at her for some time, having never seen her imposing silhouette against the backdrop of the starry sky, our bodies taking on her lean the longer we stared.

Suddenly, Joséphine pinched Angélique's backside with a peal of laughter stifled behind her palm, taking off in a gallop across the outstretched tongue of field that led to the gaping mouth of the forest. We all ran, too, gasping and shushing one another, fearful of waking the priest in his rectory, the quiet night wind whipping the linen shrouds from our hair and floating across the dry cattails like ribbons.

Our feet blackened, the soil under the canopied trees dark and lush with moisture. The branches reached out to us like children dancing at their mother's feet, wishing to be held; and they tore at our clothes until our arms lifted and the gowns were taken up into the trees. I turned my head to look back at them, the long sleeves and skirts floating like spirits and growing smaller; I never broke my stride, and I had no fear of falling.

We tramped into a cold stream and followed it to a spring, our brown bodies at last laying across the cool moss as we panted. Sister Éléonore was draped across a rock on her belly like a lizard, her thick arms spread wide and hugging the stone. Joséphine and Angélique lay clinging to one another, and I joined them by collapsing over their bodies and we all laughed and laughed. Marie-Thérèse stood waist-deep in the spring, her long hair following the line of her back as she looked up through the trees at the sliver of moon peering down on us like the Mother Superior's eye, if she were a kind woman.

"Suppose we never went back?" asked Sister Jeanne, plucking tufts of moss idly from the water's edge and rolling it between her palms. Her words hung in the air, not because they shocked us, but because she'd given voice to our own thoughts.

"Wouldn't they search for us?" I sat up beside Joséphine and Angélique, arms propped behind me and knees splayed.

"Why would they?"

"To save our damned souls." Marie-Thérèse turned to face us, gathering her mane and pulling it over her shoulder as she waded closer to where we all lay.

"No," said Éléonore, hands under her chin. "They do not care about our souls. Only about our bodies and minds and bending them to their will.

If they cared about souls, then where are our men and boys? Where are the mothers and children?"

"Suppose they are dead." Our heads turned now to Angélique, the quietest and meekest of we six. "Suppose the men and mothers are dead, and the children have been taken."

It must be so, we all agreed.

"But now Marie-Thérèse has captured the Mother Superior's affection."

"Not her affection," said Marie-Thérèse, "but her lust."

A distant frog released a low croak, and despite the somber discussion we laughed again, for there was no medicine like the sound of our own laughter. The church had taken the frivolity and joy of youth from us; this was perhaps the worst scar of all. There we could not laugh nor could we mourn, and so we sat like decoration day after day in the confines of her walls.

We lay like that for a while longer, the earliest hint of the sun breaking across the sky and casting a gray glow over our dark bodies. Joséphine and Angélique had been tangled in each other's limbs, sleeping, and the rest of we sisters dozed on and off as the morning mist settled over us.

When we at last stirred awake in full, each of our bellies were mewling as a chorus, singing the hymn of hunger. Sprouting up around us, reaching from white stalks, were crimson-colored mushrooms shiny as jewels, their domes speckled nipples. Every way we turned, there they were, set in tufts of moss like bouquets.

Sister Jeanne was the first to pluck a bunch from where they had sprung up, her thumb tracing the soft curve of its head and sticking her nail between the gills under the cap. She held it out to Marie-Thérèse.

"This is no medicine I've ever seen."

"Nor I," said Josephine. "But I am hungry, and the medicine is here. Perhaps it is a gift from Creator."

"The French do not say 'Creator.'"

"But we do," said I, and I was the first to eat.

Life overtook us. The trees shuddered and opened their canopies like wings, the heat of the sun turning our skin the color of clay. The mushrooms had given us the hollow bones of birds. We ran deeper into the forest with this sense of weightlessness, our laughter joining the distant thrum of drums that grew louder and louder in our ears until we could not distinguish our own voices, our own laughter, from that of the drums.

"Do you hear? Those are the voices of my father and brothers. That is the sound of my mother's hand weaving." Angélique kissed Joséphine breathlessly, and I lost sight of them when Éléonore's body captured my own.

Éléonore lifted me so that my feet dragged rivulets and circles into the soil. My arms fell around her, the throbbing of the drums in my ear punctuated by distant war cries. It compelled me to cry out, shivering in my sister's arms, and it was her lips against mine that swallowed my pain. I rolled my head away from her mouth, grasping her, kissing and biting her shoulder, desire pulled tight as a bowstring in my stomach.

Our skin, for a moment, seemed to stick together like the wax of two candles, our breasts covered in dew and sweat. I knelt at Sister Éléonore's feet as she stood over me, strong as a tree, holding her thick thighs in my hands and parting her legs with my thumbs. I was surprised by my own desire, tasted the sweet apple of her with my tongue. Her expression— often so stern and serious—softened, became tender as she stroked my hair. I had never noticed how long Sister Éléonore's hair was until her head fell back and she trembled under my ministrations; my fingers kneading her backside, the strands brushed the backs of my fingers like horsehair.

My dark eyes lifted to watch Éléonore's breasts heave with breath, the light of the sun catching my pupil in such a way that I felt momentarily blinded. When I recovered my sight, Angélique and Joséphine were black silhouettes suspended against the clear blue sky, bodies mirroring each other, legs draped so their groins were flush and frictive, the sounds of their moans ecstatic as birdsong. Sister Jeanne wrapped her arms around my waist from behind, Marie-Thérèse taking Éléonore, whose body was still quaking in bliss, and together we four joined the other two, our tangled mass blotting out the sun as a storm cloud, rivers running currents between our legs.

We looked down upon our bodies, pale among the moss, the empty white stalks of the mushrooms scattered around us like broken arrows.

***

It had been weeks since the Mother Superior found our bodies in the woods, and by that time much of our flesh had been absorbed by the moss or otherwise eaten away by insects and small predators; bobtailed cats and badgers. The sun remained hidden at our backs and the rain had not let up since we became one, our howls of ecstasy and laughter drawing thunder and spears of lightening, the wind of our gasping breath bearing down on St. Joan of Arc so that she creaked and moaned, constantly bending shape.

We had been interred in a mass grave some yards away from the church and scattered atop with seed. The church ledgers bearing our names were burned, as were our carefully transcribed Bibles, our linen clothing, the tangled remnants of our dark hair in the teeth of our combs. Whatever alliances the church had formed with our tribes, they were now broken and fed to flame.

The Mother Superior remained at St. Joan of Arc, and we spied on her with singular intensity day and night. We watched as she prayed, as she laundered her linens at the river's edge, as she avoided the pit in which our bodies had been thrown. We watched when she touched herself in the early hours of the morning, Marie-Thérèse's name a ghost on her whispering lips. She remembered our language badly and was unable to satisfy herself.

We played many games, our giggling a constant rumble in the gray sky. When she took her tea, we waited until the cup touched her lips, and then we erupted in laughter, loud as we could. The church shook with a sudden clap of thunder, and she spilled the tea across her breasts and lap, crying out, blue eyes rolling in her head, fists lifted as she dropped to her knees in prayer. At night we moved as one with purpose, rubbing our forms together until we made fire. We struck the church with a spear from the sky, leaving blackened marks across the roof, spindly as roots. On such nights, the Mother Superior would tear her hair, and in the morning, she would go to the priest's rectory, begging to flee this *terre sauvage.*

Each time the priest denied her, she found new ways to torment herself; a length of thin branch to crack like a whip across her pale spine, a bed of burrs in the soles of her shoes. She grew thin, jaundiced skin wilting on her face like a waxen candle, pale blue eyes overtaken by cataracts. She began to speak to us, softly at first, as if in prayer. She wished for the rain to cease, for the never-ending patter that filled her mind to allow her a single night's rest.

Though we heard her prayers, we could not grant her this. We found our satisfaction in her wanting, in the way the rain eroded her, our bodies in constant bliss.

It was the priest who found the Mother Superior hanging from the very redbud tree she had shorn for whipping branches. The force of our rain had shed the loose-hanging habit from her weathered body, exposing the many self-inflicted wounds, and he sent word to the nearest French settlement that the Mother Superior of St. Joan of Arc had been secretly wicked and was dead. He requested another Mother Superior and six new virgin Indian girls to fill his parish, for he craved souls, desperate as the Devil himself.

⁂

The arrival of the new girls caused the rain to come down hard as daggers; it no longer flowed from between our thighs, but from our eyes, the sky black as pupils. The force of our screams carried on great winds, the gales battering the church like so many phantom fists, causing the very earth beneath its unstable foundation to quiver to the core.

The priest stood at his window, gazing upon the church several yards away as it began to sway and splinter. In the distance, he saw us; a great cyclone coming across the water of the Misi-ziibi, picking up the river as a great blanket and wearing it as a shroud. Our single eye watched as he fled the rectory, stumbling over the plains to seek shelter in the forest. We scooped him up, his body as a blade of grass, taken into us with ease.

We had never before realized what a small man the priest was, short and graying with a dishonest heart. We could not hear his cries, only watched as the force of us spun him like thread, broke his bones, the skin at every joint loose and surprisingly thin. He was stretched until he came apart completely, the blood of him drenching the roof of the rectory as it too was torn away.

We turned our eye now to St. Joan of Arc. She still had a grip on the bank of the Big River, the mud sucking her foundation so that she shook like a loose tooth. Inside, the six young nuns were screaming. Their Mother Superior whipped them until they prayed.

⁂

The day broke without rain for the first time in many months. Nothing remained of the church of St. Joan of Arc; we had buried it deep in the riverbed and had laid the water over it with a promise to return should it ever be found.

Along the bank, the six girls slept in their beds, quilts pulled over their heads. The first to wake woke the others, and together they looked upon the land as it had been before the French came; before they had stolen their fathers, brothers, mothers, sisters, and children.

It was a wild land, but it was theirs. They lived alongside it as one cattail lived alongside another, each yawning toward the sun.

109

As they walked along the bank hand in hand, the smallest of the six stepped upon our bones, unearthed by the storm. Our bodies were draped across each other like sleeping pups.

The girls gathered our skeletons in their arms, one to each, stopping only to shed the linen of their habits. They stomped them into the dark mud with the tough soles of their feet, shaking out their hair and trembling with giddy laughter. They pulled their beds into the river and we, like alligators, swallowed them whole.

OUBLIETTE

by L. R. Stuart

The spider was barely larger than the pad of her thumb, and delicate, with spindly legs almost thin enough to be part of its web. It scuttled along the floorboards, searching for some poor bug to fill its belly, and instead found a toe, attached to a foot, attached to an ankle.

Maybe it was a poisonous spider. Perhaps it was simply a foolish one. Certainly it was ravenous, long starved locked away in the dusty attic with not even a dust mite to keep it fed. So it crawled over the iron cuff and onto the flesh of leg above, tickling with its dainty feet as it went, and prepared to bite.

The woman was much larger than the spider, easily able to trap it between the pinch of her fingers. Strong enough to keep the spider in her grasp in spite of its wriggling. Maybe poisonous, perhaps foolish, and just as ravenous as the spider.

She put its delicate body in her mouth and swallowed the spider whole.

<hr>

"You're moping."

Countess Maria von Oertzen—a woman, not *the* woman—looked at the crumpled heap of a person on the floor. Her hand curled and uncurled around the head of her cane, the only sign of her discomfort, though she was decidedly not looking around the room. As always, her head was tall, her gaze was firm, and she never made obvious her emotions.

"I'm allowed to mope," Odessa replied from beneath her arms. She was *the* woman, though she wouldn't like to be. "What else am I supposed to do? *Clean?*"

"It certainly wouldn't do you any harm." Maria had her skirt bunched up to keep dust from getting on the hem. She gestured around the room. "Look at the state of this place. Look at the state of *you!* Surely it is making you miserable."

"Oh, I'm sorry." Odessa unspooled herself. "You're right. Imprisonment shouldn't stop me from decorating."

Maria rolled her eyes. "You aren't imprisoned."

Odessa didn't answer. She lifted her ankle and shook it, making the heavy chain rattle.

It, as always, brought the conversation to a halt.

"Why are you doing this to me?" Odessa asked, aware that she sounded much like a child being sent to bed without supper, if not for the crack in her voice.

"Because I love you."

Odessa scoffed.

"*And*," Maria continued, "I cannot trust you. I'm fairly certain you don't understand just how much I want to, but I can't."

"I can control myself," Odessa protested, as she always protested.

"I really think you believe that." Maria almost smiled. "But one of us needs to stop lying."

Odessa slumped where she sat, one hand resting atop the iron keeping her in place.

"I'll send up a maid," Maria declared, before shutting the door behind her and leaving Odessa alone once again.

⁂

The maid was sweet. Too sweet. She reminded Odessa of trying to eat a banana that had been left to ripen in the sun for just a little too long. Her first act was to open the moth-eaten curtain—from back when there were still moths to eat it—filling the room with colors filtering through the stained glass window, and then to open the window so that more bugs could come flying in.

"Much better!" she said with a deep inhale and a loud sighing exhale.

Odessa wanted to open the window further and push the damn girl out.

"Mistress told me to bring some soup!" The maid lifted the lid off the small pot, filling the room with its aroma. She wrinkled her nose. "I have to say, it doesn't smell terribly appealing, but she said it was your favorite!"

Odessa pulled back as the maid forced her way into Odessa's space, getting almost close enough to touch even when Odessa snarled at her. She hummed some melody that Odessa instantly despised as she wiped the bed table clean of dust, a ball of it forming in her hand, before setting down the claypot.

"Enjoy!" she said, daring to give Odessa a pat on the knee.

Even the long-awaited arrival of food could not be truly savored with the maid moving around the attic, dusting and wiping and even, God above, spraying. Odessa watched her every move while slurping from her spoon, the way she used to do when she wanted to get on Maria's nerves.

Instead of asking her to stop, the girl just said, "I'm glad you're enjoying it!" and kept dusting.

Odessa didn't even have time to relish her meal, when as soon as it was done the empty bowl was torn from her hands.

"Time for me to make your bed," the maid said, smiling, before forcing Odessa out of the comfort of her own sheets.

Odessa, not one to be pushed around, gripped tightly onto her bedding and hissed at her assailant. The girl hardly seemed to notice, and certainly didn't care, pulling the sheet out from under Odessa and, to her outrage, pulling away her rugs as well.

"Now I can leave you with just the sheet"—the maid looked at Odessa's mocking victory—"or you can cooperate."

Odessa scowled. "I'll keep the sheet."

<hr>

"Everything looks much better," Maria said, deigning to let her skirts touch the floor.

"I feel violated." Odessa had lost the war and was now forced to lie in clean bedding. It was humiliating.

"Don't you like her?" Maria asked with a sly grin.

Bitch.

"'Don't you like her?'" Odessa repeated mockingly. "No, I don't like her saccharine, vapid, grating demeanor, or her—don't laugh at me!"

Maria hid her smile behind her hand. "I thought you would. She's quite pretty, isn't she?"

"I didn't notice," Odessa said, with the pride of someone who hadn't fallen to their usual shortcomings.

"You should." Maria's hand, and smile, fell. "She reminds me of you, when we were younger."

"When *you* were younger," Odessa corrected. "I have always been the same."

"No, my dear." Maria's hand clenched around her cane again. "You haven't."

<hr>

The maid—Claudine, apparently—was beautiful, and now, Odessa couldn't help but notice. Her hair was red and fine, always slipping out of the buns she put it in. Those eyes, too sparkling for Odessa's sensibilities, were a rich brown that shone in the light. Her lips, always pulled into the same, infuriating smile, were plump and well-shaped.

Damn Maria's eyes, she knew Odessa too well.

"I've brought you something to brighten your room," Claudine said happily, always happily, as she arranged some fresh flowers in a vase she had pulled from nowhere. The flowers, thankfully, weren't anything like sunflowers or daisies. If they were, Odessa would have had to kill her.

"I don't want my room brightened," Odessa complained. "I like it dark and miserable; makes me feel at home."

Claudine laughed. "You are silly. No, it's important to keep your spirits up when you're healing. It's far too easy to lose sight of what is good for you, in cases like yours."

"Is that what she told you?" Odessa asked, iron burning against her skin. "That I'm sick?"

"Something like that," Claudine answered. She paused in the middle of pruning a flower, her perfect smile turning to something more pensive. "She loves you very much, you know. I would give anything for my mother to care for me as much."

Odessa felt something horrible in her throat, something like acid slowly rising from within her. She wondered, momentarily, if she was going to be sick.

"Maria isn't my mother," she croaked.

"All the same," Claudine continued, "we could all do with someone like that in our lives."

Odessa's lip wobbled, with rage or tears she did not know. She smiled her worst smile, the one that had gotten her locked up in the first place, and said, "Hopefully someday you will."

Claudine smiled back like Odessa had given her a blessing.

<hr>

Claudine was the youngest daughter, but older than two brothers. Her parents married young, and had lost her amongst her pack of siblings, so when she was old enough, she left her small village for the big city, before leaving the big city to go to a different small village. But she was happy here, where people listened to what she had to say and asked her how her day had been.

Not that Odessa had wanted to know all of that but Claudine had told her anyway.

"Mama was always superstitious about these woods," Claudine prattled on, brushing Odessa's hair. "When I told her where I was going, she sent me all these herbs and spells to ward off fairies and goblins and witches … She still worries about me even though I've told her that the only strange thing I've seen in these woods is Monsieur Berkhardt wandering naked with an apple on the end of his … you know. I've never heard of goblins or fairies doing *that!*"

"No …" Odessa murmured. "No goblins or fairies or witches around here."

"She keeps telling me I should eat eight cloves of garlic a day to ward off evil beasts," Claudine continued. "She *also* keeps asking why I'm yet to find a husband. I don't know how I can do that with my breath smelling of garlic all the time!"

"I suppose not."

"Have you ever had a young man ask to marry you?" Claudine asked.

"No." Odessa watched the light from the stained glass dance on the wall. "No, it wasn't a concern for me."

"Oh, that must be nice." Claudine laughed. "I'm not a fan of them, if I must be honest. They're not terrible, but to have to see one every day, sleep in his bed, bear his children and raise them … it seems like an awful lot of work. But what else am I supposed to do with my life?"

"You could always live in an attic," Odessa answered.

Odessa guessed Claudine thought she was making a joke—still, her laugh, ill-fitting as it was, made Odessa smile.

⁕ ⸻⸻ ⁕

Odessa hated feeling better. She hated that Claudine's company made her life a little bit more enjoyable, that she had days where she didn't even think about her imprisonment. It was a cruel punishment to be held captive and made to enjoy it, and every day she fell further down the stairs into enforced pleasantness.

Still, when Claudine offered to clean her, Odessa didn't have the heart to argue. Now that everything else was free from dirt, it only served to highlight her own filth. No longer was she one of many things in disarray; she, and only she, was the problem. Maybe Maria was right. Maybe this all was Odessa's fault.

Claudine told her, "Well done," when Odessa let her take off her nightgown. This girl, still in the fruits of womanhood, telling Odessa how good she was to let herself be stripped. It was humiliating, in that special way that made Odessa want to cling to her, or else she was going to fall apart. Claudine, in one of her rare moments of wisdom, seemed to understand how Odessa was feeling and stayed close, with little more than the sponge she used between them.

"I know how easy it is to be stubborn," Claudine said, lightly rubbing her sponge into Odessa's skin.

Odessa had forgotten how good water felt, and her moan was inevitable. Thankfully, Claudine did not acknowledge it.

"But I'm glad to be helping you," Claudine continued. Her sponge caressed Odessa's neck. "You are too lovely to be locked up here, alone."

Odessa could feel the acid burning in her throat again, a bubble waiting to be released as a sob or a scream, maybe even a laugh. She just hummed instead. It was all she really could do.

Claudine bent down to dunk her sponge in the bucket again, and this time she began to wash Odessa's clavicle.

"You are so beautiful," she said, murmuring it as if it was a thought meant only for herself. "But it's a haunting beauty. The type of angels in graveyards."

It was not the first time Odessa had heard it. But after so long with no one except the rare spider to keep her company, she struggled to believe it. The beauty she had once used to bewitch people to their doom had long since gone to rot, like all things left abandoned in a dusty old attic.

"You think I'm beautiful?" Odessa asked.

Claudine's sponge moved lower, across Odessa's chest, until Claudine was gently washing Odessa's breast, caressing it with the sensitivity of a lover's touch.

"Yes," she answered softly, a secret between them. "I—"

The sound of the door opening startled Claudine out of her trance, causing her to jump back and knock over her pail. Water and soap suds spilled over the floor.

Maria looked at the mess with an indiscernible expression.

"I'll fetch a mop," Claudine said, dropping her sponge to the floor. She curtsied for Maria as she hurried past, looking like she was about to trip on her own feet before fleeing out the door without so much as a glance behind her.

Odessa shivered, naked and wet.

"She convinced you to bathe," Maria stated, bending down to pick up the forgotten sponge.

Odessa only grunted.

"May I?" Maria asked, holding the sponge in her hand.

"The soap—" Odessa swallowed. "It will get on your dress."

"I don't mind." Maria lifted her skirts as she stepped over the water.

For the first time in too long, Odessa could feel the heat of Maria's body against hers, and it was that which made her realize just how much it had changed. The firm plumpness had sagged slightly, and her skin felt strangely withered. While she had always held her head high, her back had begun to stoop over, and her body seemed unable to stop trembling.

Maria was getting old.

"You're staring at me," Maria said with a chuckle.

"I was just thinking about how it used to be." Odessa felt butterflies in her stomach when Maria swiped her hand over it. Or nausea. "When we used to squeeze into a bathtub together and hold each other in the water."

"And you'd get water everywhere because you couldn't keep still for a minute?" Maria moved the sponge between Odessa's legs. "I'd have to get you off just so you'd relax."

Odessa remembered. She remembered the feeling of warmth spreading through her, of lying in Maria's arms because all she wanted after an orgasm was to feel safe. It was why, in spite of how long she'd been locked away, she'd never managed to do it on her own. She had tried, but that peak never came, not when all she had was a cold bed and the ever-gathering dust.

"Oh, sweetheart." Maria wiped away Odessa's tears with her dry hand. "What's wrong?"

"Why did this happen?" Odessa asked. "We used to be so happy, and now you've …"

The carefully cultivated stone of Maria's face almost cracked, just enough for Odessa to know there was something underneath. What, she didn't know. She didn't have the heart to ask. It was easier to imagine and be happy, rather than to know and be in agony.

Odessa had been an artful manipulator once, and even Maria had been one of her victims. There was no manipulation now. It would have been less humiliating if there was. Instead she stood there, weeping quietly while her once beloved cradled her with one hand, and washed her with the other. Power was a game Odessa had so thoroughly lost that she had been removed from the board, and now all she had was the pieces of herself crumbling to dust.

She didn't know what to do, then, when Maria sank to her knees, the spilled water soaking into her precious skirts. It hurt to breathe, like the morning of a German winter, making Odessa feel like she was on the edge of hyperventilation. Maria washed Odessa's legs with a care Odessa had long forgotten, even making sure to clean between Odessa's toes.

With her thumb, Maria held up the iron around Odessa's ankle so she could wash the skin beneath it. She bathed the area like it was a wound, like Odessa might have bruised or chafed in it. There was no such injury, no need for tenderness, except that Maria wanted to give it.

"I used to think you loved me more than anything else in the world," Odessa said.

"I do," Maria answered, "though I'm not the best at showing it."

"Maybe that's the problem." Odessa ignored the squeak of the door and Claudine's soft footsteps. "None of this would have happened if you had loved me a little less."

Maria didn't look up at her again. A droplet of water splashed into the pool under them.

"Claudine," Odessa said, interrupting the girl's monologue on the love affairs between Maria's staff. "Why are you here?"

Claudine looked up from the bookcase. "I thought you might like something to read?"

"No." Odessa stood from the bed and walked towards her. "Why are you *here*?"

"I'm your maid," Claudine answered, as if she was worried Odessa had forgotten. "I have been for—for more than a year now."

"And not once have you questioned—" Odessa reached the end of the chain, pulling it taut. It made a noise, uncomfortable with being stretched so thin.

Claudine didn't even look at it. "The Countess wanted someone to keep you company. I understand how lonely you must be—I too have suffered from afflictions."

Odessa smiled sardonically. "I doubt any quite like mine."

"But we are friends now," Claudine said hurriedly, when Odessa hung her head. "Good friends. You make your jokes, but no one has ever put up with me quite as much as you before."

Odessa wanted to scoff. She didn't have friends. She used to, in days of old when she could hold galas and attend balls. Once, she had many friends.

"I'm sure you'll find a friendship with me most unfortunate, everyone does." She smiled, remembering what it was like to be charming. "Don't worry, you'll be cured of it soon enough."

"No, madame." Claudine spoke like she was making a passionate oath, clasping a book in her hands. "To me, your friendship is a most precious thing."

It had been a long time since Odessa had been kissed. She wished her last had been Maria, and not a stranger she couldn't even name but had come between them so thoroughly. A lifetime of kissing her, and Odessa could never remember what Maria was like.

Claudine was forceful, in spite of her nature. She held back her tongue but otherwise kissed fiercely, her cupid's bow gently making love to Odessa's upper lip. It was, in truth, a relatively chaste kiss, but Claudine's hands on her neck and the book lost beside their feet made it feel obscene.

They didn't make it to the bed, lying in a tangled embrace on the floor while they struggled to rid Claudine of her clothes. Both gave up once they had got her down to her undergarments, Odessa freeing one of Claudine's breasts from her stays and caressing it with her mouth.

Touch was a long-lost sensation, intimacy even more grieved, and the fire inside Odessa burned hot. The smell of sweat beading on Claudine's skin turned to a burst of flavor on her tongue, and, in kind, Claudine reached beneath Odessa's nightgown and stroked every plain she could reach.

"We shouldn't do this," Odessa said, though the remark lost its power when spoken with her lips against Claudine's flesh.

"Do you want to stop?" Claudine asked, also without ceasing her movements.

Odessa could hear the pounding of Claudine's heart, the powerful thump as it worked through her exertion. She wondered if Claudine questioned the absence of such a sound from Odessa's own chest. No, probably not. Ecstasy had a way of distracting people from such things.

Claudine moaned when Odessa worked her hand between her legs. The girl wasn't a virgin, she had admitted as such, though had never reached pleasure either on her own or with another. In another lifetime, Odessa would never have let Claudine go after such a confession, driving her to ruin then and there with Odessa's fingers and tongue and any other implement she had on hand. But in this life, she had waited, and felt proud for doing so.

Odessa understood in that moment why Maria had imprisoned her in the attic and wished, with all her heart, that she was capable of change. That Claudine writhing and bucking against her didn't intoxicate Odessa with the life within her, that the increased pounding of Claudine's heart didn't become the only thing she could hear.

The only kindness Odessa could give was that Claudine was not hurt by it. No, based on her cry of pleasure, she quite enjoyed the pierce of Odessa's fangs in her throat, and her climax was untampered by the steady flow of her blood.

Heartbreak. That's what Maria had been hiding underneath her mask. The heartbreak of being betrayed by the person you love, of losing them again and again to their worst impulses.

Odessa could see it plainly on her face.

"She was your friend," Maria said morosely, looking at the lifeless body.

Odessa didn't protest. She continued to sit slumped against her bed, dried blood on her chin, her belly full of fresh life instead of the stale bowls of it Maria had been feeding her. If only it had been worth it in the end.

"Why didn't you do it?" Odessa asked. The evening sun was making the room dance with colors. "You had the stake against my heart."

"Because I love you," Maria answered, her voice wet with tears.

Odessa looked at Claudine, her eyes still open, immortalizing the moment when she finally realized what Odessa had done.

"I wish you'd never loved me at all."

Conversations with Roe

by Alex Luceli Jiménez

My head is loud with the feeling of missing you. I can't say I expected that missing you would be so loud, or that I would miss you at all. I've never killed anyone and missed them. I miss you and I'm looking out the glass sliding door that leads out into the backyard and beyond and there you are, just beyond the fence that separates my land from your land. You're far away but I know it's you. Who else would be out there? My head is so loud with the feeling of missing you and the blurring confusion at the sight of you out there that I almost don't hear you say my name.

Nora.

I don't say anything, or turn around, and you say it again: *Nora.*

I don't want to talk to you. I don't want to know what's going on. I turn around and there you are, as if it's somehow possible for you to be alive again. Alive in your fuzzy pink cardigan.

Nora.

I don't want to talk to you. I turn away, look at you outside one more time, then go into the downstairs guest room and lock myself in there. I hear you walking around the house. I hear the stairs creak. Maybe you went upstairs to see your body.

⋅⊷⊷══════════╌⊰⊱╌⊷⊷⋅

You have to come out, eventually. You know that, right? You can't stay in there forever.

I know that and it's already the next night. I can't remember the last time I ate or drank water. When I open the door you're out there in the hallway, smiling at me. I walk past you and up the stairs, where our bedroom door is open. In there is your body, sprawled on the white sheets I used to strangle you two days ago. And there you are beside me, too, in your fuzzy pink cardigan. I look out the bedroom window, looking out into the backyard and beyond, and you're there, too: you've hopped the fence now, you're standing on my land now. But still, unmoving. A hazy figure in the moonlight.

How are there three of you?

You tell me. This is all in your head, right?

It feels real.

Maybe you're just that crazy.

Then you laugh and your laughter fills this cavernous house and my head is loud with the feeling of missing you and your laughter, and I walk past you again and go downstairs and force myself to eat cereal and drink water. You stand with me in the kitchen, still laughing. Then I lock myself in the downstairs guest room again.

⁂

A knock on the guest room door, and then:

Will you come out and tell me a story?

I don't answer you.

Come on, come out and tell me a story.

I roll over in bed and stare at the closed blinds.

Nora, Nora, Nora.

I close my eyes.

Nora May De León.

So it's like that? You're using my full name now?

You laugh. *Come on, Nora May De León. Come tell me a story.*

I stand up and open the door.

You're acting like a child. What kind of story do you want to hear?

Tell me our story.

What do you mean?

Start with how we met.

You know how we met. You were there. That's half of the event.

I want to hear our story in your words.

You say it like it's important.

Maybe you can make it sound important.

The danger of doing that doesn't evade me. My head is already loud with the feeling of missing you. I haven't gotten this far whilst being an idiot. I close the door. I pretend I don't hear you calling my name, lilting and taunting. *Nora, Nora, Nora. Nora May De León.*

⁂

You were wearing your fuzzy pink cardigan. I thought it was ugly. That's why I stopped to talk to you. I wanted to know what kind of person would go out walking in the desert at 1 a.m. wearing such an ugly fuzzy cardigan. Sure, I wanted to know about the supposed neighbor a few feet away from my backyard, but it was more about the cardigan. Maybe I'd have shown less mean-girl-clique colors if I'd known about the agoraphobia. I'm sorry I was such an asshole that day. I told you to your face how ugly that cardigan was.

I'm standing in front of the glass patio door and you're both behind me and in front of me: in front of me, you out there in broad daylight, still but closer, and behind me, the you wearing the fuzzy pink cardigan and smiling. I don't need to look at you to know you're smiling.

You remember it well.

Of course I do.

You were an asshole, but it's an ugly cardigan. What happened next?

We did, didn't we? I don't know. It doesn't feel like four years ago, but it was. You understood me so quickly. For some reason you didn't seem to mind that I didn't fully understand you. I was so proud when you finally made it to my back door.

Back then I still couldn't leave the house at all until after nightfall. Was that as hard for you as it was for me? How long did it take for me to reach your back door after we met—it was a month, wasn't it? I'd been going on my night walks for some time.

It upset me that you'd been walking alone for so long.

Yes, you told me that to my face, too. On the first night. Do you remember how, when you asked me to come in for a drink—the can't-leave-the-house-for-too-long thing hadn't come up yet—I stammered a little and said as if! Because what if you were some kind of psychotic serial killer? That's really funny now, isn't it?

Why would you bring that up?

Because it's funny, Nora. It's dramatic irony. It's funny.

This time when I retreat back into the guest room, you're laughing. I think I catch a little snort, that's how hard you're laughing.

⁕ ⸻⸻⸻ ⁕

What are you waiting for? Don't you want to get somewhere? Don't you want to make sense of it all?

I let you into the guest room, and we lie down side by side. I know the you outside is getting closer, but right now I don't want to look. I know the you upstairs is rotting, but right now I don't want to look.

Tell me how you started killing.

Maybe it started as far back as when I was born, an unwanted child in southern California with an ugly face and stringy red hair adopted by a Black mother and a Brown father. We looked out of place everywhere we went. I never had friends. I never had anyone. I didn't love my parents because I didn't believe they loved me, even if they chose me, and they didn't love each other. I wasn't beautiful until I turned eighteen and then suddenly all the doors in the world were open for me. I fell in love with my college roommate, or at least thought I did, and she let me into her bed, but she was always bringing other people to her bed too. I couldn't stand it. She made me feel ugly and unwanted again. So I pushed her down the concrete stairs in our building and she fell on her head and that was it. It was so simple. It made so much sense. Everyone thought it was an accident. Nothing had ever made so much sense to me.

It was the first time but it wasn't the last.

I got more creative after that. There were three others, two men and a woman. I stabbed, I strangled, I drowned. They were people that couldn't be linked back to me, and I got away with it every time. And then there was Margaret at the country club in San Bernardino where I was a waitress after college.

You don't have to tell me what happened. I know this was her house and I know you two were together before she died. I know all your money was her money. I put the pieces together when you told me the dead man I helped you bury before you killed me wasn't the first person you'd killed.

I want to say it wasn't as simple as that but it was. I saw my chance and I took it.

How did you do it?

I poisoned her. It had to be subtle. I'd never been that subtle but I knew I could easily be suspected. She was old, so no one questioned it. The night you and I met was the night after her funeral.

You were wandering the property that was yours now. You were vibrating with joy. You were ecstatic. I could tell even then that you were overjoyed. I thought it was strange but mostly I was embarrassed about being caught walking and I cared more about the embarrassment than I did about how strange you were acting. You were so happy but I knew that the woman who may as well have been your wife had just died.

I knew your parents died a few years before I met Margaret. She told me she didn't know what happened to you and your sister after that. I guess she didn't realize that you were still in that house, you just couldn't leave it for so long.

I didn't know you but I knew of you. My parents were friends with Margaret before they died. Adrienne mentioned Margaret was living with a much younger woman. She said she saw you at the grocery store one time she came to visit, before we had all met. She said you were beautiful. I'll never forget that.

Don't.

Why? Are we going to pretend you ever felt guilty about cheating on me with my sister?

I did. I do. You have no idea. You can't possibly understand.

We're never going to get anywhere if you lie.

I stand up and walk out of the room. I go upstairs. Our bedroom stinks with the smell of your rotting body. I fall to the ground at the foot of the bed and, for the first time since my adopted mother stopped making me pray at age twelve, I ask God for forgiveness.

Two weeks now. I've been ignoring the you inside. Outside, you're getting closer. Outside, you're also wearing that ugly fuzzy pink cardigan, but your face is rotting, like your face upstairs. Inside you look alive and you stand beside me and watch yourself standing out there in the moonlight.

When do you think I'm going to reach the door?

It took you a month the first time.

So you're talking to me again?

I don't answer you. I stare at the you outside and the you outside stares back.

I loved you, you know. Think what you will of me, and you did what you did to me, but I loved you.

I know.

We sit on the cold tile floor in front of the glass door, cold even though it's July and the California heat is burning everything up outside and sometimes the heat comes inside too. Out here in the desert with the wind howling outside we may as well be the only people in the world. Just me and the you beside me and the you outside and the you upstairs.

I loved you too, Roe.

That's the first time you've said my name since you killed me.

But you loved me too much. That's why I had to do what I did.

That's a terrible excuse.

I remember it all like it just happened. I remember the night you made it to my back door and I let you in and I kissed you for the first time. I remember it only took you two months to tell me you were in love with me. I remember you basically moved in after three months. I remember slow dancing with you out in the dark in the desert and reading beside you in bed and taking you to the beach, your first time leaving either of these properties in years. I remember holding your hand as we drove home from the beach and I remember telling you I loved you that same night.

I remember that you slept with my sister after we'd been together for three years.

Roelle.

So I'm not Roe anymore to you?

Roe.

That's when things started to go wrong.

We couldn't slow dance in the desert forever, Roe. We couldn't hide out here living some perfect life forever.

We could have. We had the money. We were happy enough. We could have stayed happy forever if you could handle being loved.

I slept with Adrienne because I'm weak and because she asked. Blame her for asking.

I blame both of you. You could have said no.

I'm weak.

You're the strongest person I've ever known.

You once told me your mother was the strongest person you'd ever known. You moved back home after college. You were already depressed and then your parents died and you couldn't leave the house for five years. You loved your mother more than you loved anyone.

I loved you more than I've ever loved anyone, and you couldn't handle it.

Stop.

Why did you lie to me when I was alive? Why did you tell me you didn't sleep with Adrienne?

Because she and I agreed we would hide it from you. I didn't want to ruin your relationship with the only family you have left. How did you even know? You were sleeping.

I heard her leave our house. The next morning you two wouldn't look at each other. You had been flirting the whole time she was visiting. It wasn't hard to figure out.

You wouldn't let it go. If you had just let it go, maybe we would still be slow dancing in the desert. Why were you okay with me killing people and not okay with me sleeping with Adrienne?

Because when you slept with Adrienne, you betrayed me. I was devoted to you. I was loyal. I loved you and you slept with my sister.

I'm so weak, Roe. You don't know. You can't know.

I stand up and leave you again. I lock myself in the guest room. I sleep.

⚬⊷━━━━━━━━━━⊶⚬

When did you know you were going to kill me?

Three weeks. You're only a few feet away from the door now. It's the middle of the day and the sun is burning down hot on your rotting head. Pieces of you are falling off, just like pieces of you are falling off upstairs. I stare at the you outside, blinking, and the you outside stares at me, unblinking.

I didn't know I was going to kill you until I killed you.

I don't believe you.

It's true. I knew I wanted to kill you but I didn't know I actually would. That day I took your keys and locked you out of my house, a year after I slept with Adrienne and you wouldn't stop confronting me about it, it was because that day I wanted to kill you so badly. But I trusted myself not to. I trusted myself to stop myself. You stood outside screaming for me to let you in all day and all night. I let you in the next morning. I thought the urge had passed, but a few hours later you were sleeping on the couch and I wanted to do it again, so badly.

That's why you went out and killed that man.

I met him at that bar on the outskirts of town. The one we went to that one time, because you'd never been to a bar, but we could only stay for ten minutes before you got overwhelmed and we had to leave. He was old. He reminded me of the pictures Margaret showed me of her dead husband.

The dead husband who left all his money and his house to Margaret and then Margaret left all of it to you.

I let him kiss me in my car. Then I stabbed him.

You drove all the way back here with his dead body in the passenger seat.

You opened the door to the passenger seat before I could stop you. You were waiting for me outside.

I helped you bury the body.

You weren't angry. You weren't even shocked.

I remembered how happy you were the night we met. The night after Margaret's funeral.

It was four in the morning when we finished digging the grave and went to bed.

Look, I'm getting closer.

I do look and outside you are getting closer. I can see your eyes, filmed over. Next to me, your eyes are still brown and beautiful.

We were lying in bed and I told you that wasn't the first time I had killed someone.

You said it might not be the last.

You said we'd just have to work on it and maybe keep me from hurting anyone else.

You started crying. Four years with you and I had never seen you cry.
You were so kind. I told you I'm a murderer, and you were so kind.
So you killed me.
So I killed you.
You strangled me.
I strangled you.
You couldn't have been more creative? You couldn't have done something you'd never done before?
I'm sorry. You deserved better.
I deserve to be alive?
I miss you. My head is loud with the feeling of missing you.
You should have thought of that before you killed me.
I don't think. That's the problem. I'm weak. So weak.
You don't know your own strength.
Why didn't you fight back when I started strangling you?
Because I'm kind.
I needed it. I needed you to fight back.
You needed to kill me and I let you.
Outside you're so close I can see you smiling.

❦

One month. In one hour it will have been exactly one month since I strangled you. You're standing in front of the glass sliding door and I'm staring back at you. Your body is bloated and your mouth hangs open in a wide grin. Your arms hang at your side, sleeved in that fuzzy pink cardigan. I lift a trembling hand to rest against the glass and you raise your bloated hand to rest against mine.
What do you think I'm going to do when I get in?
I know. I know I will open the door for you, like I opened it for you all those years ago, and you will step inside. When it's time, that's what I do: I open the door for you, and you step inside. Your cold hands touch my face and you kiss me with your cold lips and I know this is the last time we will ever kiss, just like that night you reached my back door for the first time, I knew it would be the first time we ever kissed. As you pull away, I feel your hands on my neck. My eyes are wet with tears. You are so kind. So, so kind.

Our Lady of Devouring Violence

by Cheyanne Brabo

The Court should understand, first and foremost, that I knew what the Lady was the moment I saw her. I was there when the evidence of her Devouring Soul was first noticed, when bodies appeared like limp leather hides drying on the riverbank so many months ago. A demon, a monster, a devil—she is all this Court accuses her of being and more. And today, because I have been brought before you all against my will, I will describe to you what else the Lady is.

It was early autumn when I found myself walking along the River late at night. The moon was full, and all the land was bathed in blue shadows, the water shimmered like silver gossamer beneath the dull light. I happened upon a curve in the favor-trail when, in a clearing of sweet grass and wild blackberry, I saw the dark shape of a creature kneeling on its hands and knees in the darkness.

The shape, masked in black shadow as it moved and thrashed, put terror in me as I had never known before and will never know again. My mind's eye went without hesitation to the diabolical imagery of the Devil and his demon hordes, of the beasts of fire and brimstone, of the terror of Hell below. Frozen with terror, I found myself too afraid to move for fear of being heard. Though my guilt held me asunder, the scene before me inspired a dark, awestruck curiosity within my cowering soul.

To those who hear this testimony or read these transcripts, I will attempt to impart the depths of feeling which next came over me via the poor substitute for genuine experience the human language is.

I realized that the shape was a woman, that she was crouched above a prone body, her head bent as she bit and tore into the neck of her victim, somehow involved in a ritual of predation unlike I'd ever imagined. In the night's darkness, I watched the woman feast upon the flesh of another person, poised like a predatory cat as she ate her fill.

As I watched, the Lady threw her head back, the mighty veil of her red hair tossing wildly as her lips parted in a silent moan and her face opened in awe. I knew instantaneously it was she who was responsible for the three deaths on the Riverbank, for her victim lay flat and deflated in the grass exactly as the first three bodies had been discovered. The man lay still as a bedsheet, all the material of his body pulled out of him via the bite mark on his neck, his remains like a withered fruit in the moonlight.

And then, through the mist and cool air of the blue night, the Lady locked eyes with me. I dared not breathe as we stared at one another.

Does this court know that the Lady's eyes shine like pits of fire through the darkness? Like twin suns from the smooth brown skin of her skull, the Lady saw me standing as I saw her. Two full, sly lips pulled into a smile all together sinister and sensual. In her queer, ancient-looking corset, the Lady's breasts heaved as she panted through the exertion of her kill. Of course, every muscle of my body wanted to run, to scream with fear or cry for mercy, but my heart made me do otherwise.

Only when she moved to stand and the spell between us broke, did I turn tail and run.

In my bed some hours later, in my room above the dye vats and fabric swatches for which my occupation depends, I could not but think of the auburn-haired monster on the Riverbank. In my dreams I saw the burning fires of her hot-coal eyes, her mischievous and freshly blooded smile.

When I woke the next morning, the Hamlet was irate with hysteria again. I kept to myself, mixing the dyes and weaving the garments those in this community love to wear. With my head in the vapors of the dye pits, my heart was firmly distracted by the Lady and her violent beauty.

Again, I went to the River, only a day having passed, and there I came upon the Lady. In the middle of the walking path, on the packed dirt on the banks of our beloved River, she stood devouring her kill.

She held another woman to her chest in the moon's light, standing behind a milkmaid named Florence, her mouth secured onto the girl's lower neck. The maid was tall, though the Lady was taller, and she held both her arms pressed flush to her sides as the Lady forced her to her knees. I could see the Lady gnawing on the neck of the poor maid, subduing the woman like a lioness, sending waves of excitement through me as I watched her do violence supreme. When I did not believe that the moment could become any more intense, that the night could not become any more special, the Lady met my gaze.

The moonlight set fire to her luminescent eyes. Her hair hung in red coils that framed her smooth, tanned face like the veil of a Saint. When the wind blew, the Lady sighed into it, her meal running in bloody rivulets down her cheeks and over her lips like ghastly rouge.

While I watched the Lady's performance, she slid her hands from where they were around the maid's body. Like the touch of a lover, the Lady's left hand wrapped around the woman's shoulder while the right hand slid around her waist. Enraptured, I saw the Lady laugh, her mouth full of the maid's innards, a red cavern of flesh and blood.

The Lady straightened slightly, heaved a deep breath and then, like the magic of dark sorcerers and the wrath of the Lord in the Old Testament, the maid's body seemed to collapse into itself. The woman who had once been Florence had been transformed into a hollow, decompressed, flattened object of indescribable nature and incalculable disturbance. By way of her open mouth on the wound of the maid's neck, the Lady had siphoned the inner material of the woman's body into her stomach like an infant from the teat of its mother. All the blood and bone, all the muscles and organs once within the poor milkmaid were consumed by whatever compound existed within the Lady's mouth and saliva.

I swear there is no other creature on Earth capable of doing as the Lady does, certainly not while looking so beautiful. Still, my appreciation of her physicality did not lessen the incredible horror I felt watching her. I turned and ran soon after she finished, too afraid of what might come next.

That night, my thoughts were drawn to the Lady again, though I was not as interested or intrigued as I had been. I could not stop envisioning the milkmaid, laying in the arms of the Lady as she drank her dry. When I closed my eyes, I saw the sinister smile on the Lady's ruby red lips and its juxtaposition to the great violence she was committing.

And the pleasure—I could not help but remember the Lady's face, enraptured with the greatest pleasure I had ever seen on another woman. How could something so awful, so sinful, cause someone so much pleasure?

By then I'd seen two murders, two individuals I knew by face slain, but paces in front of me. I wondered how I'd feel in the morning when news spread of yet another death. What if my customers, the seamstresses and chamber maids who came to buy my textiles, somehow knew what I'd done by the look on my face? What if everyone in town suddenly knew what I'd paid witness to that very night before?

I stayed indoors after dark for some time following my encounter. Trips to the market and around town were taken only in the daytime. I stayed away from the River at all costs.

Nonetheless, I couldn't stop myself from dreaming of the Lady. I'd been praying for a reason to see her again, though I couldn't understand why. Despite the terror she put within me, I wanted to see her more than I'd ever wanted to see anything.

Destiny works in mysterious ways. God's hand can send us down paths we never desired to go. As the members of this Court well know, last summer my home and shop burned to the ground and the trajectory of my life was changed forever.

Never shall I forget that day, for the heat made the dye pits weep with steam and I served less than three clients in eight hours. I had scarcely felt such heat in all my life, as I know you all remember. Past noon, when I was certain no more patrons would arrive, I stripped to my corset and underskirt and laid like some Grecian maid of old in the shade of my courtyard.

Relaxed in the coolness, I dozed for some time, relishing a moment of peace. When I came to, the room before me was filled with smoke.

Leaping from my seat, I pulled my textiles down from their drying racks like a woman possessed. Grabbing sheets of blue and red, black garments I'd made for the Clergy and this Court, I first tried to save my beloved inventory but ended up throwing them upon the growing blaze at the foot of my hearth. Weeping like a child, I attempted to throw buckets from the dying pits onto the suddenly sizable fire, with little success. No matter how I tried, the courtyard filled with black, acrid smoke, and I found my wall engulfed in red-and-orange fire. Flames licked up the stone and wood around me. Hundreds of hours' worth of work was destroyed, the home I inherited from my father was burning down before my eyes.

Heat was lapping at my skin, pushing sweat from my brow and bosom until it drove me into the pantry closet across the courtyard. The smoke clouded my thoughts, and I ran behind a bag of rice and pressed my body into one of the dark corners in the little room. Helpless and afraid, exhausted by my days without the Lady in my life, I put my head down and waited for the smoke to choke me. There, in the corner of my pantry, I found myself wishing I'd seen the Lady again, that I'd spoken with her even once. I cried for her with no belief that she could hear me. Resigned to my fate, I held my eyes closed tight and waited for the end.

Not even a minute passed before I heard a crashing bang reverberate through the building. In the darkness, I tried to ignore the barrage of noise echoing from the house around me before I heard a particular sound, the smashing of a door being kicked in. When I felt a great gust of air and heat blast over me, I was compelled to open my eyes.

I could not move nor speak for what I saw. Frozen and awestruck, I believe the Saints and Holy Messengers of God must have felt as I did then, sitting placid and helpless before a divine specter. Our Lady of Violent Beauty stood above me, her smile like a balm over all the fear I felt that afternoon. As hot and wild as the roaring blaze behind her, the Lady smiled down at me happily, her hands on her hips, her breasts heaving like she'd run all the way from the River to save me.

Without care for the blaze raging behind her, the Lady rucked up her skirt and squatted in the doorway. "Are you alright, dear?" the woman asked as I blushed in the heat.

Her voice was as deep as the well at our town's center, its timber as rich as hard liquor. Unable to speak as I was, I nodded my answer, to which she smiled again. "You must be awfully scared. Come, let's get you out of this place."

She came to stoop over me, her arms wrapping around my shoulders and beneath my bent knees. Hoisting me up as if I weighed no more than the bags of rice and flour behind me, she stood with me in her arms. I nearly fainted as she pulled me out of the closet, her face silhouetted in the orange firelight; the flames illuminating her red hair as if she wore a halo. Like a bride in the arms of her bridegroom, the Lady carried me confidently through the house, out the back door, and into the green space between my home and the woods.

In the sun of the hot day, she set me down in the green grass and brush weeds, her hair shining as though the flames of the courtyard had followed her. One hand on my shoulder, she stilled me with a gentle hand, as if she'd carried a hundred women out of a thousand burning homes.

Afraid and entranced and awed by the Lady, I stood before her speechless and horrified, my home destroyed behind her. Both of us in only our corsets and skirts, I watched the lady as she watched me, afraid of what might come next between us, ecstatic about what she was capable of. All the emotion of the previous few weeks welled to a head inside of me as I panted through the horrible, smokey air. "I saw you!" I blurted in the silence of the day, "I saw you kill those people by the River."

The Lady smiled and shrugged. "But you didn't tell anyone what you saw."

Confused and exhausted, I continued stammering, "No, I didn't. Why would I? Why would I when … when—"

"When no one in this Hamlet cares about you anyway?" the Lady added with a sly and sympathetic smile on her lips.

"Yes, when it wouldn't have mattered what I said in the first place."

The Lady hummed and nodded knowingly. "I saw what happened to that Ranchero last month. The Court waited for his widow to make a mistake—one miswritten tax form, one missed signature on the deed left by her husband and they punished her for it. Men went and killed all her cattle, said she had no claim to her property. Now the woman has nothing. Such is their world."

I shook my head then, anger flaring suddenly inside of me. "Such is their world?" I repeated.

Stepping so close to the Lady that our chests touched and I felt the heat of her breath across my face, I spoke freely, my anger a righteous force that spurred me on. "Such is their world! It's *my* world! It's *God's* world—it's God's entire damned, forsaken existence! Miss, do you dare propose an alternative?"

The Lady seemed not only unphased by my yelling, but in some way delighted by it. I thought I saw her stifle a laugh before she answered me. "Why, yes! Yes, I do, my darling viper of a girl."

Admittedly surprised by her answer, I stood silently before the red wreckage of my home and the woman who'd saved me from it. I could hardly comprehend what the Lady had said to me, my capacity to do anything but react completely subdued. "Of course," I told her. "You live your life of sin so freely, you've no obligations to hold you back. You kill and destroy, and you live *outside* of their world, don't you?"

The Lady's smile wavered, and her gaze sharpened as she looked at me with the intensity of renewed focus. "If I offered you that same life, to share that sinfulness with you, what would you do then?"

"Miss!" I finally shouted. "I would insist that I do not believe you! I don't understand you! And my home—my little home is gone!"

Before I could say any more, the Lady was throwing her head back and letting out a loud, boisterous laugh. Between snorting shouts and breathless giggles, the Lady insisted, "But you do believe me! How can I make you more sure? What can I do to prove my willingness to share this life with you?"

"Take me!" I was shouting before I could stop myself. "Take me back into the forest with you! Take me to your witch's lair, bring me to your shack by the River. Prove to me that you can keep this ravenous hellhole away from me!"

So near me, the Lady's fiery, exuberant excitement and my subdued, tired anxiety were drawn to each other like polarized magnets. When the Lady took my chin between her two powerful fingertips, tilting my head so that I could not look away from her, I felt as breathless and faint as I had in the home full of fire behind me.

"I can do that—I'll do just as you ask," she told me, her voice quiet and deathly serious.

"I know exactly how you can share your world with me," I added.

The flames danced behind her and fury fluttered in my heart as the soft, velvet plushness of the Lady's lips pressed against my own. Yes, the Lady and I kissed as a man and a woman might, as a husband might kiss a bride while my home burned.

And why shouldn't I have shared that moment with the Lady? Already, I'd witnessed her murders, her stealing of the souls of my neighbors. What more sin could I commit, already damned in the eyes of the Lord as I was? Besides, she'd promised to save me—the Lord refused to save me, and I did not care if Christ would love me more than the Lady could, right there, in the grass behind my home.

To answer the probing questions of this Hamlet, to address the rumors of this God-fearing Court, I have been absent from both town and church because I followed the Lady, my Lady of Divine Violence, into the forest on that summer day. I had no home or livelihood, and the Lady offered me her heart and shelter with open arms.

In the freedom of the unholy wilderness, in the dens of the beasts which every Godly soul has learned to fear, the Lady and I agreed on how best she could prove the existence of my freedom to me. All the while, we knew that the brutish men and jealous women of this Hamlet would not allow us our privacy, no matter how we had found our happiness and wanted nothing to do with their entitled suffering. We devised, just in time for this trial, a way for the Lady and I to live unbothered and for the Lady to prove to me that there is a life more fulfilling than that which this community provides.

My Lady of Devouring Violence has lived upon this Riverbank since before God put man on Earth, since before the beginning of time. Above our human religion, my Lady is an elemental spirit which words cannot adequately describe, she is the Goddess of a netherworld that only I have been invited to join. Already she knows that none in this Court or this Hamlet has a heart pure enough for us to spare.

Here, I have come to your Holy Court, the emissary of my Lady of Devouring Violence, the portal through which you seek to punish my lover. I relish to say that you are wrong. You men know almost nothing of the way in which the world works. My Lady had lived a thousand years before she tasted the ugly souls of men, now she and I shall live another thousand years free from man's unquenchable desires.

Is the whole Hamlet not here, in attendance within this very building? My Lady is a predator, and I am a creature of revenge. I know the Alderman and his sons are the ones who burnt down my home for the crime of refusing his marriage proposal. I know the citizens of this Hamlet ignored the Alderman's arson and attempted murder because it agrees with him, because I have been called unholy and harlot for years upon years and many of you would be happy to rid the world of me.

Now, you all will know the violent indifference of your God, who loves your unproven souls too much to save your obvious mortal bodies. My Lady waits with oil and torch and when she hears that my testimony has concluded, she shall save me and burn you all alive. We will hold each other as lovers do while this courthouse ignites in righteous flames with all the Hamlet inside it.

FAMILY PLANNING

by Luc Diamant

The neighbors have a baby.

He's very cute, all dark brown eyes and long lashes. Laina and I are jealous, to be honest. But he does cry a lot and especially at night. I feel bad for the parents, who must be getting even less sleep than we are. And we've been getting very little. The neighbors' bedroom is directly above us, and the walls and floors are not thick.

All that is to say I don't understand why Laina is looking at me so confused now that I've brought out a box of earplugs right before bed.

"What are you doing?" she asks me.

"I … thought we would sleep a bit better this way," I say, unsure if I'm understanding her question right. It should be obvious what I'm doing. I hold out the box to her, but she shakes her head, still looking at me with that strange expression.

She almost seems … hurt, I think. I frown. She's not the type to get upset over nothing.

"Are you okay?" There must be something else going on, unrelated to the earplugs. Sometimes she'll see an upsetting article on the news right before bed and it won't let her go.

She shakes her head. Her face doesn't change, though.

I decide to leave it for now. I'm tired and it's probably making me read into things. I do that. My therapist calls it rejection-sensitive dysphoria. I usually wake up the next day wondering what I was on about. So I kiss Laina goodnight and put in the earplugs, excited about getting a good night's sleep for the first time this week.

I do feel better the next morning. "I slept like a baby," I tell Laina. "Or maybe I should say, *unlike* a baby."

She doesn't react to the joke, doesn't even roll her eyes, and I feel a new pang of anxiety. "Are you okay, Lai?"

She nods, but she doesn't look at me.

"Is it the baby thing? We can go over our options again this evening?"

We've been over our options a lot already. Enough that lately, I've seen Laina look up videos on manifesting when she thinks I can't see her phone screen. God knows how she hopes to manifest her way out of our situation, because it's a complete stalemate. Laina's family has a history of complicated and sometimes fatal pregnancies. Her own mother died giving birth to her. She is, understandably, scared that a similar thing will happen to her.

I don't love the idea of being pregnant myself, but the point is moot because I have been infertile my whole life. A complicated chromosomal issue that affects, among other things, my womb and ovaries. When I realized I was gay, I thought that would make my infertility irrelevant, but it hasn't worked out that way.

The obvious solution would be to adopt, but I just can't get behind the idea. I've read too many studies on the adoption industry and its deep-seated corruption. I know there are plenty of adopted people who are perfectly happy, but the whole concept of essentially buying a child just doesn't sit right with me. I can't help but think that the happy ones must be a minority.

Laina doesn't say it in so many words, but I know she thinks I should get over myself. She's probably right.

She smiles a thin smile now. "Sure," she says, "let's go over it again."

She's still not looking at me, though.

"Are you sure you're okay?" I ask.

She nods again, in exactly the same way as before. Nothing about it is reassuring to me, but my therapist says I need to take Laina at her word.

If you keep asking people if they're upset with you, eventually they will be.

So I let it go.

***

That evening, as always, the topic of surrogacy comes up, and as always, it's swiftly discarded. The only person we know well enough to ask for something so big is Laina's older sister—and she obviously has the same family history as Laina.

So the conversation is the same one we've been having for over two years now.

"Think about it," I say. "Would you want to be flown halfway across the world before your first birthday, to a mother you've never met who doesn't even really condone the practice? Would that be a good start in life?"

Laina turns the orange stone pendant on her necklace over in her hands. "I'd prefer it over a dead mother."

I sink back into the couch. I know she's right. And of course I don't want her to risk her life. I think about the girl I used to play with as a child, brought here at two years old and never really able to bond with her adoptive parents. "I just keep thinking there must be another way," I say.

She looks at me with a sad smile. "I know, Dee," she says. "And maybe we'll find one. But if we don't—if adoption is the only way—just promise me you'll at least consider it?"

I feel the silence stretch out, feel it pull at something between us. Finally I nod, but too late and with too little conviction. Laina is looking at me differently.

"Well," she mutters, turning away from me, the color draining from her knuckles as she clasps the pendant in one hand, "that's that, then."

I stiffen. "What did you say?"

She turns back to me, her smile bright and untroubled. "I said let's go to bed then."

⸎

"Lai, have you seen my earplugs?" I'm staring at my nightstand where I left the box this morning.

"Wha?" Laina calls from the bathroom, her mouth full of toothbrush.

"The earplugs!" I repeat, getting down on my knees to check under the bed. Nothing.

"'Aven't 'een 'em."

I rummage around for a few more minutes while Laina finishes getting ready for bed. She looks at me from under the covers as I search, uselessly, through my sock drawer. "Come on, love," she says, "I wanna turn off the light."

I don't want to turn off the light yet. I want to look through every drawer in the house until I find the damn box. But I've already looked in every place I can reasonably think of, plus some that I *can't* reasonably think of, and I don't want to keep Laina awake. Her shift starts earlier than mine tomorrow. "You're *sure* you haven't seen them?" I ask one more time.

She shakes her head, and for a moment, the gesture reminds me of her reaction when I asked her if she wanted some earplugs.

I fight down the urge to press the issue. *Take her at her word*, I remind myself. I nod and turn off the light.

"I'm sure you'll find them tomorrow, Dee," Laina says into the dark.

Above, the baby begins to cry.

I wake up in darkness, staring at a ceiling I can't see.

I'm so used to this by now that it takes my half-sleeping mind a second to realize that the baby isn't crying. Why did I wake up then? I try to listen for the sound that must have disturbed me. It takes a few heartbeats before I feel Laina's breath on my ear.

It's warm and familiar—but why now?

Then I notice her lips are moving and I am immediately wide awake. She's not just cuddling up to me—she's whispering in my ear, in a staccato rhythm, barely pausing for breath. I don't know the words, don't know the language. Neither should Laina—she speaks Greek, but this is *not* Greek.

I want to turn my head to the side, to look at my wife, but I am frozen in place. I try to open my mouth but my lips won't move. I can't blink. My heart is pounding in my ears, a steady beat to Laina's unending mantra. Her voice is unmistakable, low and coffee-colored, but it sounds *hollow*.

The words, though, are solid and dense. I can feel them worming their way into me, trying to take hold. They are pulling at threads of thoughts and feelings and I know with a deafening certainty that if they find purchase, they will unravel something inside me and spin something new in its place.

I fight it with all I have. I can feel different parts of my psyche sitting inside me, taking cover. My gymnastics training. My germaphobia. A memory of my mother, singing to me. I hold on to these as hard as I can.

Laina seems to notice my resistance. She's speaking louder now, in that hollow voice, more urgently. I feel something in my stomach shift and twist. Tears roll out of my frozen eyes, onto my cheekbones and my ears. I wonder if Laina notices, if she will see me cry and stop.

As if reading my thoughts, Laina pauses. Her mouth reaches even closer, lips pressing against my earlobe. I feel the warm wetness of her tongue as she licks up my tears and though I still can't see her, I swear I can feel her mouth twisting into a smile.

When she resumes her incantation, something in me cracks.

How could you? I think, and I feel the shape of a long-held belief begin to come undone in the pit of my stomach.

And then, suddenly, I feel a wave of calm washing over me and I know everything is okay.

It's a lovely day.

Laina is rocking the baby in her arms on the terrace, singing a lullaby I haven't heard before. He was crying earlier, but now he's sleeping peacefully against her chest. I smile at her through the window, wordlessly letting her know I will join them soon—right after I finish cleaning up.

The apartment upstairs is much nicer. In our old one, we only had a tiny balcony, not even big enough for a single seat. Nothing like the large space where Laina now reclines in a swinging chair with our beautiful boy, all dark brown eyes and long lashes.

Adoption wasn't such a big deal after all, I think as I wipe the last of the stains off the floor. I can't remember why I ever had any doubts about whether it would work out.

I drag the two large, heavy bags across the floor into the hallway. Taking them out can wait—it's still too light outside now. I amble back towards the terrace.

On second thought, I don't think I ever really had any real doubts. Just the nervousness that comes with entering a new phase in life. No, our little family is perfect, I think as I sit next to my wife and son and gently run my hand through his small tufts of black hair. Just the way we had planned it for years.

And if there is a small twinge of doubt somewhere in the back of my mind, it's a simple matter to push it away. After all, I know for an absolute fact that this is exactly what I've always wanted.

UNGRATEFUL DEAD THINGS

by Alyssa Lennander

London, 1889

Under the veil of darkness, punctuated by gas lamps lining the streets at the edge of the cemetery, Victoria pushes her shovel into the ground. Sweat coats her brow and dirt cakes under her fingernails. The air hangs heavy with the scent of damp earth. Gravestones and obelisks silhouette against the lights of London, haunting her as she digs. More than once she thinks she sees movement in the cemetery, but when she looks, no one is there. No one she can see, anyhow.

Victoria fancies herself a scientist. She's studied books and dissected cats in secrecy and bribed anatomy professors to give her lessons. She believes in what she can see and touch, but she can't dismiss the world's possibilities. Maybe ghosts do exist. Maybe they're watching her right now.

Why must coffins be buried six feet under? She thinks as she jabs her shovel endlessly into the freshly packed soil. *It's so needless.*

Her palms blister the faster she digs, screaming at her to cease, but she can't stop. She only has a few more hours of darkness, and she still has to transport the body to her lab before anyone notices. Her neighbors are pesky creatures. They sniff around her house, probing her with questions, peering over Victoria's shoulder when she answers the door. You would think they would have something better to do than wonder about Victoria's daily life. But Victoria is the neighborhood's oddity, and oddities are to be studied. It's human nature.

Her shovel connects to the coffin with a deep *thunk*.

Quickly, Victoria removes the remainder of dirt and then grabs the crowbar she brought with her. With a couple hard yanks, the coffin lid pops.

She lifts the lid. Inside lays a young woman, dressed in a white satin gown, her pale face resting in a small, permanent smile. Victoria caresses her cold cheek with a gentle finger.

"Hello, my love," she whispers.

Death is finite. Except, of course, if you're Victoria Frankenstein.

Back in Victoria's lab, the woman lies on a metal table. She is dreadful looking in death, with bluish skin and an unnatural stillness, made worse by the harsh lights shining upon her. Victoria would turn them off if she could. When she was alive, the woman never had a hair out of place, and it's a shame death has changed her appearance so drastically.

Her name is Ellen.

The woman Victoria loves. The woman Victoria is going to defy the laws of nature for.

Ellen's family had buried her earlier in the day, forcing Victoria to watch the workers lower Ellen's coffin into the ground, knowing she would be back under nightfall to dig her back up. She wishes she could have taken Ellen's body when it was still warm, or even above ground, but between the family and the undertaker and the church, there was simply no opportunity.

Victoria steps up to the table and brushes a blonde lock of hair out of Ellen's face. From what her family told her, Ellen had simply dropped dead. There were no warnings, no way to prepare. Perhaps something with the brain, the undertaker had thought.

When she learned of her death, a piece of Victoria died with her. She loved Ellen with her entire being, every drop of blood, and she knows Ellen had loved her, too. For years they had hidden their love affair behind a shroud of friendship. Such things are not permitted in regular society, and Ellen's family is not the sort to accept any divergences. Victoria has no family left; she'd wanted Ellen to live with her, to live as wife and wife, but it would not have been possible.

Until now.

Victoria retreats from Ellen's lifeless body and consults the long-abandoned journals of her ancestor, Victor Frankenstein. She flips through the brittle pages, pouring over the details one last time, running her fingers across soft paper. It's essential that she fully grasps the process.

She squints at the barely legible scrawl, made worse by almost a century of wear, the ink almost invisible in some spots. But Victoria has studied these words a hundred times, and then a hundred times more. She practically knows these journals as well as she knows her own name.

If her ancestor could bring the dead back to life, so could she. It is her legacy.

But Victor had taken bits and pieces from many bodies. Victoria has one, and she refuses to cut Ellen up for parts and turn her into a monster like Victor did.

Once she's through with Victor's journals, Victoria skims her own, not wanting to risk waiting much longer, but hers are updated with current medical knowledge and thus the process requires tweaks to Victor's original findings. Only then does she feel prepared to begin.

The process is simple and yet it isn't; she needs to be precise, to be perfect. One mistake and Ellen's body will be ruined forever and then Victoria will never get her back.

First, Victoria flushes out the embalming fluids preserving Ellen's body.

Second, she puts fresh, warm blood into her veins—courtesy of a medical student she's paid handsomely for such things—pumping it throughout Ellen's vascular system with an apparatus Victoria designed herself.

And third, before the blood has a chance to coagulate, Victoria electrifies Ellen's body.

A different sort of electricity runs through Victoria. A thrill races down her spine—this, *this* is the very heart of science. This is everything Victoria wants to do. To bring the woman she loves back from death, to be able to hold her again … it's a marvel few have the skills to do.

Bulbs flicker as electricity buzzes, so loudly that Victoria resists clamping her hands over her ears. Ellen jolts with the force, her limbs loosening as her muscles begin to relax and it's almost lifelike. Blood coats Victoria's hands, but she pays no mind to it, even as her fingers stick together and her skin feels stiff. A miracle lies before her.

Victoria turns off the electric device, then presses two fingers to Ellen's pulse point in the neck. There—a heartbeat. It's faint, but it's there.

Victoria sags with relief, tears pooling on the edges of her lashes, which she hastily blinks away. There had been a chance it wouldn't work, but it did.

Ellen has a *heartbeat*.

With a small laugh, Victoria grabs either side of Ellen's face with her dried bloody hands and kisses Ellen's cold gray lips.

Now all she has to do is wait.

***

For hours, Victoria stares at Ellen. At first, she double and triple checks that she did, in fact, feel a pulse, and once she's satisfied the pulse is strengthening, she watches for the telltale rise and fall of Ellen's chest. It's so slight at first it appears hardly there but then it becomes more obvious, and Victoria leans against the cabinetry behind her, resting her hand on her own warm chest.

One hour bleeds into four. What if Ellen won't wake up at all? And if she does, can she accept her second chance at life?

But then she opens her eyes.

"Ellen," Victoria breathes.

Her lover does not hear her, and Ellen blinks against the bright bulbs above her but Victoria can't make herself move to turn them off. She's frozen as she watches Ellen come back to life. Ellen's breath grows faster, heavier, and she moves her fingers, then her hands, raising one to her pale face and staring at her palm as though she has never seen it before. Her body shakes, horror crossing her lovely face.

Victoria breaks her reverie and sweeps forward, clutching Ellen's wobbling, ice-cold hand between both of her own. Her skin is still stiff, though it gives way the tiniest bit under her touch. "Shh," she murmurs. "You're all right, Ellen. You're all right."

Ellen's eyes flick to her. They had once been as blue as the deep sea, but death and reanimation has turned them milky blue, filmy. Ellen flutters her lashes and squints, as if trying to clear away a mist. "Victoria?"

Hearing her name on Ellen's tongue makes Victoria's heart batter against her ribcage. Her voice is low and scratchy from disuse, but it's Ellen's voice. Victoria smiles, remembering the first time the two of them had exchanged their first *I love you*'s. She'd studied the way the words fell from Ellen's lips until she dreamed about it.

"It's me," Victoria says, clutching Ellen's hand to her body. She can't stop the tears this time; they leak from the corner of her eyes, spilling down her cheeks even as she's smiling. Her own voice is rough with emotion. "You gave me quite a scare, my love."

"Victoria," she says again, gasping. "I feel strange."

"That's to be expected. Your body went through something traumatic. It will take some time to adjust."

Ellen doesn't respond. She moves to sit, and Victoria gently grabs her shoulders, easing her up, watching Ellen wince as her skin pulls and stretches, listening to her joints crack. Ellen swings her legs to the side, dangling them off the metal slab table. Victoria trails her hands down her arms, then grips her hands. She doesn't think she could ever let go of her hands again.

"What happened?" Ellen whispers.

She tightens her grip on Ellen's fingers, swallowing. "You died. You were walking from your bed to your vanity and just … died. But you're back now and that's all that matters. You've come back to me."

"I died," she repeats.

"Yes."

"And now I'm … alive."

"Yes."

"How?" she asks at last, glancing around the laboratory.

Victoria has never brought Ellen here, never let her see the glinting sharp instruments, nor the rusted stain surrounding the drain on the floor, nor the shelves of preserved specimens lining one wall. Ellen is a gentle soul; seeing hearts and kidneys and fetuses floating in jars when she was alive the first time would have given her nightmares.

"Victoria …" she says slowly. "What did you do?"

Victoria frowns at the slight accusation in her tone, and she can't help but grow irritated. She's defended her scientific interests all her life, to her parents and teachers and peers, and the way Ellen questions her, like she's done something wrong, brings back those memories, those feelings of being *other*. "I saved you. I brought you back. You think I could survive without you? You think I wouldn't have done *everything* in my power to get you back? I love you, Ellen. You're mine."

"Brought me back?"

"From the dead."

"No." Ellen yanks her hands from Victoria's and clenches them into fists. Her breathing escalates, her lungs wheezing with effort. "No, you didn't. You can't. No one can bring people back from the dead."

"Well, I can." Victoria retrieves one of Victor's journals and hands it to Ellen. "Just like my ancestor did. You are not the first to be reanimated, and it *is* possible. You're proof."

Ellen flips through the pages, though Victoria doubts she can even understand what Victor is saying; she was never a scientist like Victoria, never understood half of what she said to her about the articles she'd read and the anatomy lessons she'd had. She never faulted Ellen for that. Ellen is the one person who accepts Victoria's strange nature.

A shudder runs through Ellen as she reads, her lips tightening into a thin line. Victoria gives a small sigh.

Or rather, she *was* accepting. Perhaps not anymore.

Ellen snaps the journal shut with enough force that it blows back her hair. She shoves it into Victoria's arms, as though the touch of it scalds her. "I am a monster."

"No," Victoria says harshly, tossing the journal on the counter behind her. She takes Ellen's shoulders firmly, willing her to see herself for what she is. "You are not a monster, Ellen. You are special. You are a *miracle*."

"You brought me back from the dead. Is that not the definition of a monster?"

"A rabbit believes the fox is a monster and yet it is not. It is simply a fox."

Ellen chews on her bottom lip as she stares into Victoria's eyes. She expected a certain level of apprehension, of fear, when Ellen woke up. But she refuses to let Ellen believe for a moment that she is anything but wondrous.

"My parents—" Ellen hastily jumps up from the table, but her legs are rigid and she nearly topples over until Victoria leaps forward to catch her. "I have to see my parents."

"No." Victoria shakes her head. "It's too early for that. We'll discuss it with time, perhaps, but not now."

"At least let me contact them so they know I'm … alive." Her last word comes off hesitantly, as if she doesn't quite believe what she's saying.

"Let's wait until you've adjusted, all right?" She can't expose Ellen to the world—not so soon after Victoria got her back, or before they can have the life they've always wanted to live. This is their chance. Their *only* chance. Once anyone learns of what Victoria has done, everything will be ruined.

Her lungs squeeze as she holds her breath, waiting for Ellen's agreement, and at last she nods.

"Come," Victoria says gently, relieved. "Let's get you upstairs to bed. I'm sure you're tired."

They manage to make it to the spare bedroom upstairs as Victoria half-drags, half-carries a stumbling Ellen around the house, and despite Ellen's pulse, Victoria feels no warmth. Victoria peels off Ellen's burial gown, studying the Y shaped rows of stitches on her body from where the undertaker cut her open, and dresses her in a silk nightgown. Golden sunlight streams through the windows, bouncing off Ellen's hair and forming a halo, like she's an angel.

"There you go." Victoria helps Ellen into bed and pulls up the blanket, then gives her a kiss on the forehead. "Sleep well."

She moves to leave, but Ellen grabs her arm, sitting up, eyes wide. "What if I don't wake up? What if I die again?"

Victoria pushes her back down and shushes her. "You won't," she reassures.

They never do.

Victoria walks into Ellen's room to see her sitting in front of the vanity, dabbing rouge over her powdered face. Victoria admires her from the threshold. She looks almost like her old self, before she died, with porcelain skin and rosy cheeks, and for a moment Victoria forgets what the cosmetics are truly hiding: a sickly bluish complexion, lips the color of dark wine, the sharp sting of her cool skin.

But for now, the only thing that appears different are her eyes.

"Do I look all right?" Ellen asks, turning to face her fully. She's curled her hair and pinned it back into the fashionable updo she always wore before.

"You look beautiful," Victoria answers with a smile.

This is what she had envisioned in those days between Ellen's death and her reanimation. The past few weeks had been rough on her as she adjusted to her new life, keeping Victoria at arm's length and confining herself to her room most days. As much as it pained her, Victoria let her. But it seems Ellen is coming to terms with herself.

She hopes, in time, Ellen will tell her she loves her again. That she will kiss her. Perhaps even come to her bed, as she once did.

Until then, Victoria is patient.

"You look like you're expecting someone," she teases Ellen, wandering further into the room. She picks up the nightgown Ellen hastily threw on the bed, running her fingers over the cool silk. A light, sickly sweet scent perfumes the air—the smell of decay. Victoria gives Ellen another smile through the mirror. "What's the occasion?"

Ellen touches a curl. "There is none. I just … want to feel like myself again."

"Good—that's good." Silence envelopes the air until Victoria can stand it no more. "Breakfast is ready."

"I'll be there soon."

Victoria waits to eat until Ellen comes down fifteen minutes later. She watches her pick at her food from the corner of her eye. Since her rise from death, Ellen has eaten nothing, though it appears she has lost no weight. Maybe she *can't* lose weight. Victoria makes a mental note to write down this observation in her journal later this morning.

They make small talk, though it becomes harder and harder to come up with something to say. *It's just temporary*, Victoria thinks. *Once Ellen is ready to venture outside, things will be better.* But doubt lingers at the back of her mind.

A knock comes at the front door.

"Stay here," Victoria says. She'd given her maid time off while Ellen settles into her life, which means Victoria has to answer the door herself, a little unorthodox for a wealthy woman. "I'll get it."

When a series of knocks comes again, Victoria scurries to the door and opens it with a sweep of her arm—and freezes.

"Mr. and Mrs. Dawson," Victoria says pleasantly, subtly moving the door to reveal less of what could or could not be behind Victoria. Like the Dawsons' undead daughter. "To what do I owe this honor?"

Mrs. Dawson frowns. "We received a letter from *you*, Victoria. Asking if we could visit."

She mirrors her frown with one of her own. "You must be mistaken. I did not send any letters to you."

"I did."

Victoria's heart skips a beat, then pounds erratically. Ellen pops up behind her, widening the door, revealing herself fully to her parents. She gives Ellen a hard stare; neither of them has discussed when or if she should contact her parents again, and now the Dawsons are standing in the doorway staring at their daughter they buried a month ago, their mouths hanging open.

Ellen is not ready. Her parents are not ready. Victoria is most *certainly* not ready.

"Come in," Ellen says, gently moving Victoria away as she ushers her parents into the house.

Victoria clenches her jaw and shuts the door behind them. How—how had Ellen gotten a letter to her parents without her knowing? She's been watching Ellen closely, practically beside her all day, every day.

"How is this possible?" Mr. Dawson asks in a trembling voice as Victoria enters the drawing room. He rubs his shaking hand against his forehead as though he's about to faint. "You died. We saw your body."

"I know this is a lot to take in." Ellen smooths her peony pink skirts, keeping her filmy eyes lowered. "I *was* dead. But now I'm not. I wanted you to know, and I … I wanted to see you."

Victoria shakes her head ruefully, and Ellen cuts her a look. This is going to end disastrously, she knows it. There is a reason Victoria never contacted the Dawsons to begin with, why she never brought Ellen outside before she was ready. The world isn't prepared to see someone as magnificent as Ellen.

"You're back … from the *dead*?" Mrs. Dawson chokes out. Her hand clutches the jeweled pendant hanging from her neck.

"I am." Ellen steps forward and, at last, raises her eyes to them, and they gasp. "I want to go home."

A sharp pang slams into Victoria, but she quickly hides her hurt. Ellen's home is here now—why would she want to leave?

Mrs. Dawson shakes her head, her other hand latching onto her husband's arm, knuckles turning white. She's staring at Ellen like she's grown horns. "No. Whoever, whatever, you are, you are not my daughter. My daughter is *dead*."

Despite her hurt, Victoria's heart cracks a little when Ellen gives a broken, "It's me, Mother."

But her parents are shaking their heads, backing away from Ellen, refusing to look at her milky eyes. Mrs. Dawson spits out, "You're a monster."

With a flurry, the Dawsons turn and escape the house, and Victoria has half a mind to wonder if they will call the police over this issue, if she needs to pack a bag and flee before they get here.

Ellen screams through clenched teeth, clutching her hair with fists, locks coming loose from her scalp. Her eyes shine with tears, though none fall. Victoria isn't sure if they're tears at all, actually.

"It was too early for them," Victoria says softly, drawing nearer, though she's not sure how much she believes her own words. "They weren't ready, that's all. Give them more time."

She touches Ellen's arm, but she jerks away from Victoria, casting her a vicious glare. Ellen has never looked at Victoria with such hatred.

"They're right," Ellen says. "I'm a monster. An undead, cold, heartless monster!"

"Ellen—"

"You did this to me!" She backs away, her fingers curling into claws, and a second later, she hurdles a lamp at Victoria's head. She dodges just in time, and the lamp shatters on the floor, scattering a hundred ceramic pieces. "You made me into this, Victoria! You think you can just bring the dead back to life? You think I can be who I was before? You're wrong. I *am* a monster."

Victoria winces, and she swallows down the words she wants to yell, even as her chest swells with fury. "Don't say that, my love. It's not true."

"It is. And I am not the only monster here."

The accusation forces Victoria back a step. "What do you mean?"

Ellen spits out her words, each like a nail hammering straight into Victoria's heart. "You are no god, Victoria. Only a monster would do this to someone they love. You should have left me *dead!*"

Is it monstrous to breathe life back into the dead? Is it monstrous to want the woman she loves to be with her no matter the cost? If these questions make her a monster, then that is something Victoria can accept. She has defied the very laws of nature. She is unstoppable, and she'll be damned if she lets Ellen discredit her work, no matter how much she loves her.

Something snaps inside Victoria.

"I thought you would be different," Victoria whispers. A tear wells up and falls, and Ellen watches it spill to the floor, finally quiet. Her next words are cold. Rigid. "But you're just like the rest of them."

Ellen's brow crumples. "What do you mean?"

How many times had Victoria hoped someone would be grateful for what she did for them? But they never are. They are all ungrateful dead things. Even Ellen.

Victoria snatches Ellen's arm and drags her across the house to the basement door. Ellen claws at her fingers, pleading for her to let her go, to stop, but her grip is too strong, and Victoria forces her down the stairs wordlessly. She marches past the metal slab Ellen had awoken on, to the door in the shadows she keeps locked. She fishes a key from her pocket and unlocks the door.

A dozen pairs of milky eyes blink at her.

"You're just like *them*," Victoria says.

"What is this?" Ellen whispers.

The other dead women Victoria has reanimated—all blonde, all blue-eyed, like Ellen—are tied to the walls with short chains, barely long enough for them to lay on the floor. She gave each of them a chance when they reawoke, and each of them turned on her, ungrateful for the life she gave back to them. So be it. If they don't want their second chance, then Victoria will keep them for her research. She's learned so much from each reanimation.

"These are my specimens," Victoria answers. She hauls Ellen through the damp, rot smelling room, and chains her to the wall. She trails the back of her finger along Ellen's cheek. "And now my collection is complete."

Straight Flush

by Anya Leigh Josephs

They say the devil deals at Sapphire's Saloon.

Most nights, the saloon is a pleasant spot, miners and farmers and tradesmen swapping stories, sipping ale, and making good work for Sapphire and her ladies. Some man or other might bring a set of dice or a deck of cards and deal out a round of Faro, but the stakes are low and the game is fair, no one winning or losing more than a few pennies. But on winter nights, when the moon is dark, it's the devil who deals.

No one can quite say what she looks like, in the flickering light and thick cigar smoke of the saloon. Probably tall, with long dark hair. Probably beautiful. But all they really remember is her hands, at once still as a painting and always in motion. Her slim white fingers wrapped around a cigarette. Her soft palm curving around the deck; long, red nails tapping staccato on the table.

You can win a lot, when the devil is dealing. But you have a lot to lose.

Men come from all over to play a hand at her table. Word spreads fast, even out here on the edge of the world. It has to, with the sorts of stories that swirl through town after one of those long, moonless nights.

Edward Pinkton's barren farm blossomed with fresh fruit—cherries and apples and peaches—in the dead of winter. Josiah Lee Howard's barren wife blossomed with twins, a boy and a girl, and though some folks whisper the boy was born with a tail, everyone agrees they're as obedient and beautiful children as any parents could want. Maynard Pierce's leg, lost decades ago in the war, grew back strong and sturdy, and now he walks without even a cane. Jimmy Lawry started courting with the beautiful Beulah Harris, and now they're married even though Jimmy is pock-marked and not five feet tall and has not a penny to his name, and that was ten years ago and Miss Beulah hasn't aged a day.

None of these men, and none of the others who've gambled at her table, deny how they won their happiness. They even boast about it, about the night they beat the devil at her own game. So now, winter nights when the moon is waning, men set off from all over the state, even just over the border. They ride or walk for hours or days, and they find themselves at the doorstep of Sapphire's Saloon.

Miss Sapphire takes their money for board (two dollars a night, an outrageous rate, but they all pay it uncomplainingly) and serves them drinks while they wait in the waning winter sun. When night falls, and the devil arrives, Sapphire and her girls will be long gone.

Sometimes one of the younger girls will ask if she can stay. "Surely there could be a good night's custom, ma'am, with all these men away from home, spirits running high."

But Sapphire didn't go from tupping twenty men a night standing up in the cribs to sleeping alone in a featherbed in her own fine house by being a fool. She doesn't gamble for dreams: she sells them—and she knows what gossamer-fine and worthless things they are. She keeps her girls away. Because it's men the devil deals with but it's women she wants.

On the nights when the devil deals, no man walks alone into Sapphire's Saloon. Spring, summer, and fall, a lady would never let herself be seen there, but on moonlit nights they come. They've been bullied and persuaded and bribed and cajoled by brothers and fathers and husbands and sons—for the devil won't deal to any man without a lady on his arm. Nobody knows why. No one knows why the devil does what she does.

I did not have to be begged or tricked into coming. I demanded my husband Johnny make the long journey up from the mountains. Our daughter is sick. Four years old and like to die before her fifth. We've tried syrups and tonics, tried doctors, tried prayer. There's only one thing left to try.

I have never been in a public drinking house before, and certainly not a parlor house. None of the ladies have. We enter gingerly, holding our skirts a scant quarter-inch above the floor, clinging to the arm of whatever gentleman we are accompanying. Our husbands and fathers and brothers and sons whisper reassuring reminders.

"You won't have to do anything. Just watch the devil deal a hand," Johnny tells me, and that's true.

As long as he wins.

Night falls over Sapphire's Saloon. Inside, there is silent, breathless anticipation. They'd left one table empty, the rest pushed against the wall. Men and women form a ring at the edges of the room, as far from the devil's table as they can go. There is no chatter. No one drinks. If they pray, they do so in silence as they wait for the devil to walk through the door.

She wears a man's suit and her hair unbound, and she's holding her deck of cards in her hand. "Sure are some fine-looking ladies here tonight," says the devil, and a hot shudder runs through me. I tell myself it's fear.

The devil saunters across the room. I feel Johnny flinch back. I feel myself lean forward. I see the devil smile.

She sits at her table and lights a cigar. She smokes a while, flipping through her deck of cards. And then she says, "Any of you fellas want to give me a game?"

I've never seen poker played before. I'm a lady, it's not suitable. But somehow, I imagine it's not always played like this. Three men crowded around a table, their hands shaking. Three ladies standing behind them, as pale and silent as ghosts. And the dealer, smoking and shuffling and smiling, her face bright as dawn and her lips red as blood.

"All right, boys. What would you like to win?"

One man asks for money. Another for his sick mother to get well. A third for his thieving brother not to be hanged.

"And what can you wager?"

The bets start small. I almost expect the devil to laugh when one man bets a dollar. Surely that means nothing to her—but she just nods, and takes a drag on her cigarette, and deals.

She wins.

"Another round?"

Her voice is cold as ice and makes me feel hot all over. They play another round. She wins. Five dollars, then twenty, then a hundred. She wins. Then the clothes off a man's back. His shoes. The silver pocket watch his father left him. She wins. And when they've nothing left to gamble away, the devil smiles.

These men started out desperate. They came with all the money they have, hoping to win a reprieve, and now they've lost that too.

"Doesn't have to be money," the devil says.

They offer her years off their life. They offer her their good right hands. They offer her their souls.

That makes her laugh. "What use have I got for men's souls? I'm drowning in the damned things."

Sooner or later, the men make the offer. The women standing behind them, the pale silent ghosts, do not flinch. They knew, even if no one had told them, that they dealt in mortal danger here. None of them are surprised that it should come to this, that the men who love them should set a price on their lives. They do that anyway, when they pay our dowries or our passage from back east, when they pay a doctor or don't while we bleed after childbirth, when they spend their coin in houses like this one. We would be fools if we did not see that we are bought and sold.

The devil smiles. She looks at the ladies in question. They stand still and terrified, like virgins on their wedding nights—aware of the danger of desire. The devil flicks a little ash from the tip of her cigarette. And she says, "I fold."

The men leave, in their breeches and stocking feet, to limp their way home without the prize they'd come to win. Their women follow them. Maybe they'll speak of this night when they have walked, or ridden, for hours or days with no shoes on their feet and no coat to keep away the winter chill. Maybe the men will say they're sorry, in the half-hearted way men do. Maybe the women will say they forgive them, the way that women lie.

But I think I see, as a man offers his arm, as his sister walks away without taking it, the weight of this night growing between them, heavy as lead.

"Who's next?" the devil asks.

One man wants his eyesight back. Another, forgiveness for his sins. A third, three hundred dollars.

The blind man wins the first hand.

"I'll give you one eye back," she offers. "Or you can play me for the second."

"I'll take it," he says, and the devil simply nods.

The man does not cry out. There is no blast of light or shimmer of magical power. But the blind man turns to his daughter, who is standing silently behind him, and I can see that he sees her. He does not bet again.

The other two men lose, and lose, and lose. The devil takes, and takes, and takes. She takes their money, and their horses, and their land, and finally they make the offer all men do. Emboldened, perhaps, by her concession in the last round.

The blind man's daughter puts her hand on his shoulder and squeezes, gently. The other two women do not move. I think perhaps one is a wife, the other a sister. Both are like statues.

"Very well," says the devil, and deals another hand. She wins.

For the first time since taking her seat at the table, the devil gets to her feet. Her footsteps ring like church bells on the tiled saloon floor. She walks up to the sinner's wife, a pale mouse of a woman with cherry-red hair. The devil reaches out to her with her long, thin hands, and with her red, red lips, and the sinner's wife flinches.

The devil sighs and snaps her fingers, and the mousy woman falls to the floor like a puppet with all her strings cut. Her husband cries out for her, and turns to her, and then blood is oozing from his fingers, from his eyes, from his open mouth, and within an instant he is falling from his chair, hitting the ground with a thud of finality.

I've seen men die before. My father died when I was thirteen. I was the only girl, set to the task of nursing him back to health, but an infection set in his broken leg and he died roaring, a fever driving him near to madness. I've cared for dead and dying men since. But I've never seen anything like that.

The devil turns to the last man.

"Let me fold," he says, quietly, pleadingly.

The devil nods, and the man runs. He does not stop to take his woman's hand.

He does not make it to the door. He screams as he catches on fire, burning blue flame enveloping him 'til he is nothing but ash. His woman stands there, not moving, looking straight ahead.

The devil kisses her, hard. She does not kiss her the way a man kisses. She is not hungry, not demanding, but something else entirely. The kiss goes on a long, long time, and the woman's lips are swollen as red as the devil's when she finally pulls away.

"Go on then," the devil says to her, and she goes.

Then Johnny is called up to the table. I figure I should stand beside him, as the other women have done, but it doesn't seem right. Instead, I pull up a stool.

"You playing, ma'am?" the devil asks.

"No, ma'am," I answer back, in my best Sunday-school tones. "Just figured I'd be comfortable while I watch."

The devil throws her dark head back and laughs. Her throat is very white, and my lips itch looking at it. When her laughter passes, she says, "Well. Let me know if I can deal you in."

There are two other men playing. One asks to become mayor of some small town I've never heard of. An older woman, perhaps his mother, is standing behind him, looking fierce and proud. Another asks for his food stores to be refilled for the winter. His wife is very young, and stands so close behind them that they nearly touch.

The devil deals my husband in.

Johnny is a good card player. If he were dreadful, I'd have told him not to risk this. But I reckon the devil doesn't deal too fairly. I can't begin to guess what game she's playing, but I don't think it's five-card draw. It's something much more complicated and much, much older, with rules probably known only to herself.

The first round, Johnny loses fifty dollars. No sense starting small, I figure. I know I'll be up on that table, metaphorically speaking, soon enough. The second round, he bets the deed to our house (I'd told him to bring anything of any value he could carry). He loses that too.

"What shall we play for now?" the devil asks.

"My mother," the would-be mayor says, and the other offers his wife, Susan. I give Johnny an expectant glance.

"I reckon I'm out," Johnny says.

Stupid martyr of a man, I think, kicking him hard under the table.

"You sure about that?" the devil asks. "I've got a good feeling for you this round."

"I've got nothing left to bet," Johnny replies, always stubborn as a mule.

I think about how it would feel to stand and walk out of here. The relief that would go through me, like a breath of air after nearly drowning. The freedom I would feel, away from this strange place and this stranger woman.

I think about my little Rose, dying alone in a house we no longer even own. I imagine watching her turned out on the street, too poor to buy her food, helpless to do anything but listen to her last little gasping breaths.

"Johnny Pembrose, I swear to God, you better not be turning into a coward now," I say, not caring that a room full of people have just heard me take the Lord's name in vain.

The devil's smile turns a little crooked. "Suppose you ought to mind your wife," she says. "And I don't just say that on account of how I like to play at a full table."

"Patience, I—" Johnny tries to say to me, but I lack the virtue that is my namesake.

"You better play."

Johnny turns back to the table. I know he can't look at me while he does this, and I can't blame him. "I'll bet my wife, Missus Patience Pembrose."

"And you're playing for the life of your little girl?" the devil asks. As if she could have forgotten.

Johnny grits his teeth and nods.

I feel cold and clear inside, like my soul is a stream in springtime. I am not afraid as the cards are dealt, each one snapping precisely down on the table. Nor as the players arrange their hands, nor go in rounds to trade out cards. I'm not a brave woman by nature, but the devil's dark eyes have wrung all the fear out of me.

They play. One man folds, then the other. It's the devil and Johnny playing now.

"Before we all show our hands," the devil says, "I'd like to offer you a bargain, Mister Pembrose. The kind of bargain you don't get offered twice."

Johnny nods at her. "I'll hear you out."

"Why don't we both fold and keep each other's wagers? Your daughter lives. Your wife stays with me."

Johnny looks at her, at her beautiful, unseeable face. He looks at me, at the barely contained rage there, as I mouth, "Do it," at him. And then he looks at his cards.

"Check," he says, and the devil laughs.

"You're a brave man, Mister Pembrose. Well, let's see, then."

Johnny lays out his cards on the table. Four aces and the King of Spades.

The devil places hers down too, one at a time, precisely. The Two of Hearts. The Three of Hearts. The Four of Hearts. The Five of Hearts. The Six of Hearts. "Straight flush," she says, her voice like a banked fire—low and hot. "Seems like I win."

I pray Johnny has the sense to get out of here quick. I pray he makes it home to Rose before she dies. And then I can pray no more, because the devil's hand is on mine. My breath stops in my throat, and I feel my skin flush from my lips to my nether parts. I should yell to my husband to run. I should beg the devil for mercy for my daughter.

Instead, I tip my head back, and I set my lips against hers. Her long, thin fingers tangle in my hair, tugging my hat pin free from its careful confines. She kisses me as my hair cascades down my shoulders, as her hands find my breast and my waist. She tastes like ash and fire.

"Stop," Johnny says, like a fool, and she says nothing, but I feel heat surge around me, the same heat that burns within me.

As the room catches aflame, as the saloon burns, as men scream and die around me, she kisses me. She does not pull away until we are standing on the bare, snowy ground, only ash where once walls and men stood. Her swollen lips are redder than ever. She looks at me, brushes my cheek with her ever-moving hand.

"I win," she says.

A Mirror Has Two Faces

by Lindz McLeod

Every afternoon, Miss Havisham lay on the low couch while I sat on the love seat, gazing at the street below. She compelled me to describe the populace in the meanest possible ways—deriding this lady's plain green dress, that man's dark coat—before switching to my most charming self and describing those same things with lavish praise.

"Duality is the key, Estella," she often said. "A coin has two sides, has it not?"

When she tired of this game, she ordered me to escort her through the rooms of Satis House, performing the same trick. The fireplaces, therefore, were at once grand and imposing as well as sooty and unswept. The walls were beautifully adorned with wallpaper, yet the paper had been ripped and gouged in unseemly ways. The ceilings were high, elegantly corniced, yet they were tinged a pallid, smoky yellow. The windows were large but they were barred with rusted iron and the lower ones often bricked up entirely. The rooms were large but airless, the atmosphere oppressive yet enticing. Every clock in the house was stopped at precisely twenty to nine—the exact moment she had received a letter informing her that her wedding would never take place.

A couple of years ago, she asked me to perform this trick on her. I'd refused. "Perhaps you love me too much to utter criticism," she'd said, circling me like a hawk, keen to spot movement in the grass below. The faintest mouse-flutter of weakness and she would have been upon me, shaking me, rebuking me in the sternest of terms; reminding me what evils and treacheries the world outside holds, and what I must become to endure it. "Perhaps you hate me too much to utter praise."

"Neither," I'd said, holding myself steady.

She'd moved in front of me, smoothing thin hands over her ragged wedding dress. It had once been white, I supposed, though my memories of it being any such thing had faded entirely. Stains of varying shades littered the front. She never took it off, even to bathe, but preferred to submerge herself in a bath of tepid water while the lacy material billowed around her. A pale cloud, obscuring a gathering thunderbolt.

"Am I mother to you, girl, or sister?" she'd asked. The jewels at her throat were bright, round rubies, each the color of a fresh wound. The white flowers in her hair looked like scattered snowflakes, forerunning a storm.

"Neither," I said, slightly puzzled.

She had never displayed the slightest bit of maternal affection to me, nor a sisterly comradeship. I was but a child of two or three when she adopted me, and my education—while appropriate for a young woman of reasonable means under a guardian so rich—had tended in the opposite direction from most girls my age. They wished to be married. I wished nothing of the sort. Miss Havisham had been a relentless teacher for all of life's miseries. People were capable of the greatest betrayals, the worst vices, and the deepest, most corrupting greed. She had raised me to disdain affection, to distrust amiability, and to reject the notion of love entirely. She had succeeded well in her task to replace my heart with ice, to infuse my soul with a glacial chill.

She stepped closer. The faint scent of lilies wafted through the air, momentarily overpowering the familiar doughy stink of the uneaten wedding cake on the table to our left. "Am I god or monster?"

This answer I had hesitated over. She did not rebuke me for it, however, but instead smiled. "You have learned a great deal, Estella."

Pumblechook's boy first came on a chill, rimy day, when frost still clung to the ground like a drunk man afraid to stand. I showed him to Miss Havisham and listened at the door while she asked him questions. He had no ear for subtleties, that was plain, but answered what was put to him in an honest manner. Afterwards, she told me that the boy would make a fine challenge of my skills. "Make him fall in love with you," she ordered. "Break his heart."

It was no great feat, though I did not voice this opinion. The boy visited often, spoke politely, gazed upon my beauty with willing eyes. I acted out my part with a little relish, for we received very little in the way of company and this at least was a diversion, and came and went as I was ordered to do. The boy escorted her on a turn around the rooms when desired, though I could see discomfort written on the lines of his body. Had he been a tree, one might have sliced him open—not to discover his age, but to confirm what words were scrawled upon his soul. *I do not understand this woman. I am at sea in this earthly place.* Miss Havisham stood slightly lop-sided, wearing only one shoe, as was her custom. The silk stocking had worn away at the sole, and when she walked, I could hear the slap of her bare flesh on the dirty wooden floors.

How many times had she warned me—nay, rejoiced savagely in the fact—that a man's love could be won in a moment, a single glance coquettishly shot his way. Yet one afternoon, while the boy dealt cards for yet another game of Beggar Thy Neighbor, his eyes flickered to Miss Havisham rather than me. I followed his look, wishing to see what had caught his attention when I, the clear object of desire, sat plumed and perfumed mere inches away. The moment was etched upon my mind forever; Miss Havisham, frowning at her spread hand. I saw her for the first time not through my own eyes, nor through a smoky fire or guttering candle as was our usual. A striking woman of thirty and three. High cheekbones, presiding sternly over sunken hollows. A thin nose. Dark eyes fringed with dark lashes. Hair so pale it looked white in the dimness, though I had once boldly drawn back a curtain while she slept and examined her to my own satisfaction. In fact her hair was yellow, though the knowledge was my secret alone. I rather thought she no longer knew her own self, though she dressed every day with the aid of a large, gilded looking-glass.

She held herself stiffly, strangely, as if expecting any moment to be dealt a blow rather than a card. When we were alone together she was less affected, less prone to sudden outbursts. The boy brought out the worst in her, reminded her that she had made a vow to wound the world threefold what had been done to her so long ago.

The boy left Satis House that day carrying unspoken words in his mouth like a loaded applecart. I listened to the sound of his footsteps fading, and I realized I did not care if he loved me or not. The boy and I were merely pawns to be pushed around; two pebbles dropped into the same lake, or perhaps two rats cornered by the same cat. In her chamber, Miss Havisham asked me to remove her jewels while she talked of the boy, how his every look and word had seemed designed to court me. No reigning queen ever rejoiced over such a victorious battle. I was barely listening. Her neck smelt of forgotten lilies, of something sharp and hot and yellow, and something else that did not quite—

"Is that not so, Estella?" Her voice was a claw, currently sheathed. Her eyes were two unstruck matches. "You do not flinch from the idea of hurting him now, I hope?"

"Of course not." I placed the last of the jewels on the table, arranging them in a loose circle. "I am looking forward to it."

In bed that evening, I mulled over the problem. A boy could be won so easily. A man would doubtless be the same. What challenge was it, really? I had beauty, wealth, charm. Even a woman, I thought—at least for those for whom the notion was more than a passing fancy—would be easily won over by these same qualities. The word *satis* came from the Latin for *enough*, Miss Havisham informed me at least once a week. It was enough for her to have me live out her revenge. What would be enough for me?

I pored over the answer for hours and yet when it dawned on me, it was as clear as if I had always known it. The only true challenge was to seduce Havisham, the only person in the world for whom love was neither a sport nor a hunger. I thought of the way she spoke of her groom; a love which had once burned brightly enough to blister, which had cooled into a thick, sticky hatred, drowning everything in its path. A strange new emotion simmered inside my belly. Dark as the gloom which penetrated every corner, as jagged as the rents in the wallpaper. If I could usurp the groom's place, then surely I would have conquered all. Proven myself, at last.

I sent the boy away when next he came, and lied to Miss Havisham that he had been unavoidably delayed by something or other. I used every trick she had taught me and every trick I had learned besides, in books or by my own arch means. I was beside her always, breathing in the lilies, watching the vein in her temple pulse, brushing my ungloved hand against her cheek when I took off her jewels in the evening. I was attentive and sharp, noting her every breath, tasting the color of her mood as it shifted from moment to moment. Her emotions reverberated like plucked strings under the bow of my tongue. Was it any wonder that a woman deprived of real attention, severed on her wedding day, was powerless to resist a single focused ray of light? Over dinner each night she ate less and less, instead devouring my every flush, every coy smile.

I gave her no time to think in my presence, only to react to some new device, some cunning ruse of batted eyelash or brief clasps of fingers. Men do not woo in such ways. I was willing to bet her groom had never been so subtle, so tender, so able to build the swell of desire into a tremendous deluge. Having spent the last decade of her life preparing me to deliver such warfare, she was entirely unprepared to endure the onslaught herself. Her castle, thus besieged, withstood my attacks for weeks. It fell, eventually, as we both knew it would. She had encouraged me too much, imbued me with such confidence that I never once considered failure a possible outcome of my endeavors. I was a soldier well-trained in the art of love, a knight pursuing an unholy quest. A hound on the trail, running down her quarry.

I picked my moment well that night. She trembled on my approach, though she resisted my first embraces. Demanded me to explain myself, while color flushed high on her cheeks. Parried my following thrusts. Relented under my cajoling, my persuasion, my whispered words of adoration. I took her to bed and unwrapped her wedding dress. I captured what the groom had never uncaged, what Havisham had always promised never to give and now gifted to me willingly.

Afterwards, I dressed, feeling and looked down upon her. "Where are you going?" she asked. "Stay with me."

I could barely see her face in the low blaze of the firelight. Her voice sounded different—younger, as if she had stopped growing at one-and-twenty years just as the clocks had stopped at twenty to nine. The sneer curled up through my thighs, blossomed in my belly, burst into flower on my lips. "You have succeeded, madam. I must congratulate you."

For a moment, she did not understand me. The realization dawned quickly, a candle bursting into flame. She had not created an ice queen, as she had once imagined, but a full-blown winter. Terrible, beautiful, unforgiving. "No," she said. "No, Estella. Please, I—"

I straightened my dress, crossed to the window and opened it. The night was cool, with a faint green scent drifting on the air. Spring, perhaps. A hundred thousand seeds, budding at this very moment, ready to erupt through the ground at the slightest provocation. The estate below was a dark abyss, untouched by moonlight. Below, there were uneven flagstones, paving a path through the garden.

Quite a fall. Quite a jump.

Choking back a sob, Miss Havisham stepped out of bed, gathering her crumpled dress to her chest. She crossed to the window. I held out my hand, and helped her up onto the ledge. She did not look at me before she stepped out, nor did she wish me farewell.

I watched her pale body flutter down, down, down into the dark aisle of the night. Watched it collide with the altar of her resolution. Watched it twitch for a moment, then still. I stepped back from the window. I smoothed down the sheets, still warm from her body. Returning to the window, I stared down at the body and prepared a suitable scream, which would alert the staff to what had just happened. Quite without meaning to, I instead performed my usual trick instinctively, comparing the way our bodies had moved against each other, the sweat-slick of a carnal desire. The beauty of her lips on mine. The repulsion of shared heartbeats. The utter grotesqueness of love. The sheer glory of loathing.

The Turner House Heritage Tour

by Caitlin Marceau

Claire drums her fingers against the surface of the ancient desk, her nails tapping loudly against the scratched wood as she waits for the landing page of her Facebook business profile to load. She takes a sip of her red wine, the large glass filled well past where it's meant to be filled, and she tries not to get frustrated as the computer struggles to get her where she needs to go.

This is why we should have paid the extra fifteen a month for the high-speed, she thinks, trying to win an argument in her head that she'd lost when they'd changed service providers a few months back.

But we don't have *an extra fifteen a month*, she hears the memory of her wife whisper to her, worried that someone might overhear their conversation and ashamed that she'd admit to poverty in public. The way she spoke about money was how she knew Elle had spent her life—or her life until marrying Claire—middle-class.

As the header of her page comes into focus, *The Turner House Heritage Tour*, she can hear her kids and wife downstairs, laughing and playing and no doubt leaving messes in their wake. She already knows she'll have to play the bad guy when she comes downstairs and finds their belongings scattered around the rooms she just finished cleaning.

It feels like they've forced her to play the bad guy a lot lately.

She scrolls down to view her page's insights, the knot in her stomach tightening as the advertisement comes into view. She'd maxed out her last credit card boosting the post, desperate for people to hear about the new tours and activities that her family's heritage house had to offer.

Although over a thousand people had seen the post, only two people had bothered to like it and she'd been one of them.

She slams back the rest of the boxed Merlot in her glass and wishes not for the first time that her mother was still around.

You always knew what to do.

"Claire, have you finished your homework?" her mother asks her, stirring the spaghetti sauce as it simmers and sizzles on the burner. The smell of cheap beef and canned tomatoes fills the kitchen as her mother cooks the same thing she always cooks whenever money is scarce.

"Almost!" Claire lies, flipping open her math workbook and turning to the right page, hoping her mom doesn't notice that she hasn't taken out a pencil yet.

"Mhmm."

Her mother beats the wooden spoon against the edge of the red Dutch oven, trying to get off any stuck-on sauce, before setting it down on a clean plate nearby. She puts a massive pot in the sink and turns on the water, letting it fill up, when the phone rings.

"I'll get it!" Claire says happily, looking for any excuse to get out of doing math.

She crosses the small kitchen, her cotton socks slipping and sliding on the freshly cleaned floors as she rushes to answer the landline before her mom.

She's too slow.

Sit, her mom mouths silently to her, pointing to her pile of work on the kitchen table as she picks up the receiver.

"Hello?" she says pleasantly into the phone. "Hey Mom! Perfect timing, I was just going to call and ask if your garlic butter uses one or two—"

Claire knows something is wrong the second she looks at her mom.

Her brown eyes are wide and look like they're about to bulge out of her head. Her mouth hangs open, lip quivering as she listens to the woman on the other end of the call. She closes her eyes and shakes her head, the movement getting faster and faster until she finally cuts the woman off on the other end.

"No, Mom, you can't! We can—No, listen, we'll find another way! You don't—STOP! Mom, please, I need you to—Mom? MOM?" she screams. The line is dead, but soon it begins to beep loud enough that Claire can hear it at the table.

"Mom, is everything okay?" Claire asks, worried at her mother's sudden silence.

It takes the older woman a moment to answer, her voice hoarse and rough, like her mouth is too dry or her throat is too tight. "Just do your homework, sweetie."

Claire takes a pencil out of her bag and starts on one of the equations while her mom shakily punches a number into the phone. She waits as the line rings, leaning against the wall for support as she breathes heavily through her open mouth until someone picks up on the other end.

"Dad," she says, voice cracking as she speaks, "Mom went into the house alone."

Claire's not sure what her grandfather says, but it doesn't matter. All that fills the kitchen now is the sound of her mother sobbing.

⁕

Claire runs her hands through Elle's hair, watching as the other woman kisses a trail down her chest, over her stomach, along her hips, until the woman's soft lips find softer folds in the darkness of their bedroom. Claire doesn't want to close her eyes, but she can't help herself as she arches her back, head pushing against her cheap pillow as she pushes herself against her wife's tongue.

Claire bites her lip, trying to keep quiet as Elle enjoys her body, her breathless moans and whispers for more as intense and desperate as they were the first night they explored each other. She gasps as Elle pushes a finger inside her, slowly slipping it in and out as she tastes the nectar between Claire's thighs.

Elle works her open, works her deeper, and for the first time in a long time, Claire lets herself fall apart and come undone.

⁕

"Why do we need to go *now*?" Elle asks her quietly, spitting the last of the toothpaste into the sink. She runs the water as low as she can, mindful of the children asleep in the room next to them.

"Because you know how they are. If we go during the day, the kids will want to come too," Claire whispers, brushing her hair off of her face. "And there's no fucking way we're letting them come to the Turner House with us."

"No, of course not. But we can just leave them in the car."

"And what if May decides she doesn't want to wait and follows us in? Or, God forbid, she gets Jordan out of his car seat and brings him in with her?"

Elle rubs her eyes with the base of her palm, the dark circles under her eyes looking darker in the cheap yellow light of the small room.

"Okay, so we get them a babysitter and we go—"

"Elle, we can't *afford* a babysitter. But if we go now, while they're asleep, we won't need one."

"I just don't feel good about leaving them alone in the middle of the night. What if—"

"For fuck's sake. It's a broken pipe being held together with duct tape and old bedsheets. If it bursts for *real* this time, we're fucked."

I'm fucked, she thinks, trying (and failing) not to picture herself as a mound of twisted flesh and broken bones. She thinks of the rotting walls in the basement, the peeling wallpaper that hangs unglued in every room, the way the foundation is cracked and broken, and wonders how that neglect and ruin will be reflected on her corpse. She thinks of the family before her, all dead and gone, and wonders how they ever lived comfortably with the axe that is the Turner House hanging above their heads. How could any of them sleep knowing that if the house fell to ruin and was left to starve, its fate would be theirs too?

Why would anyone marry into this family? she asks herself.

She looks at Elle and her heart aches, knowing that if the roles had been reversed, Claire wouldn't have loved her wife enough to marry her. Not if it meant tying her fate to a house.

"Our *kids* are fucked," she says, knowing it'll be enough to convince Elle to leave with her.

She's right.

***

Claire pushes open the door of the Turner House and is somehow overwhelmed and underwhelmed by the sight of it all at once. The house is massive and the oldest in the area, something that's not hard to believe based on the derelict state of the building. The hardwood floors are scratched and chipped, the furniture is covered with grime, and the stone bricks that hold it all together are beginning to crumble.

Claire notices a deep crack in the wall that runs from the door to the entrance of the parlor, and she can't help but trace her finger along it as she follows it deeper into the house. She frowns, staring at it, trying to figure out if the crack is narrower than she originally thought, or if her eyes are playing tricks on her. She watches as the crack shrinks and the white paint smooths over where it used to be.

At the end of the hall a woman screams and begins to run, her shoes loud on the solid floors. She looks up just in time to see her mother scoop her up into her arms as she barrels towards the door, desperate to get Claire out of the house.

Once they're in the parking lot, her mother sets her on the ground, holding Claire's arms with tight hands as she looks her over.

"What did I tell you about going into this house without me?"

"But I didn't go in without you. I saw you leading a couple of people in and I wanted to—"

"How many times do I have to tell you, Claire? Kids grow up fast in the Turner House. Everyone does! I told you that I always, *always*, had to be next to you and that you couldn't just wander in here alone. Jesus Christ, Claire, this house is *dangerous*!"

"But what about the people still in there?" she asks, now worried about the tourists still inside.

Her mom drags her towards their car and pushes her in front of the passenger's side mirror. Claire looks at her reflection, not recognizing the face that stares back at her. Her face is thinner, but her lips and nose are more full. The skin on her face is dotted with acne that wasn't there a moment ago and her gums hurt, her loose teeth now bigger and permanent. She looks down and is surprised to find her pants are too short, her once oversized sweater is now tight across her chest, and her feet ache from her suddenly too-small shoes.

"Everything needs to eat, Claire. Even the house. But not you. It should *never* be you. And it won't be, as long as you bring it what it needs."

* * *

"How much time do you think we've got?" Elle asks her nervously. The two of them move quickly through the labyrinth that is the basement of the house. Claire's mother always said it was built that way to keep the rats away from the food.

Claire always thought it was to keep them in.

"Until the pipe bursts or until—"

"Until."

"I don't know. I say we get in, see the damage, and get the fuck out."

Claire undoes the lock on the heavy door that sections off the storage tunnel and opens it for Elle. Against the walls are tables and chairs that were once used for parties and receptions. Now, they lie folded up and forgotten, the wood rotten and sprouting mushrooms that thrive in the dampness and the dark.

She knows there was a time, long ago when she was younger, when business was good. The Turner House could see hundreds of visitors in a week and each one would be allowed to leave a few weeks older, but none the wiser.

But now …

"Do you remember which end the leak is on?" Elle asks her.

"The left? Or, no, it was the right, right? Or, fuck, I really don't know. You go left, I'll take right, okay?"

"I don't know. I don't like the idea of us splitting up."

"The faster we find it, the faster we're out of here."

It's clear Elle wants to argue, but she nods instead and heads down her side of the hallway.

Once she's far enough, Claire exits the storage hall and locks the door behind her. She covers her ears with her hands and runs for the exit, Elle's screams for help following her through the house and all the way home.

• • • •

"They did a great job with your mother, don't you think?" someone, Claire's not sure who, asks her.

"Yeah, they really did," she lies.

The person keeps talking to her, but Claire isn't paying attention. She's too distracted by the old woman in the coffin that rests in front of the crucifix on the altar at the front of the room. The woman is old and withered, her back rounded and shoulders hunched, her once bright hair grey and listless, her brown eyes grey and milky with cataracts. The woman in the coffin has to be in her late eighties, but Claire knows her mother was only sixty-one when she died.

Part of her is disappointed that her mom chose to die at home. If she'd let the house finish the job and have her, she could have bought Claire a bit more time.

Part of her is happy to be able to say goodbye, even if her mother looks like a stranger now.

"She must have had you very late in life," someone tells her.

"Yeah, I guess," Claire says dismissively, knowing her mom gave birth to her when she was only twenty-one.

"I didn't realize how old she was, but you know how secretive Lauraine was about her age."

"All us Turner women are."

• • • •

When Claire returns to the house the following afternoon, she's happy to see that the brickwork outside is once again intact. The cracks that ran along the front door are gone and the shingles that were missing are back

172

on the roof. She opens the door and peeks inside, smiling when she sees that the hardwood floor is unscratched and the familiar cracks leading to the parlor are gone.

Elle must have had more years left than she'd thought.

Claire hurries to the basement, knowing that while the Turner House *probably* won't feed on her so soon after eating, she's better off moving fast in case it's hungry for dessert.

She unlocks the storage hall's door, her breath catching in her throat when she sees the dark spot on the floor that marks where Elle's body once lay. She imagines her wife growing old, years leaving her body in the blink of an eye, and she wonders if she looked anything like Claire's mother when her heart finally stopped beating. She wonders how she died, wonders which part of Elle gave up first, and tries to hold back the tears that want to come knowing that even her bones were picked clean and turned to dust.

Claire makes her way to the end of the tunnel, finding the broken pipe in the dark of the basement. She strips the bedsheets off and unwraps the duct tape, seeing that the metal has fused together like she hoped. As she turns to leave, she hears a familiar sound behind her.

Drip. Drip. Drip.

The pipe is fixed, but not entirely. She knows it's only a matter of time until the pipe bursts and the Turner House falls into ruin again. She exhales shakily through her lips.

"Is everything okay, Mom? Can we go home now?" her daughter asks, her hand wrapped nervously around her brother's.

"Not yet, May, but soon," she lies, the key to the storage door heavy in her hand. "But first, I need you and Jordan to do Mommy a favor and wait right here."

Enamored

by Shelley Lavigne

As the client entered my apothecary, the alligator on the ceiling swung from its chains in holy ecstasy over her nearly translucent pale skin, doll-like features, and lustrous chestnut hair.

I tried to guess what she would buy. She looked to be the age of debut, and wouldn't need rouge or fragrance to extend her season like my usual clientele. Her dress looked expensive enough that she should be able to afford a doctor, ruling out most cures. I settled on a sleeping aid; doctors gave their patients the first taste of laudanum but never could satiate the hunger they created.

I gave her a capable but deferential smile; a servant who knew more than the master.

"Good morning. Welcome to Watson and Sons. I'm Mrs. Josephine Watson. May I help you find what you are looking for, Miss …"

"Cora Metcalfe."

I knew of her from Ottawa's society papers. You need only walk Metcalfe Avenue to know their importance. And wealth.

With her patronage I could say goodbye to this backwater town of lumberjacks and mosquitoes. Travel again. Or pay off creditors who had turned threatening after the police investigation.

"How can I help you today?"

"I'm looking for rouge and perfume."

I'd been wrong.

Her eyes wandered the displays, lingering on an illustration of a ghostly pale girl with blue veins on her neck like fractures in a teacup, ready to shatter.

Cora traced the girl's neck with a delicate finger. I wished she'd do the same to mine. Miss Metcalfe looked more tempting than the advertising. Her essence was the very thing companies promised to sell. *If someone could distill her*, I thought, *they'd make a fortune.*

"What's this?" she asked.

"Enameling, it's the newest trend, very popular in Paris. It will make you more resplendent, while hardening your skin against future damage. I can offer a sample, free of charge."

"Will it hurt?" she asked, eyeing the creams and pots I had already begun placing on the countertop. She ungloved slowly, popping each white silk finger. Heat settled in my middle.

"You're in safe hands." I dipped my index into the white lead cream and reached towards her.

She pulled her hand away. "Can you use a brush?"

"The finish won't be as smooth."

She said nothing, just stared. I left her to rummage in the back room for some old brushes. When I returned, she placed her hand daintily on the counter, a reward for my good behavior. I smoothed the white over her skin, erasing freckles from a youth spent outdoors.

I painted into the crevices between her fingers. I left her fingertips nude, to let the skin breathe. Several months ago, a duchess had failed to leave exposed skin and fainted dead away. A friend had to smash her open like a hard-boiled egg.

Cora giggled as I painted her wrist. "It tickles."

Cora's heart raced as I painted over her pulse point.

"You're doing beautifully."

When the white was applied, I pulled out a light blue ink and painted where her veins should be, where blood was coursing warm, wet.

The surface lost its sheen as it hardened into a porcelain-like finish.

Cora brought the immobile hand up to her face, marveling at it, at the pristine skin without a single variation in tint, at the blue veins crossing her hand like rivers in the countryside. "Is it permanent?"

"No, it will break if you move it or tap it hard."

She ran the hand along the exposed skin of her neck. My eyes followed her route.

"You can do this to more than my hand?"

"Of course! Face, neck, and hands are typical. We cover only the exposed areas, any more than that can be dangerous. The full procedure is expensive and—"

"I would like this done as soon as possible."

"Next Tuesday?" I proposed.

She smiled widely. "Perfect."

"A full procedure is fifteen dollars."

It was a gamble, setting the price that high, but a worker's yearly salary was a drop for her.

The door swung open and a dowdy servant woman charged in.

"Miss Cora! I thought you'd been taken!"

"I will be here next Tuesday at twelve sharp," she whispered before turning to the woman, tucking her hand behind her back.

"We are going to be late for supper with George," the servant whined. "Your mother is sick enough without having to worry about you."

"I had completely forgotten."

She hurried to the door, where her chaperone waited anxiously. I held my sigh of relief until the door had closed.

It seemed my luck was turning. I could make a tidy sum, maybe try gathering a couple of her friends in my net, and rebuild my nest egg.

My late husband had opposed my suggestion to broaden our cosmetics offering, saying it would cheapen us. It was a shame he wouldn't witness me making more in a sitting than he had made in six months.

⁂

She arrived as the church bells rang noon. I blinked as if sun-blind before her beauty.

"The tub is in the back room. You'll soak in a special mixture of Arabian salts and flowers to set your skin before we can proceed."

It didn't really do anything, just gave me a chance to check her pockets for easy-to-miss items I could sell.

Cora drew off her gloves and hat as I led her through a small door. I had spent the last days clearing the remaining traces of my late husband's detritus of boxes and vials—good riddance. I'd turned the storeroom into an imitation boudoir with candles and fabric and been proud of my work until her presence made clear how shabby it was.

Cora smiled as if this was some great adventure. She stripped, waving off my assistance.

"You're a merchant, not a maid."

The candlelight made the pale expanse of Cora's back and ass glow as she stepped into the tub. I resisted the urge to dig my fingers into the roundness of her flesh to see it bounce, to bite into her breast, leaving my mark.

Alchemists had once thought there was something in the young that, if consumed, returned one's vitality. Looking at her, I understood why. She had the suppleness of youth no one appreciates when they have it, convinced of their own hideousness. Time, the only true mirror, reveals beauty only in hindsight.

Nothing could make her more beautiful, paints and tinctures ruined the skin, requiring greater and greater amounts to hide the damage they cause. It's a great business model, one that feeds on and amplifies anxieties.

I'd permit myself one taste of her money, then set her free.

She sunk into the water, pink nipples catching my eye before plunging below the surface. The water dipped and rose like a fan at a cabaret, hiding and revealing her.

When I looked up, Cora watched me with coquettish mirth.

I swallowed my need. My collar was too tight to let it pass.

"I need to prepare the treatment. I will be back in a moment."

I nearly ran out.

Cora's arms had become gooseflesh when I returned an hour later.

"Is it time?" she asked.

I wrapped her in my late husband's bathrobe, while I'd removed the embroidery at the lapel, a dark, ghostly WW was visible in harsher lights. She sat primly, like she was posing for one of those new photographic portraits.

"Shall we start with your hands?"

I scrubbed off what remained of the previous treatment—a patch on the front, dusting around her nails—with the caustic solution that I used to clean my countertops. There wasn't much, water and time had done most of the work.

I applied the white paint across her inner wrist, preoccupied with images of what I'd rather be doing with her hands.

Aimless chitchat might fill the thickened silence. I asked, "Are you attending any balls soon? Any special suitors?"

"Let's not talk about that," she said firmly.

But I was curious about her, fascinated at being so close to wealth. I wanted to take advantage of this rare opportunity for learning how to cater to those like her.

"But if not for your suitors, surely there are other ways to spend time. Playing piano or embroidering?" Rich women enjoyed those things in novels.

"It's armor."

I resisted the urge to point out how delicate the enamel was, leaving a silence for her to fill.

"It keeps hands off me, hands of suitors, tailors, parents—all valuing and assessing me. I'll no longer feel their pinching and petting, like I'm some kind of settee."

But she didn't comment on *my* touch as I brought down the robe so I could paint her neck and upper chest. She tilted her head, revealing more skin. I imagined the brush was my mouth, licking under her ear, sucking her earlobe.

"I'll never be as beautiful and free as I am now. Especially with such a dimwitted chaperone. But when I'm married, I'll need to be accounted for, surrounded by staff. My time will belong to my husband and children."

I imagined her enameled body as her future husband thrust into her. The cracks spreading out from her pelvis. His uncaring violence as her body fractured into pieces underneath him. He still did not stop, thinking his gluey semen could hold her together.

"Don't you want to find love?" I asked.

"I hardly think I'll find love in marriage … I'm sure you understand, Mrs. Wilson."

She stripped me barer than I'd done her, seeing right through the mask I'd worn since my hastily arranged marriage. It had been an easy way to cover up a scandal, after I'd been found performing unsisterly acts upon the woman I'd called my spirit sister.

Cora moved on as if she had not implied anything noteworthy. "I don't quite have the luxury of waiting, like you, for the death of my husband, even if that might happen sooner now that I have access to your discrete assistance."

I was surprised she'd heard rumors about my shop's other business, but maybe her visit to my pharmacy was not an accident; she, like the police, had sought out the source of arsenic—inheritance powder—which had started flowing through the region like logs on the Ottawa River. After my husband's death, the police's eye had fallen on me, especially since I was the purveyor of creams and tinctures for many of the recently widowed. There hadn't been enough evidence to convict, but the bribe for my freedom had extended further than my own pockets. Creditors were quick to help but also quick to demand repayment. With interest.

Cora laughed bitterly, lost in some private memory. "Beauty fades, as does health. Being weak, sick and vulnerable is seen as beautiful. But I've seen sickness, how it hollows you, takes your loveliness, your joy. I don't want to decay. I want to be forever as I am now."

I flinched. Not because of the anger in her tone, but because of her words. I was probably old in her eyes—yet I had so much life left. I never felt more in control of myself, more capable than I did now in my forties. Life is a death sentence but aging doesn't need to be.

Her pulse beat frantically in her neck. I smoothed over it with the white paint.

She suddenly pushed me away. I toppled over my stool, sitting stunned on the ground for a moment before I realized she was coughing, chest-shaking, rattling hacks that I felt from the floor.

The fit passed and she tucked away a spotted handkerchief. "Sorry about that," she said.

"Just warn me next time."

She nodded, creating cracks on her neck. I righted the chair and sat.

"Will I die, Josephine?"

"We all die eventually, Miss Metcalfe. Please hold still."

For the rest of the session, she was so still and silent I could imagine her as a doll, a pretty thing I was making for myself. I reddened her lips and cheeks with rouge.

"Perfect," I labelled her.

She couldn't smile lest she mar the finish.

⁂

I did not see her again for seven days, but I constantly wondered how she was doing, what she looked like now.

How her warm, hardened skin might feel.

The alligator swam around the ceiling when the door flew open.

Cora's face was fractured around the eyes and hinged around the mouth like a marionette. The skin between the cracks was red and inflamed, pushing up between the uniform matte white. It looked like something was trying to emerge, a monster covered by a crumbling disguise.

Cora's shattered face repelled me. It seemed impossible for someone so beautiful to have broken down in such a way. But I couldn't tear my eyes away, she was still magnetic, awe-inspiring.

"It wasn't enough," Cora wailed.

She lurched and her bag thudded against a display with a metallic rattle. There was something in there; money, jewels, something of value. She would make it worth my time.

"Wait in the backroom, I'll close the shop."

When she left, I allowed myself a deep, steadying breath. *I have nothing to fear, I am in control.* I repeated it like a prayer as I locked the door and flipped the sign. I closed the blinds, even though the street was empty. I found Cora weeping in the chair, bag at her feet. I approached her, unsure what she wanted or needed and was surprised when she grabbed me, pulling me in.

Loud messy sobs erupted as she pushed her face into my chest, flecks of white and tears streaking my bodice. I stroked her hair.

A flap of enamel was torn half off her cheek, holding on by a thin flap of skin, revealing the raw pink and yellow flesh beneath.

She pushed me away again as she coughed into a spotted handkerchief.

I had no cure for what ailed her, nothing that could do more than temporarily ease the pain.

"Cora, you should go to a sanitorium."

She shook her head. The piece of enamel clinked as it tapped her hardened cheek. "That's not why I'm here."

"Why, then?"

She closed her lips as if that was the only thing that could keep her secrets in. I held her warm porcelain cheek. She nuzzled into my palm.

"Let's get this off of you," I suggested, but she shook her head.

"Just fill in the cracks."

I no longer wanted to play her sick game of self-destruction; I wanted her to live. Sensing my hesitation, she kicked forward the jangling bag. It was heavier than I had imagined and when opened, the contents glimmered even in the dim light. Jewelry, all polished metals and sparkling gems, glinted next to red velvet. The sheer opulence dazzled me. It was worth at least a couple hundred, maybe more. I closed it, placed it on her lap.

"I cannot accept this as payment. Everyone will think I stole it."

"Who cares? Pawn it."

"Where do you think the police will look first? And the brokers will be happy to turn informant when questioned."

"Then … don't sell them here."

She was right, I could leave, maybe go to Paris where I'd be quite comfortable amongst others like me. Start fresh in comfort.

"One more treatment," I agreed. She returned the bag, its heft similar to an infant. I couldn't help but look down at the jewelry. "These don't really look like your style."

"They were my mother's."

I noticed the past tense. No wonder Cora was distraught.

But this was good, in a way. With the flurry of a funeral, it might take time for someone to notice Cora's absence. Could I entice her to run away with me?

No. I couldn't maintain the level of luxury she was accustomed to. She would slow me down.

This was my big payday. My chance. I couldn't ruin good business because of sentimentality.

"I'll get the bath ready and put some salve on your wound. Then we can start."

"Is it time?" she asked when I placed my hand on her shoulder.

The pruned skin at her fingertips looked so normal compared to her cracked face. I focused on the rosy tips as I guided her out of the water, small sharp flecks of the remaining enamel biting into my hands.

She emerged from the water like a siren, calling me to fall to my knees and worship her body with mine. I pulled up the robe like a shield between us, but she shook her head.

"Paint my whole body."

"That will kill you."

"Was my payment insufficient for the treatment?"

"I'll be charged with murder."

"Then make sure they don't find us."

"Cora—" I tried to stand my ground, but she tore the robe out of my hands and prodded me hard in the chest.

"Do not treat me like a naive girl."

I collapsed onto the chair.

She continued. "This is how I will own my body, decide what is done with it. I won't waste away or live at someone else's whim."

I could see tomorrow's headline if I said no. *Beautiful grief-stricken young lady throws herself off bridge holding a king's ransom in jewels.*

"Okay," I said, "I'll do it."

She smiled and waited patiently as I ran the robe along her body, following the soft curves and dips and folds, an introduction to the flesh I'd be painting soon.

"Where do you want me? Shall I pose in a particular way?"

A sculpture and a muse all in one.

"Hop on the table."

I started by patching the hole in her cheek. She whimpered as I brushed over the oozing sore.

"Shall I stop?" A dare as much as a plea. It wasn't too late.

"No."

I patched the cracks around her eyes but avoided her lips, I couldn't bear to silence her yet, couldn't seal away that part before I'd had a taste. I started at her feet, running the brush along the delicate arches, carefully circling every toe. I crept up, painting the ankle bone and Achilles tendon with care.

Her soft calf and dimpled knee.

If I went higher, I'd have to split her legs. Normally in this position—a woman naked, lying down in front of me—this would not be an issue. I knew the role she wanted me to play, a consummate professional at her service, but I wanted more, wanted to spread her open and devour her bodily.

"What's the delay?" she asked.

I put my hands on her knees, gently pushing them apart.

She opened herself.

I dragged the brush up her inner thigh, watching the hairs on her legs rise and hearing her breath hike in her throat. She moaned as I ran the brush between her legs, painting her folds.

"Paint inside of me."

I dipped my hands into the cream and slowly glided in.

She sat up suddenly.

"No," she closed her legs. "Don't you have a tool?"

She did not like being touched.

Why would this have been any different? If I offended her now and she walked out, she might still die and they could prove I was the culprit, unlike with my husband.

I needed to fix this.

"Sorry Miss, yes Miss. I'll be right back."

I wiped my hands on a towel, shame making me tremble.

"Hurry back."

I ran upstairs for the pestle I kept at my bedside for when I wanted more than the touch of my fingers inside me—it did quite well.

"Is this better?" I asked, showing it to her.

She nodded, reopening her legs. She watched my hands as they covered it in white paint. I slowly pushed the rounded tip into her.

She gasped, moaning on the exhale. Her fingers curled around the side of the table, knuckles going whiter than the cream I was applying.

Her nipples were like two berries dipped in cream. I found the brush, mimicking with it what I wanted to do with my tongue, flicking and circling the tip. Her hips bucked into my hand.

I heard the set enamel crack as her toes curled. She pushed into me. I pushed back harder, set equal parts on pleasure and pain.

Her stomach seized and she fell back on the table with a cry.

I wanted to touch that soft skin of hers with my own, feel it's warm pliability. I longed to kiss her mouth, but knew I couldn't.

I looked down at the ruined mess of her feet, the cracked enamel I'd have to fix, but also the beautiful darker flesh below, at the reddened chest streaked with a mess of white. It seemed a shame to desecrate her in this way.

"Are you sure you want to proceed?"

She laughed sharply at me, so sure of herself. Her coldness had returned. "Why wouldn't I?"

Because there was still so much for her to experience and—cockily—so much more I wanted to show her.

But I never was a savior. I've always been a destroyer, a runner.

I settled back at her feet, fixing my work, nothing but a professional now. I moved her body without shame and fear, painting her torso and arm before turning her onto her side, arranging her in a goddess-like pose.

Next came the inks and creams, the blue veins, the rouge darkening her nipples, the coal to redraw a heart-shaped beauty mark on her clavicle.

Her body froze slowly, the enamel losing sheen as it hardened. Toes first, then feet, then ankles.

I put a mask of it over her hair, sealing her completely to prevent the smell once she died, which was now inevitable. She hummed in pleasure as I stroked down into her scalp. I smoothed her hair back into a bun, leaving tendrils tickling her neck where I wanted to place my lips, taking my time.

I looked down at her face. Her eyes were closed. Was she already dead?

"Cora?"

"Yes, Josephine."

She opened her eyes slowly—relaxed or dying.

"I'm going to finish now."

I placed my brush over the cracks near her mouth.

"Take care of me, will you, Josephine? Forever."

I kissed her unpainted lips. She leaned into my kiss, as if she finally felt safe enough in her shell to allow contact. Her mouth burned as if all her body's heat was concentrated at that single point. I wanted to climb onto her, pin her to the table, shatter the porcelain, digging my fingers into her soft flesh.

Instead, I sealed my kiss with white paint.

I closed her eyes, painting over the lids, and placed dollops into her nostrils.

I held her hardening hand until I felt only my own warmth. When I awoke in the morning, she was cold.

I tapped at her flesh. The solid ringing sound was a little like a china bowl filled with soup.

I'd have to be careful not to shatter her in transit; she'd make a beautiful window display for an apothecary. An advertisement for the beauty you too could achieve. with the products inside.

I packed her like a relic, placing my few gowns and decorative fabrics in the bottom of a large supply crate. I wanted only the softest of fabrics touching her skin, to keep the finish clean and honor her sacrifice.

I chose an emerald necklace from her bag and pulled on her gown. I'd let it out a bit when I arrived in Montreal, but it fit well enough for now.

No one questioned me when I hailed a cab, nor did they complain about my oversized crate. No one looked twice when I bought a ticket for Montreal and insisted that they place my luggage in my private compartment.

Of course, a rich woman would be particular with her things.

I bought a newspaper to amuse myself. It included an obituary for Cora's mother, Mary. I wondered if I'd see something about Cora's disappearance soon.

Once on the train, I remembered the handkerchief she had stuffed in her pocket. I pulled it out. The initials on the corner were MM. I looked back over the obituary and realized the handkerchief and illness had likely never been hers.

I drew down the train window and let the handkerchief be carried away by the wind.

LAGNIAPPE

During a staff meeting one gloriously stormy night, the idea of having a section titled "Lagniappe" near the end of anthologies published by Brigids Gate Press was discussed. The staff unanimously voted in favor of the idea.

Lagniappe (pronounced LAN-yap) is an old New Orleans tradition where merchants give a little something extra along with every purchase. It's a way of expressing thanks and appreciation to customers.

The Lagniappe section might contain a short story, a poem, or a non-fiction piece. It might also feature a short novella. It may or may not be connected with the theme of the anthology.

⋈━━━━━⋈

The extra offering for this anthology is "The Call of the Sea," by Eric Raglin, a beautifully talented writer of dark fiction.

Enjoy the tale!

The Call of the Sea

by Eric Raglin

Rafael has escorted for millionaires before, but never a billionaire. Mr. Davies will be his first. The man's seaside castle is the size of a football field. Thankfully, there's no alligator-infested moat to cross—just a pink marble pathway leading to rosewood double doors, a guard on either side. They have AR-15s slung across their body armor. As Rafael approaches, the one on the left taps his headset, whispers something, and nods. Rafael has never encountered this level of security for a client before, but it makes sense that a literal castle would have a military checkpoint.

"Who are you?" the guard on the right asks.

"Mr. Davies's masseuse," Rafael says.

The guard motions for Rafael to lift his arms. The inspection is thorough, but thankfully doesn't involve bending over, spreading the cheeks, and coughing. When the guard gets to Rafael's upper thigh, a crinkling sound draws his attention. He opens the pants pocket to find condoms and lube packets.

"That's not for—" Rafael starts.

"You know the password, right?" the guard interrupts, wincing as if he's pinched a nerve.

"Oh, um, yes. Gumbo."

The guard steps away from Rafael and inhales sharply. He tugs at the body armor on his back as if reaching for a terrible itch.

Rafael breathes, glad the strange man is no longer invading his personal bubble. Sweat drips down his brow, and he wipes it away, not wanting to look disheveled for Davies.

With some difficulty, the frisker opens the right door while his partner opens the left.

Inside the castle, crystal chandeliers worth more than Rafael's tuition light the long arched corridor, glinting off tile patterned with coral pinks and tropical blues. The sight is so dazzling that Rafael doesn't notice Davies approaching.

"You're late," the billionaire says, his voice echoing through the marble arches.

Those words freeze Rafael in place. He has an excuse but isn't sure Davies will buy it. These rich assholes always look for some reason to cut pay. Dock him for tarnishing their silk sheets with cum or failing to live up to the youthful twink advertised on his website.

He can't afford to lose this money. Not with a student bill past due. Hopefully, Davies will be understanding.

"I'm really sorry," Rafael says. "When I was driving here, there were a bunch of pile-ups on the interstate. People swerving off the road for, like, no reason. I saw some guy sprawled out on the pavement, all red and flattened. Didn't get a good look at him, but he was screaming. No idea how he was still alive. Anyway, you probably don't want to hear—"

"Right. Don't talk so much," Davies says.

In a few broad strides, the man reaches Rafael and gazes down at him from an imposing height. He extends a bear-sized hand. Rafael shakes it, hoping Davies will notice the softness of his skin and not the sweatiness of his palm. Davies holds Rafael's hand a moment too long, then grins and breaks away.

"Well, we best get to it then," he says. "Follow me inside. It's a bit of a walk, and I don't want you getting lost."

Before they get even five steps in, Davies turns to address the guards.

"If you want to keep your jobs, you will not interrupt us. Under any circumstances," he says. "I don't care if the board calls or the CFO comes knocking. I don't care if the world is ending. Whatever it is, it can wait. This is my time to relax. Understood?"

The guard with the headset nods, but the frisker's response is more bizarre.

"Yes, sir," he hisses through gritted teeth, clawing at his back like it's a scratch ticket.

Something is wrong with him, but it's not Rafael's job to care. All that matters now is the money. Without another word, he follows Davies deep into the castle.

⚜ ═══════ ⚜

Lying naked beside the billionaire, Rafael gazes out the massive window at the sparkling white sand and shimmering turquoise ocean. There's no sign of human activity, not even an abandoned Corona bottle or the ashes of a snuffed-out bonfire. It's as if no person other than Davies has ever set foot on this stretch of beach.

"Aren't you a sexy mystery man," Rafael says, burrowing into Davies's chest hair and caressing his firm pecs.

"You tried looking me up, didn't you?"

Davies smiles and runs a playful finger up Rafael's ass crack. The finger feels prickly, like a torn-up callous, but Rafael pretends to enjoy it anyway, making an mmmm sound.

"I always research my clients beforehand," he says. "Helps me get to know them better." He kisses his way down Davies's chest to the stubbled happy trail. "And the better I get to know someone, the more easily I can satisfy them. Couldn't turn up a single thing about you though."

Davies laughs, then pulls down the sheets to expose his cock. He props himself up against the cushioned headboard and laces his hands behind his head.

"I have enemies who'd love to destroy me." He moans as Rafael's lips envelop his cock. "It's safer to use a fake name … oooh … when I book services with someone like you."

Rafael opens his mouth wider, teasing Davies's cock with only the warmth of his breath. "Enemies?"

"Keep sucking. Environmentalists. Liberals. Shit like, ooooh, god yeah."

Ah, oil money. Not Rafael's first, but certainly his richest.

A sound stops him from bobbing his head. Faint but undeniably present. Someone screaming?

"Whas tha sau?" Rafael asks, struggling to form words around Davies's cock.

"Probably seagulls, flying fucking ocean rats." Davies groans, stroking but not quite pushing the back of Rafael's head. "Don't stop."

Rafael licks the man's glans, tongue snagging slightly as if caught on the sharp edge of a scab. He shudders but doesn't stop, trying to focus on the sound instead. It can't be seagulls. The screeches are too throaty, too full of terror. They're getting closer.

Rafael lifts his head, a string of saliva connecting the bottom of his lip to the tip of Davies's cock, swollen purple with pleasure. He knows he shouldn't stop to listen, but that sound is just too—

A pillow smacks him in the jaw, too soft to hurt but sudden enough to surprise. This is no sexy pillow fight; it's a billionaire's horny temper tantrum.

"I told you not to stop," Davies says.

The screaming outside gets louder, more guttural.

"Listen," Rafael says, holding up his hands as if calming an aggressive dog. "I'll give you the greatest head of your goddamn life if you just give me one second to—"

Davies shushes him and points out the window.

Rafael sees it. Outside, the frisker is howling. He staggers and stomps across the formerly immaculate beach, tosses his AR-15 in the sand, and frantically rips at the clips on his body armor.

"Is he … going for a swim?" Rafael asks, unnerved, but on the verge of laughter.

"He's losing his job is what he's doing," Davies says, marching naked to the window and pounding the glass. "Goddamn idiot! What did I—?"

Rafael can't see the frisker with Davies blocking his view, but something cuts the billionaire's sentence short. Rafael wriggles out of bed and joins him by the window. What he sees stops him dead.

The frisker is facedown, writhing in the sand. His body armor is still on, but the side straps are stretching outward, fibers popping as his chest expands. Within seconds, he's twice as wide from shoulder to shoulder and flattened out in the middle. His transformation shows no signs of slowing. Even through the glass, Rafael can hear bones crunching and expanding, strips of flesh snapping like rubber bands and shedding to unveil a new form.

"What the fuck is happening?" Rafael asks, gripping Davies's arm.

When Davies turns to yell at him, Rafael hears none of his words. Davies's lips move, but all Rafael can focus on is the man's left hand. It's seared crimson, like the worst sunburn imaginable on just one part of his body. Then there are the spikes, poking a few millimeters out the skin but looking sharp enough to cut. Rafael remembers the rough feeling of Davies's fingers along his asshole.

"Did you hear me?" Davies says, shaking Rafael's shoulders. "Go. I need to deal with whatever this shit is, and you didn't make me cum, so … get out."

"What's wrong with your hand?" Rafael asks, not registering that he won't get paid for services partially rendered.

Before Davies can answer, his fingers spasm and smoosh together. The skin sizzles and bubbles, welding the gaps between digits until only one thick finger and a thumb remain. Both men scream. Steam that smells of iron and salt rises to greet them.

Davies runs out of the room, his panicked footfalls reverberating through the corridor.

Another shriek outside steals Rafael's attention.

The frisker's rib cage is exposed now, but his bones stretch together, twenty-four ribs merging into one. Calcium white darkens to crimson, and it isn't blood. The bones themselves are changing color.

Rafael thinks back to the interstate pile-up, the man he only half saw on the asphalt, all flattened and red and screaming. Whatever happened to him is the same thing happening to both the frisker and Davies. They all look like—what?

The screaming outside stops. As if following some natural instinct, the frisker scuttles toward the water. His legs look less human with each passing second. They bisect with a thunderous crack, exposing marrow, becoming multiple. The gushing splinters become autonomous.

When the frisker disappears into the ocean, Rafael realizes what these people have become: crabs.

A fever boils between his eyes and a hysterical laugh rises in his throat.

"What the fuck, what the fuck, what the—"

A shriek from within the castle.

Rafael knows he should get the hell out of here, but Davies and the frisker touched him. He could already be infected, if that's even how this disease—is it a disease?—spreads. He feels his hands—still smooth and sweaty. He runs fingers along his back—still soft and blessedly human. Maybe he got lucky.

"Help!" Davies calls. Wherever he fled to, he's coming back now, the slap of his footfalls getting louder. "Help, goddamnit!"

Rafael won't risk his life for this asshole. He needs to find somewhere safe.

As he runs into the corridor, it's hard to tell which direction Davies's voice is coming from. The castle is a labyrinth, endless curving hallways branching off into rooms with functions only a billionaire could contrive.

"Stop!"

Davies is close—too close. Rafael whips around, trying to find his way back to the exit before—

A hand—no, claw—clamps down on Rafael's arm. He tugs and kicks, desperate to free himself. The skin of his wrist peels like an orange in Davies's grip.

"Let go, motherfucker!" Rafael says.

"You have to help me!" Davies says. His left arm is almost fully transformed, the flesh above his elbow hardening into chitin and crackling as it climbs. His dick is changing, too—red and barbed and the wrong kind of hard. "Take me to a fucking hospital!"

"Fuck"—Rafael pulls hard, his hand flaying—"off!" Another jerk, his skin slipping loose like a glove. Adrenaline blocks out the pain, but he has enough sense to change tactics before he peels himself completely. He swings his foot high and kicks Davies in the armpit. Once, twice, three times, and then—

The fourth kick severs Davies's arm from its socket. The pinching claw releases Rafael and falls to the tile with a clack. No blood spurts from Davies's wound, but thin translucent fluid dribbles from the white bulbs of crab meat.

Davies is speechless for a moment until he sees more crimson chiton hardening along his shoulder stump. He lets out a hopeless wail—Rafael's cue to run. Davies makes chase, but the slap of his bare feet soon morphs into a staggered clicking sound. His screams and pleas fade to silence. He doesn't need a hospital anymore. He needs an ocean.

The city will be swarming with crab people by now, so Rafael doesn't bother driving home. Thankfully, an old client has a cottage deeper inland, far from cell reception and civilization. Hopefully, the man still keeps his key under the potted violets.

Taking the interstate isn't an option. As Rafael approaches an exit, he surveys the blacktop carnage. Tipped-over semis block multiple lanes and cars belch black smoke. Shell shards and detached crab legs decorate the road's shoulder. Drivers must have hit some crab people as they scuttled across the pavement toward the sea beyond.

Despite there being no living drivers behind him, Rafael puts on his blinker and checks his rearview while exiting the interstate. Something in the mirror catches his attention: his left eyeball. It's completely black, as if the pupil has dilated far enough to consume the whole surface. Did he burst a blood vessel? No, this is worse. In real time, he witnesses the second pupil expand like a drop of black ink. Two spheres of pure darkness stare back at him.

He slams on the brakes and puts his car into park. Tears leak from his transformed eyes. He's not special, not the lucky exception. He's just as fucked as the rest of the world.

He sits and waits for the call of the sea.

About the Authors

Hatteras Mange is a speculative author, poet, and founding editor of *Diet Milk Magazine*. His work has been featured by *The NoSleep Podcast*, Ergi Press, Hearth & Coffin, and Ram Eye Press. Find him on twitter @HatterasMange and at hatterasmange.com

Anastasia Dziekan is an emerging queer American horror author. Her writing can also be found in anthologies such as *Moonflowers and Nightshade: an Anthology of Sapphic Horror* and Eerie River's *Fire (Elemental Cycles Book 2)*. Outside of her own writing, Anastasia teaches high school English and creative writing. Anastasia also enjoys stage magic, comic books, scary movies, and her two dogs. She has a passion for female representation in horror and an appreciation for the weird and wonderful. She can be found on Twitter @ahdmagic and on Instagram @stasiadz.

Ariel Marken Jack lives in Kespukwitk. Their fiction has appeared in *Beneath Ceaseless Skies*, *Bikes in Space*, *Canthius*, *Dark Matter Magazine*, *PseudoPod*, *Strange Horizons*, and more. Their nonfiction writing on speculative literature appears in *Fusion Fragment*, *Interzone Digital*, and Psychopomp.com. They also curate the #sfstoryoftheday. Find their work at arielmarkenjack.com.

Maerwynn Blackwood is a mother of three based in the swamps of Southeast Texas. She is the author of the children's picture book *P is for Plants: An ABC and Plant Care Primer* and is currently working on her debut novel, a queer dark fantasy for adults loosely inspired by Bram Stoker's *Dracula*.

Avra Margariti is a queer author and Pushcart-nominated poet with a fondness for the dark and the darling. Avra's work haunts publications such as *Vastarien*, *Asimov's*, *F&SF*, *Strange Horizons*, and *Reckoning*. Avra lives and studies in Athens, Greece. You can find Avra on twitter (@avramargariti).

Grace R. Reynolds (she/her) is a native of the great state of New Jersey, where she was first introduced to the eerie and strange thanks to local urban legends of a devil creeping through the Pine Barrens. Since then, her curiosity with things that go bump in the night bloomed into creative expression as a dark poet, horror, and thriller fiction writer. She is the author of two poetry collections, *Lady of The House* and *The Lies We Weave*, both released by Curious Corvid Publishing.

By day, **Evelyn Freeling** is a nomadic troll coming to a bridge near you. By night, she's an author and editor of the dark, gruesome, and horny. Her short fiction has been published by Flame Tree Press, CHM, *The Arcanist*, *NoSleep Podcast*, *Dark Void Magazine*, Ghost Orchid Press, and more. She is also the editor of the erotic horror anthology, *Les Petites Morts*. Stalk her on Twitter (if it still exists at time of publication) @Evelyn_Freeling, on IG @Evelynfreeling, or at her website www.evelynfreeling.wordpress.com.

Hailey Piper is the Bram Stoker Award-winning author of *Queen of Teeth*, *No Gods for Drowning*, *The Worm and His Kings* series, and other books of dark fiction. Her short stories appear in *Pseudopod, Vastarien, Cosmic Horror Monthly*, and other publications. She lives with her wife in Maryland, where their occult rituals are secret. Find Hailey at www.haileypiper.com.

T.O. King wanders the woods like a lost soul and looks for inspiration in the natural world. When she's not writing or wandering, you can find her buried between stacks of books and haunting her local library.

M.S. Dean is a graduate student studying genetics in Massachusetts. Her short stories have been previously published in *Anathema, Beneath Ceaseless Skies, khōréō*, and elsewhere. She can be found on Twitter @MyrceneDean.

Minnesota native **Chloe Spencer** is an award-winning writer, indie gamedev, and filmmaker. She is the author of *Monstersona, Duality*, and the upcoming paranormal mystery-romance *Haunting Melody* and adult horror novellas, *Vicarious* and *Mewing*. In her spare time, she enjoys playing video games, trying her best at Pilates, and cuddling with her cats. She holds a BA in Journalism from the University of Oregon and an MFA in Film and Television from SCAD Atlanta.

Mae Murray is a writer and editor hailing from Arkansas, now living in eerie New England. She contributes essays and criticism to horror-centric websites, including Fangoria and Dread Central. She is the recipient of a 2022 Brave New Weird award for the Superior Achievement in Short Fiction, and has been published in horror fiction anthologies and nonfiction collections. *The Book of Queer Saints Volume I* was her editing debut. Volume II is expected in Fall 2023. Her debut novel *I'm Sorry If I Scared You* is due Spring 2024. She can be found across social media platforms as @maeisafraid.

L.R. Stuart loves all things abject, relishing in what lies between boundaries. Too introverted to live out a murderous queer romance, she prefers to write about them instead.

Alex Luceli Jiménez is a queer Mexican writer and school counselor in training living in Marina, CA. Her fiction has appeared in *Berkeley Fiction Review, Southwest Review, Moonflowers & Nightshade: An Anthology of Sapphic Horror,* and others. She can almost certainly be found listening to Phoebe Bridgers and drinking an iced latte while reading or writing. Visit her online and read her work at alexlucelijimenez.com.

Cheyanne Brabo (she/her) is a fiction writer and proud Californian. Her fiction is slated for publication in Warning Lines Lit and is a finalist in Crystal Lake Entertainment's *Shallow Waters* Flash Fiction Competition, her work has also been featured in Kingdoms in the Wild and Raven Review. When she's not writing, she enjoys taking her cat for walks in his leash and harness. Find her on twitter @cheysectoplasm.

Luc Diamant is a writer, translator, and perpetual student from Amsterdam, where he lives with his partner and their imaginary pets. He has writing out or forthcoming in *The Deeps, Tales to Terrify,* and *Dark Moments,* among others. When not writing, he enjoys spending time with the aforementioned partner, watching the plants on his balcony grow, and thinking about lemurs. You can find him on Instagram and (for now) Twitter @lucdaniel94.

Alyssa Lennander is a writer and a children's librarian in rural Minnesota. She holds a BA in English as well as a Master's in Library and Information Science. While she reads sweet stories to littles during the day, by night she enjoys writing dark speculative fiction with a historical bent. When she's not doing either of those things, you can find her snuggling her three cats.

Anya Leigh Josephs holds a BA from Columbia University and an MA from UCLA, both in English, and a MSW from NYU. Raised in North Carolina, Anya now works as an artist and psychotherapist in New York City. When not working or writing, Anya can be found seeing a lot of plays, reading doorstopper fantasy novels, or worshiping my cat, Sycorax. Anya's writing can be found in venues like *The Magazine of Fantasy and Science Fiction* (forthcoming), *Fantasy Magazine*, tor.com, and many others. Anya's debut novel, *Queen of All*, a fantasy for young adults, was published by Zenith Press.

Lindz McLeod is a queer, working-class, Scottish writer and editor who dabbles in the surreal. Her prose has been published by Apex, Catapult, Pseudopod, The Razor, and many more, including prior issues of Assemble Artefacts. Her longer work includes the short story collection *Turducken* (Spaceboy, 2023) and her debut novel *Beast* (Hear Us Scream, 2024). She is a full member of the SFWA, the club president of the Edinburgh Writers, Club, and is currently working on a PhD in Creative Writing at Manchester University. Lindz is represented by Laura Zats at Headwater Literary Management.

Caitlin Marceau is a queer award-winning author and illustrator based in Montreal. She holds a Bachelor of Arts in Creative Writing, is an Active Member of the Horror Writers Association, and has spoken about genre literature at several Canadian conventions. Her work includes *Femina*, *A Blackness Absolute*, and *This Is Where We Talk Things Out*. Her novella, *I'm Having Regrets*, and her debut novel, *It Wasn't Supposed To Go Like This*, are set for publication in 2024. For more, visit CaitlinMarceau.ca or find her on social media.

Shelley Lavigne is a purveyor of moist literature, usually queer horror. Their words can be found at The Dread Machine, If There's Anyone Left and others. They live in Ontario where they roam their neighborhood in search of haunted houses and cool bugs. You can also find them on twitter @shelleysghoul.

About the Editors

Rae Knowles (she/her) is a queer woman and author of dark fiction including *The Stradivarius* (May 2023) and *Merciless Waters* (November 2023). Her short fiction has been featured in *Dark Matter Ink, Ghoulish Tales, Seize the Press, Taco Bell Quarterly,* and *Nosetouch Press,* among others. Rae is an active member of the HWA and is represented by Laura Williams at Greene & Heaton.

April Yates (she/her) is a writer of dark and queer fiction, living in Derbyshire, England. Her longer work includes the novellas, *Ashthorne, City of Snares* and the novel *Lies That Bind* (co-authored with Rae Knowles) due for release via Brigids Gate in 2024

About the Illustrator

Daniella Batsheva is a self-proclaimed "Illustrator with a design habit" whose aesthetic straddles the line between underground and mainstream. Her art boasts the beautiful intricate linework of traditional Victorian illustration mixed with imagery inspired by horror films, 90's toy packaging, and macabre history.

Batsheva's art has been published internationally. Her work can be seen everywhere from "Whole Foods" to London's biggest punk venues. She has worked with brands such as Kerrang!, Pizza Girl, and multiple musicians from Paris Jackson and Ben Christo (Sisters of Mercy). Her work has recently been featured at ArtExpo, New York, and The Crypt Gallery, London.

While her work can comfortably fit in multiple contexts, Batsheva's work is always recognizable. Her main motivation is fostering local alternative communities and contributing to the future of illustration in Goth/Metal scenes. Batsheva is also passionate about researching obscure folklore from across different cultures in an effort to preserve legends that are at risk of being lost.

Content Warnings

Gladys Glows at Night by Hatteras Mange
Content Warnings: Body horror, references to religious-based disordered eating

You Oughta Be In Pictures by Anatasia Dziekan
Content warnings: blood and gore, sexual references, relationship violence, voyeurism

The Lady of the House on Legs by Ariel Marken Jack
Content Warnings: blood, death, cannibalism, self-harm

To Wilt a Flower by Maerwynn Blackwood
Content Warnings: gore, death of an intimate partner, dubious consent, sexually explicit content, self-inflicted injury, necrophilia

Teratoma, Cacodaemon, Erinya by Avra Margariti
Content Warnings: body horror, queerphobia

Torbalan's Gift by Grace R. Reynolds
Content Warnings: blood/gore, death, homophobia, profanity, violence, sexually explicit scene

Her Tongue, A Slippery Slope by Evelyn Freeling
Content Warnings: Gore, vomiting, sexual content, allusions to incest and rape (not on page), forced pregnancy

Modern Art Curse, Mixed Media by Hailey Piper
Content Warnings: Gore, violence, alcohol use, self-inflicted harm

The Flesh Grows Fonder by T.O. King
Content Warnings: mentions of death by poison, sexual content, portrayals of blood (meat), and flowers made from living flesh, body horror

Pilgrim of Worlds by M.S. Dean
Content Warning: Murder

Gingerbread Red by Chloe Spencer
Content Warnings: blood, gore, child death (mentioned), cannibalism, domestic violence

Buckskin for Linen by Mae Murray
Content Warnings: Intergenerational trauma, colonialism

Oubliette By L. R. Stuart
Content Warnings: Imprisonment (at the hands of a former romantic partner), murder (at the hands of a current romantic partner), non-graphic violence, mild sexual content, power imbalances, large age gaps (all characters are above 20), and implied ableism (in the form of imprisoning someone under the guise of it being for their own good).

Conversations with Roe by Alex Luceli Jiménez
Content warning: Partner violence

Our Lady of Devouring Violence by Cheyanne Brabo
Content Warning: Religious trauma

Family Planning by Luc Diamant
Content Warnings: Off-page death of a parent, Discussion of infertility

Ungrateful Dead Things by Alyssa Lennander
Content Warnings: dead bodies, death of a loved one, blood, scientific experiments on a body

Straight Flush by Anya Leigh Josephs
Content Warning: Murder

A Mirror Has Two Faces by Lindz McLeod
Content Warnings: manipulation, pseudo-incest, sexual content, suicide

The Turner House Heritage Tour by Caitlin Marceau
Content Warnings: Death of a child (suggested)

Enamored by Shelley Lavigne
Content Warnings: Body horror, bodily autonomy, character death

More From Brigids Gate Press

Dangerous Waters: Deadly Women of the Sea

Malevolent mermaids.

Sinister sirens.

Scary selkies.

And other dangerous women of the deep blue sea.

Dangerous waters takes us deep beneath the ocean waves and shows us once more why we need to be cautious about venturing out into the water.

Featuring stories, drabbles and poems by Sandra Ljubjanović, John Higgins, Patrick Rutigliano, Candace Robinson, Emmanuel Williams, Desirée M. Niccoli, L. Marie Wood, Samantha Lokai, Christina Henneman, Gully Novaro, Christine Lukas, Alice Austin, Dawn Vogel, Victoria Nations, Mark Towse, Kristin Cleaveland, Ben Monroe, Kurt Newton, E.M. Linden, Eva Papasoulioti, Ann Wuehler, Rachel Dib, A.R. Fredericksen, Daniel Pyle, Megan Hart, Ef Deal, Katherine Traylor, Juliegh Howard-Hobson, Simon Kewin, Elana Gomel, Lauren E. Reynolds, Grace R. Reynolds, René Galván, Marshall J. Moore, Ngo Binh Anh Khoa, Roxie Vorhees, April Yates, Kaitlin Tremblay, T.K. Howell, Kayla Whittle, Emily Y. Teng, Briana McGuckin, Tom Farr, Cassandra Taylor, Steven-Elliot Altman, Paul M. Feeney, Lucy Collins, Marianne Halbert, Rosie Arcane, Antonia Rachel Ward, Steven Lord, and Jessica Peter.

Musings of the Muses

Sing O Muse, of the rage of Medusa, cursed by gods and feared by men …

From the mists of time, and ages past,
The muses have gathered; hear now their songs.
A web of revenge spun 'neath the moon;
A poet's wife who breaks her bonds;
A warrior woman on a quest of honor;
A painful lesson for a treacherous heart;
A goddess and a mortal, bound together by the travails of motherhood.
And more.

Listen to the muses, as they sing aloud … HER story.

Musings of the Muses, 65 stories and poems based on Greek myths, is an anthology of monsters, heroines, and goddesses, ranging from ancient Greece to modern day America. They, like the myths themselves, cast long shadows of horror, fantasy, love, betrayal, vengeance, and redemption. This anthology revisits those old tales and presents them anew, from her point of view.

Daughter of Sarpedon

Medusa.

Cursed by the gods.

Slain by Perseus.
A monster.

So the poets sang.

The poets got it wrong.

Daughter of Sarpedon: A Tempered Tales Collection is an anthology of short stories, poems, and drabbles, ranging from retellings to completely new stories, from ancient to modern day.

Featuring the talents of Eva Papasoulioti, Laura G. Kaschak, Linda D. Addison, SJ Townend, Christina Sng, Ann Wuehler, Amanda Steel, Ellie Detzler, Elizabeth Davis, Katherine Silva, Megan Baffoe, Rachel Horak Dempsey, Romy Tara Wenzel, Stephanie M. Wytovich, Die Booth, Rachel Rixen, Federica Santini, Thomas Joyce, L. Minton, Catherine McCarthy, Ai Jiang, Katie Young, Lyndsey Croal, Elyse Russell, Deborah Markus, April Yates, Theresa Derwin, Jason P. Burnham, Claire McNerney, Marisca Pichette, Gordon Linzner, Patricia Gomes, Stephen Frame, Sharmon Gazaway, Kayla Whittle, Alexis DuBon, Sam Muller, Avra Margariti,

Christina Bagni, Kristin Cleaveland, Eric J. Guignard, Marshall J. Moore, Owl Goingback, Renée Meloche, Cindy O'Quinn, Eugene Johnson, Alyson Faye, Jeanne Bush, and Agatha Andrews.

Blood on the Soil, Terror on the Wind

Whether in an old weathered mine shaft, somewhere off the beaten path, out in the woods, or right here in the middle of this ghost town, danger awaits. We're going to take you way back, drop you right smack dab in the middle of the Old West at its finest. But we're not just going to give you shootouts and bullet wounds and blood splatter. Yes, those things are prominently featured, but there's so much more to this anthology of western horror.

Maybe it's a well-known creature popping in for a visit, or some new creepy crawly monster sucking out your soul, we're going to turn the Old West inside-out and explore its guts to the fullest. There are new adventures to be had, monsters both familiar and unfamiliar to be thwarted … and we're not always going to be the victors. Life in the Old West is hard, trying at its best, and it can wear you down quick.

So, prepare yourself to be transported back in time. Get yourself up on that rickety stagecoach, draw your guns, and let's get going. There's vast territory to cover here, and your journey begins now.

Featuring the talents of Antonia Rachel Ward, Nick Kolakowski, Villimey Mist & Damascus Mincemeyer, Jonathan Kemmerer-Scovner, Sean Eads & Joshua Viola, Craig E. Sawyer, Lana Elizabeth Gabris, Joel McKay, David Niall Wilson, Ej Sidle, Brennan LaFaro, Michael Bailey, Amanda J.

Spedding, Taylor Rae, P.L. McMillan, Wen Wen Yang, Ben Monroe, and Chad Lutzke.

Visit our website at: www.brigidsgatepress.com

9 781957 537900